“Now will you have a drink with me?”

The audience screamed encouragement for her to say yes.

Matilda’s face stilled, lips pressed into a line. The wait lasted a few seconds, though it was just enough time for Jared to doubt being so public in his request.

Then she nodded. “I suppose I can make room in my lane.”

The audience cheered; Jared’s knees almost gave out in relief.

“What’s your poison?” he asked when finally offstage. He waved down the bartender.

He felt a squeeze against his fingers and met her eyes. “Do you really want to know?” she said, just loud enough for him to hear.

He tipped his head down. “I’m down for anything. Another song? Dinner? Or maybe tomorrow if that works better. I’m here a few days...” he began, his adrenaline flying high.

But he was stopped by the move of her hands up his chest to his shoulders. Her fingers gently pressed against his lips. “Let’s have this drink at your place.”

His answer came as swift as his next heartbeat. “Let’s go.”

Dear Reader,

Welcome to the Spirit of the Shenandoah series! Set in Peak, Virginia, in the gorgeous Shenandoah Valley, this series blends love, family and friendship all in one swoop. Add this first book, an age gap and a secret relationship between Jared and Matilda, and I hope it convinces you to stay a while!

Thirty-year-old Jared has a blooming career as a chef in an Asian-fusion restaurant in Louisville, Kentucky. But it all comes crashing to a halt when public criticism of one of his dishes causes him to question his entire identity. He is desperate for answers, and his search leads him to Peak and the Espiritu family, the proprietors of the Spirit of the Shenandoah B & B, where he hopes to find his extended family.

Forty-year-old divorcée Matilda Matthews has been by the Espiritu family's side for almost five years, when she had boomeranged back to the town and found solace living in her small cottage and working as the B & B manager. After a long day, she meets a curious stranger at her favorite bar. Jared is sweet and unguarded—but he's ten years her junior. Yet after a drink and karaoke, she heads back to his place, only to find out the next day at work who he really is.

Jared and Matilda now have some decisions to make and secrets to keep. I hope you enjoy their journey as they manage it and their newfound attraction and, dare I say...love?

XO

Tif

IT STARTED WITH A SECRET

TIF MARCELO

Recycling programs for this product may not exist in your area.

ISBN-13: 978-1-335-59465-5

It Started with a Secret

This is a work of fiction. Names, characters, places and incidents are either the product of the author's imagination or are used fictitiously. Any resemblance to actual persons, living or dead, businesses, companies, events or locales is entirely coincidental.

For questions and comments about the quality of this book, please contact us at CustomerService@Harlequin.com.

Harlequin Enterprises ULC
22 Adelaide St. West, 41st Floor
Toronto, Ontario M5H 4E3, Canada
www.Harlequin.com

Printed in Lithuania

Tif Marcelo is a veteran US Army nurse and holds a BS in nursing and a master's in public administration. She believes and writes about the strength of families, the endurance of friendship and heartfelt romances, and is inspired daily by her own military hero husband and four children. She hosts the *Stories to Love* podcast and is the *USA TODAY* bestselling author of adult and young adult novels. Learn more about her at www.tifmarcelo.com.

Books by Tif Marcelo

Harlequin Special Edition

Spirit of the Shenandoah

It Started with a Secret

Visit the Author Profile page at Harlequin.com.

To Cooper and Greggy, my Virginia boys!

Chapter One

Three Months Ago
Louisville, Kentucky

It had been sixty-four days since Jared Sotheby's last serious kitchen injury.

Having worked in restaurants from the age of sixteen and long before that in his mother's kitchen, he'd endured his share of minor knife mishaps and splatters of hot oil, sometimes from inattention, and other times from plain old negligence.

This time, though, the slipup was due to hearing the food critic's statement blaring through the Bluetooth speakers.

Sotheby's re-creation of this dish isn't...what I could call authentic.

After setting his chef's knife down, dumbfounded by the strike of those words as well as the slice of the powdered steel blade, he stepped up to the sink, flipped the faucet on and dunked his bloody pointer finger underneath the cool stream of water. A hiss escaped his lips as he watched the blood rinse away to reveal a gash that, thank goodness, wouldn't need stitching. It, however, did nothing to prevent the start of anger.

He cursed under his breath and said, "I can't believe it—"

"Hey, you okay?" His neighbor Darren appeared next to him and offered a kitchen towel. Cuban American and tanned deeply from his recent vacation in Costa Rica, Darren's default bright smile had slipped to a worried expression.

"Yeah, totally fine." Jared's voice croaked at the lie, and he spread his lips to what he hoped was a passing grin. "Butterfingers, is all."

With raised, disbelieving eyebrows Darren said, "Where's the gauze and tape? I'll grab it for you."

"Thanks. In the bathroom closet." Jared released a breath while he thumbed pressure against his cut, glad for the moment's peace to think. Yesterday, he'd received a last minute request from his highly connected boss, Chef Tay Yamamoto, of the famed restaurant Sizzling Platter, to appear in a cooking segment with CBN's *Good Evening Louisville*. Sizzling Platter's executive chef, who had been originally booked for the segment, had fallen ill, and its head chef had a temper unfit for television.

As Sizzling Platter's newest sous chef, the ball had been passed down to Jared.

It would be a great way to make his mark in the Louisville food scene, Jared was told. Much more, it would help advertise the restaurant.

It was supposed to be a win-win situation.

The taping was eight hours ago, when, in front of a studio audience, Jared had cooked up sisig, a Filipino appetizer traditionally made with grilled pork, fried with calamansi, onion, soy sauce, chili flakes and vinegar and served on a sizzling platter. Except he'd made it *his* way, with smoked chicken thighs, fried with onions, garlic, lemon, soy sauce and topped with a fried egg—not unheard-of in the evolved recipes he'd tried.

It was one of his favorite appetizers to make and eat; sisig had also become the rage among Filipino food trucks in the South.

Jared had thought the segment was successful. Not a single *um*, *uh*, or filler word had escaped his lips. Neither had he spilled an ingredient, and despite his initial nervousness, he'd been articulate.

The dish itself, when he'd tasted it, was perfect.

So confident was he in his first media segment that he'd invited his sister and closest friends for a watch party.

Apparently, no one at CBN had bothered to mention to Jared that they'd served up his dish to the other guests of the show well after Jared had left the studio. Nor did they think to mention that one of those guests was Will Gonzalez, a Filipino television food critic there to promote the newest season of his competitive cooking show, *Pressure Cooked.*

Or that Will would be offering feedback in the form of a hatchet job.

Otherwise, Jared would have stuck around the studio to wait for the verdict before he invited a houseful of friends over to watch his food get insulted.

Jared turned away from the sink, steeling himself to face the guests he couldn't hide from. Not only because his quirky rented historic flat in the Highlands was a mere thousand square feet, with a great room that was actually the size of a postage stamp, but because all of the twelve people in attendance would be able to see right through him, being that they were his ride or die friends.

Now, they were all looking at him with slack jaws and raised eyebrows.

"What a jerk!" Emma, his half sister, jump-started the room. She picked up the remote from the ottoman and shut the television off with a dramatic press of the thumb. After tossing the remote onto the couch, she dug her fingers in her blond hair. "What makes him the barometer of authentic Filipino food? There are a dozen ways to cook a dish."

Jared grimly kept smiling, feeling as though his lips had frozen stiff because what was he to say to encompass the range of thoughts coursing through him? The critic had a right to his opinion, right? Even if Jared agreed 100 percent with his sister. Authenticity was a buzz word thrown around in the industry that needed longer than a TV show segment to unpack, because it was linked directly to identity, to history and to the very core of who he was as a chef.

Which meant that the term was subjective.

Even if the critic's words stung like hell.

And frankly, if he didn't calm Emma down, the rest of the room was sure to follow suit and flip the vibe of what was supposed to be a chill get-together. Emma was about three years younger, and at twenty-seven, she was charismatic and convincing, aka pushy. A musician known for her empowering lyrics, she could round up a boycott in no time flat.

"It isn't a big deal. He's a purist, is all," Jared said, taping up his finger with the gauze Darren had handed him. "While I am not."

At all levels, Jared continued in his head. His culinary passion was fusion; he loved mixing up methods and inspirations. He was also biracial—Filipino and Greek, and with an English-derived last name, inherited from his stepfather who'd adopted him. From conception he wasn't quite one or the other. Though admittedly, growing up with white American family members in the South for the entirety of his life had given him that specific life experience. And sometimes, and exactly at moments like this, he wondered if he should have tried harder to figure out his other side…

Nothing's stopping you, the devil on his shoulder reminded him.

"Still. Your food is phenomenal," Emma said, knocking Jared out of his thoughts.

He met his sister's eyes, seeing the sincerity in them, though at the moment, he was reminded once more how blue they were, whereas his were a deep mahogany. Though they shared a mother, he was so different from the rest of the family. From most of Kentucky, to be honest. But these were deep thoughts, and he was a grown man hosting a dinner party. He wanted his friends to have a good time.

Jared donned a latex glove on his left hand to protect the cut and snapped it with a grin to move the moment forward. "I'm just saying. You can't satisfy everyone. I'm happy so long as *you* all think I make a kick-ass sisig." He scanned the faces of his observant friends. "Right?"

The crowd answered with *hell yeses* and cheers of agreement.

Relief spilled from him. "That's what I like to hear! Darren, top off everyone's drinks. I'm almost done slicing this up."

"On it!" Darren lifted a couple of beers from the cooler, the perpetual frat boy he was. He pushed an icy bottle of his home brew stout against Jared's hand. "Who else needs a cold one? We have to toast, to this man's first media spot."

Emma raised her bottle seconds later. "Here's to my big brother. Onward and upward."

Onward and upward. It was in every single Sotheby toast. It was a reminder not to sit still and wallow. And right this second, Jared repeated it with gusto.

They all took sips. Others tossed words of encouragement, and buoyed, Jared stepped up to the kitchen island and set down his beer. Then, he narrowed his focus to his work that had been previously interrupted: slicing hanger steak. He breathed out through his pursed lips, forcing his attention to the blade. Concentrating on satisfying his real fans—the people in his room. On ignoring the critic's statement. On not getting hurt once more.

Still, the room felt too hot and he was coming out of his skin. He couldn't shake the unease of the moment, of the critic's declaration: *Isn't...what I could call authentic.*

Who made that call, about what was authentic and what was not?

And why did it bother him so much? He knew he was a great cook. He was working at Sizzling Platter—full stop.

He knew who he was.

At that moment, his phone buzzed. It was sitting on the countertop microwave, and with a quick peek, saw *Mom* flash on the screen.

Not totally, the devil whispered from deep inside him.

The devil didn't let up, rendering the party a blur, and when Jared finally bid the last of his friends good-night, he leaned back against the front door and heaved a breath to steady the dreadful drumbeat of his heart.

The unease he'd been feeling all night was just short of intolerable, an itch that couldn't be scratched.

And all he wanted was something sweet so he could work through his thoughts.

"It's impressive that you can throw a huge dinner from this tiny kitchen, Jared. And believe me, I have been in some fancy kitchens owned by people who can't turn on a toaster," Emma said, waking him from his thoughts. Armed with a bottle of cleaning spray, she wiped down the island with a semiscowl on her face. From when they were kids, she had hated cleanup, of any kind. Sometimes Jared didn't know how she survived living on her own, albeit only two streets down.

"Magic." He grinned, snatching up a fallen dish towel.

"Nah. It's you making the best of a situation." An eyebrow rose, a sure precursor that a serious conversation was forthcoming.

But he wasn't in the mood for it, whatever it was. Cleanup, a snack, shower and bedtime was his agenda.

He swung the towel over his shoulder and sidled up to the stove, piling the pans into a stack. "I do think I should add a little more sweet chili sauce to the steak marinade."

"I have a better idea. How about we talk about it?"

"About how it's completely unfair that I did the cooking and am now also doing the cleaning? Keep up, you." He scrubbed away the oil splatters on the stove and avoided her laser stare digging into his back. Truth was, his sister, above all, also had this uncanny instinct to detect any blip in his mood.

She surely had noticed that in the last couple of hours, questions had resurfaced from the deepest layers of his soul to join his already jumbled thoughts. Questions that he'd buried down deep, now exposed by that critic's judgment.

"Jared." Emma snatched his attention like a pull on his shirt collar. "I know you're upset. You might have put up a good front with everyone else, but I can tell you're shaken."

The stove was spotless from Jared's determined efforts, and he had no choice but to turn around. "Look, I know you're searching for inspiration for your next ballad, but girl, it's not me."

She leaned against the counter across from him and narrowed her eyes. "That grin of yours might work for other people, but you forget we shared a room through elementary school. Something else is going on, and I wonder if it has anything to do with what you and Mom are in a fight about."

He groaned, throwing his hands up. "What is this, a one-person intervention?"

Their mother, Sharla, was going through a *thing.* Since she and his stepfather, Fred, moved to Asheville a couple of weeks ago, she'd been sensitive about everything. She called Jared daily, requiring proof of life.

Her nostalgia also had been on overload.

Emma's voice softened. "She said you were angry with her when she tried to hand you a box with some of his stuff in it. That when she tried to talk to you about him, you all but walked out of the house."

Jared wiped his hands on the kitchen rag, a repetitive motion that provided him with some comfort. Feeling the crosshatch of fibers tamped down the beginnings of the rise of unease.

Him. As in, Louis Espiritu. His birth father. A required distinction, because Jared's real father was Fred, the man he'd known from the beginning of his existence. Louis had been a sperm donor.

"First of all, that guy has nothing to do with today. And secondly, I wasn't angry. I ended up taking the box because she was making such a fuss. I was…shocked that she'd want to give it to me in the first place."

Shocked was the filtered version of the disgust he had felt. Because why would he want to have possession of his birth father's things? Louis Espiritu never mattered. Especially since he'd never been in his life; he'd died long ago, according to his mother. So even if he had a desire to find out more…

"Where is it now?"

"I stuck it in the trunk of my car."

"That black hole of a mobile storage unit?"

"Hey. Don't disrespect the Kia."

She snorted. "Aren't you even mildly curious about what's in it?"

He shook his head, lips pressed into a line. And yet, something was unfurling inside him. Perhaps it was the way his sister was looking at him. Or what that food critic had said about authenticity. Or every little thing that had lodged itself in his core memories, of being the only dark-haired, brown-eyed boy in a family of blue-eyed, blond-haired people, and with all its inherent little nuances, that only he could feel. "Fine, so I wondered a couple of times, but he's dead. What's the point?"

"That maybe, there's more to find out about him?"

"More to find out about Louis Espiritu? That sounds like hell. Why would I do that to myself?"

Saying his name loosened something in his chest, and his stomach gave way, like when he looked down from a rooftop bar or an open-view elevator. Of not being able to catch his breath.

This was why he didn't say his name often, or think of him in any capacity. From the age of seven when Jared truly understood who his father was, he categorically pushed the notion of the man and those dreadful feelings aside, and forced himself to look only at the bright and the optimistic.

But sometimes little things came up. Like the food critic's statement. Like when he'd interviewed for Sizzling Platter and had been asked about his Filipino food repertoire and realized that he didn't have one. Sure, he had several dishes he knew off the top of his head, like sisig, but a repertoire?

It was because he wasn't raised eating Filipino food on the regular. He'd learned the dishes on his own.

Despite all this, Jared had thrived. Had he lived in denial of his birth father? Maybe.

But his mother *had* to bring him up; she *had* to give him Louis's things.

And now his stuff was in the back of his Kia, and he couldn't ignore it no matter how hard he tried.

Emma's eyes shut ever so briefly. "Because…it's part you."

"Nah. You know what's part me? Mom, Dad and yeah, even you and that's enough for me."

Her face softened so a hint of a smile graced her lips. "I appreciate that. But I agree with Mom. It feels like the whole thing is something you keep avoiding."

"So you're in cahoots with Mom now?"

"No. It's you and me, silly. But why won't you talk to Mom? You've known her and Louis's story all your life…why take it out on her?"

He groaned, because the pressure in his chest was increasing. Not even during his most tense moments in the kitchen did he feel this…heavy, and unsure. But he blew out a breath, and reached for the first thing to say. "You should have really been an attorney. Your nagging skills are wasted on being a rock star." He balled up and threw the kitchen towel at her and grinned.

"No. No. Nope." After swiping the towel from the air, she tossed it on the countertop. "Distraction failed. I'm not done with you. When Mom told me about you refusing the box, it got me thinking. Have you ever wondered who's out there? As in, blood relation?"

"Okay…you're out." This was it. He rounded the corner, took his sister gently by the shoulders and guided her toward the front door. "Might I remind you that I cooked for thirteen today. Thirteen, and without my own sous chef. I'm ready to put my feet up."

She was quiet for a minute. Silence from Emma was never a good sign. And when she finally spoke, her words landed like an anvil in an old cartoon. "Did I tell you that Gage swabbed for My Family Tree?"

Gabe was the drummer in Emma's band.

"And," she continued, as she bent down to lace up her Doc Martens, "he discovered that he was Dominican and Danish."

"Danish?" That was interesting, in spite of his opposition to even thinking about his birth father. Gage had identified himself as Dominican and Puerto Rican, and had deep brown skin and dark features.

"Yep. He went down the rabbit hole of researching Danish culture and where the family tree intersected. He even started learning the language."

Jared nodded at what he realized Emma was getting at, so he grabbed her coat from the closet, along with her scarf and beanie. The difference between Gage's situation and Jared's was that he'd known about Louis. His parentage was never the issue.

Louis's story was a fable Jared grew up with, and his birth father was simply a representation of the kind of man he wouldn't be.

He stuffed the beanie on Emma's head, and started winding the scarf around her neck.

"He found cousins!" she yelled, before he made a loose bow in front of her face.

The silence was heavenly.

Though the thought of the family tree was compelling.

He opened the door to swing those thoughts out of his head, and with one gentle push, set Emma over the threshold. "Love you. Text me as soon as you get home."

"You having ice cream after I leave?"

"I've got brownies in the freezer."

"See. I knew this was serious." She lowered the scarf just as he was shutting the door. "Make one promise."

Jared rolled his eyes. "What's that?"

"Just keep me posted on what's up. You have the tendency to, I don't know, keep the serious stuff in."

He blew out a breath. "Whatever."

"Promise."

"Yes, of course. I promise."

"Okay then." She took one step back. "Onward and upward..."

"Onward and upward." But as he shut the door, Jared had yet to figure out what that meant.

Chapter Two

Present Day
Peak, Virginia

It wasn't that Matilda Matthews didn't believe in promises. It was just that promises always seemed to bite her in the butt.

Case in point: her declaration to her family and friends as a twenty-one year old that *I promise you won't see me set foot in this damn valley again*? Broken. She'd landed back in her hometown five years ago, properly humbled.

Another: her ex's vows of a happily-ever-after? Smashed to bits by his infidelity. And she was still single.

In her experience, expressed promises led to disappointment rather than joy.

Instead of promising the thing, she just did the thing to the T, and all aboveboard. She was dreamy, still, at times aided by the books she read. But when her heart was set on finishing a task, she did so to completion.

It was why, despite boomeranging back home, she had a reputation for her hard-nosed work ethic and had been hired as the general manager of Spirit of the Shenandoah B & B. Doing, rather than promising, had allowed for her to catch up in life.

But in the last few days, she'd said "I promise" more than she'd felt comfortable with. To the B & B guest who'd complained about her runny scrambled eggs and had wanted a promise that she would be provided the gourmet foodie experience as touted by the B & B advertising. To her best friend and B & B chef, Allie Lang, who was eight months pregnant and had wanted a promise that her replacement would be arriving soon—a replacement chef Matilda had yet to find. To her boss, Evangeline Espiritu, who was counting on Matilda to ensure the successful running of the B & B through two upcoming big events, who'd required a promise that everything was on point.

Which it all was—sort of.

And finally, a promise to herself not to scratch that itch to click on the voicemail from a cell number she recognized intimately. A curiosity that surely would be the thing to kill her after her long week at work.

You make too many promises, her conscience told her.

"Well, there's no choice but to follow through now," she answered back.

A headache began at Matilda's temples, and she rubbed her fingers against them. She'd just pulled the parking brake of her geriatric Bronco in front of Mountain Rush, one of three local bars that she and her friends frequented.

It was Friday, which meant karaoke, and though part of her wanted to crawl under her covers, the one sure thing that could cheer her up was belting out a tune with her closest friends. Besides, she'd promised to be there.

She sighed.

With a deep breath, and after one quick swipe of lipstick against her lips, she shoved her booted foot against the indestructible SUV door. It swung open to the echoing, croaking voice of a passionate soul belting out Cher's "If I Could Turn Back Time."

As predicted, some of the tension in her neck loosened. Drawn to Mountain Rush's entrance, gravel crunched under her boots, lifting her spirit with each step.

You'll make things right.

You're doing a good job.

By the time she was greeted by Lo, the bouncer just inside of the bar's door, Matilda was ready to let her troubles go, even for a couple of hours.

She entered the dimly lit room. Not too many folks were present at the moment—it never really did get crowded before 9:00 p.m., so it was easy for Matilda to spot her group of three friends in their usual booth in the back right corner. At the sight of them, the knot in her chest unfurled.

After grabbing her usual bourbon sour from the bartender, she weaved through the small round tables arranged in a semicircle around the stage. Currently, the spotlight was trained on the raised platform, where pharmacist Lily Kiu was belting out the chorus, going for gold despite the occasional screech.

Damn, respect. Matilda cheered her friend on. "You get it, Lily!"

God, she was grateful for this place. Not just Mountain Rush, but Peak. How quaint the town was, and unusually diverse for the Shenandoah Valley; and how, if she'd had a question about any medication for example, she could probably ask Lily after her performance and she would do everything in her power to help Matilda.

It was in the safety net of these people that she'd begun to heal after returning with her tail between her legs and a broken heart.

To the locals, Matilda was the reformed party girl. The late bloomer. The slightly grumpy one, because she no longer had time to suffer fools.

And it was all good. Matilda understood where she stood here, and it was by and large better than living with the unpredictable. She preferred knowing the sure thing, rather than hoping for empty and shallow promises.

Peak and its inhabitants were as reliable as the sunsets.

Matilda loved that she could encounter a friend or neighbor at each turn, that she could walk into a restaurant alone and be invited to sit with a group. That on Friday nights, her girlfriends gravitated toward the same corner of their favorite bar, and they'd always save her a spot…

Matilda halted, stunned out of her thoughts with the odd sight. Drops of bourbon sloshed out of her glass.

Her spot? It was taken. A handsome stranger was in the midst of her three friends. The group was engaged in a spirited conversation, their voices stacked upon one another like Jenga pieces, teetering into laughter.

Matilda inwardly winced. On any given day, this sight would have been welcomed. A little fun and flirtation with a tourist was a perk for being the only single person in her friend group. But tonight…tonight she wasn't fit for unfamiliar company.

"Oh finally. There she is! Mat! Get over here." Krista Rey, a hairstylist, prowled toward Matilda. As usual, her reddish-brown hair was curled impeccably into beach waves despite the humidity in the bar. Her makeup was perfect too; she worked that eye shadow palette against her blue eyes and pale skin so it looked effortless.

Still, Matilda could read what was in her eyes. Mischief. Matchmaking mischief. She had half the mind to turn around with an excuse, but Krista wrapped an arm around hers. She looked over Matilda's shoulder. "Allie's not coming?"

"No. She's had it for the day."

"Phooey." Krista leaned in. "Well, you can still have some fun. This one is so cute. He's even here a few days."

"Is that supposed to be a positive?"

Krista tugged her into step, sighing. "Quit being a brat. Just come and say hi to him."

Reluctantly, she followed Krista's instructions, and she was met by a guy with light golden-brown skin, a square jaw and a bright, confident smile. But his brown eyes, rimmed in black, met hers with a smoldering, intense gaze. It was a brave move, if she thought so herself, and excitement pricked her senses. As she neared, she could see the barest of crow's-feet at his temples and the corners of his lips.

Her breath hitched. *Ooo-la-la.*

Matilda shifted her gaze to the two other women who were across the booth: the ever-cheerful brown-haired, brown-eyed Bess Chance who was practically bouncing in her seat with excitement, and dark haired and dark complected beauty Helen Singh waggling her eyebrows.

Too excited for their own good, if Matilda had a say in it.

Then, the guy stood with an expectant expression.

Oh no.

Matilda made to turn.

But Krista had a death grip on her arm. With a singsong voice, she said, "Jared. This is our dearest friend, Matilda. Matilda, Jared's here from Louisville for um—" she peered at him "—what are you here for?"

He cleared his throat. "Doing some research. Into…history."

"So interesting, right?" Bess chimed in, her cheeks darkening with mischief. She tucked her natural curls behind her ear. "And he's staying at Kite Flyer."

Kite Flyer was a short-term rental on the outskirts of town. The thought of its privacy, of the possibility of working out some of her stress in another way besides karaoke woke the butterflies in Matilda's belly, but she smothered them with a sip of her bourbon sour.

It wouldn't work out, not even for the night. This Jared seemed so…happy. And she was far from it right this second.

A nudge at her side brought her back to the present.

Right, she hadn't responded.

Her shoulders drooped, because she would need to be the bad person in all this. "History, huh? That is…interesting.

I'm really more of a fiction kind of girl, but good for you." All four pairs of eyes blinked back so she kept going. "And speaking of books, there's not a single one in Kite Flyer… which I find strange, and an FYI, the grill has a tendency to light on fire. Also, did you know that the owner is one of the bartenders here?"

Matilda had no idea why she couldn't stop talking, except that something in the way Jared was grinning at her made her feel giddy. Her cheeks were ablaze; she could just feel it.

It was time for her exit.

"Now if you'll excuse me y'all," Matilda said. "I'm going to finish this up at the bar and watch Lily hit her notes." She gestured to Lily, who was now practicing her scales, indicative of only one thing. "U2 must be next on the playlist." Then, she gave her friends the *you're in trouble* expression, and after one, final apologetic smile to Jared, Matilda turned away.

From behind, her friends clucked their disapproval, no doubt apologizing to Jared for her rudeness.

A killjoy, a party pooper, a grouch. That was 100 percent what her friends were thinking. But the threatening guilt was squashed down by the sight of a set of empty stools on the other side of the bar.

Her phone buzzed as she slid onto the open stool. It was a text from that familiar phone number she'd ignored earlier. Matilda, it's Noah. Listen to the voicemail. Call me back.

Curiosity reared its ugly head and clamored for attention.

You promised, her conscience reminded her.

It was too late; her thumb was already a traitor, scrolling her voicemail messages and pressing on the most recent.

Her ex-husband's voice sang in that same smooth alto: "Matilda, it's Noah. To get to the point—I'm going to be a dad. I thought you should know, since, well, the town will know soon enough. You know my mom. She thinks just because she had one part-time job at the radio station that she's got permission to talk about everyone's business," he half laughed. Matilda imagined him running his hands through his dark wavy hair. "You know how she always wanted to have a grandkid. Anyway. Call me."

It took a moment for Matilda to gather her thoughts, dumbfounded at the news, besieged by the image of Noah Philips and a nameless and faceless pregnant woman, with his mother, Finola, doing her damnedest as the town gossip.

Matilda covered with her mouth with a hand, and she was unsure whether she was going to vomit or cry. A tsunami of emotions assailed her.

Noah was going to be a father.

Noah, who'd kept her under his thumb.

Noah, who'd told her she wasn't enough.

Noah, who didn't want kids. Or so he'd said.

A squeak of wood against wood snatched her attention, and with her mind still squarely on her text, she turned her head to the person seating next to her.

It was Clark Seabird, the B & B landscape manager. A former Southern California beach bum, he was permanently tanned by the sun, and he such had a mild demeanor that he was considered the nicest person in town.

Matilda rallied, blinking rapidly to bring herself back to Mountain Rush. "Clark, how can I help you?"

"No 'Hello, how are you? What are you drinking?'"

"Are we playing this game?" She steepled her fingers together on the bar top. Clark didn't drink alcohol, and his hangout was the sports bar across town that had a massive TV set up and a bona fide menu. Which only meant that he was here for her, and for work, and it was important.

Matilda took back her previous thought. Sometimes it would be nice not to see someone familiar, and especially, someone from the B & B.

"*Someone* hasn't destressed from her shift." He waved down

the bartender. "An order of curly fries for my hangry friend, please."

Speaking of, she glanced once more at her girls and Jared, who'd resumed their conversation. Then, as if clued into her, Jared's gaze slid to hers. His lips curved into an inviting grin, and for a beat, she longed to be back there. She wanted to unhear Noah's voicemail. If she could've have rewritten history, she would have.

But there was no such thing. Especially not with Clark as a reminder that she'd reinvented herself, and she wouldn't let anyone down again.

"You're stalling, Clark." Matilda fished out a greasy fry from the basket that had been placed in front of them. Minutes had passed since and he had been going on about the weather—which in his case was a valid topic of discussion. But the fries were clearly an offering. Everyone in town knew that Matilda was ruled by her stomach.

"It's about the SE. We have an issue, with the landscaping."

The SE was what the staff had begun to call the total solar eclipse event, scheduled in a couple of weeks. The B & B was on its direct path of view, and the Espiritus had decided to open the B & B's outdoor space to the public, with admission.

The solar eclipse was the first of two events ruling Matilda's conscience and to-do lists. The other: a wedding a short week later. Both blessedly ensured the B & B had no vacancies, but required all hands on deck.

Not an issue on any given day, except for the small issue of Chef Allie being weeks from giving birth.

She crunched against the fry to mitigate her rise in panic. Her current plate of stress couldn't have one more crisis.

"Oh, Clark, don't do this to me," she said. "Don't say there's an issue. You're the landscaping whisperer. Hell, you're the weather whisperer."

The crowning glory of the B & B was its grounds, banked by seasonal blooming wildflowers and trees with leaves that changed colors at each season. Its maintenance was all attributed to him.

His expression was sullen. "We have an overgrowth of plants that are encroaching on vista point number two."

For the SE, they'd planned for four ticketed areas within the B & B's property limits with perfect views of the stars. Each was located on higher elevation and clear of tall foliage, especially trees, and was spacious enough to accommodate thirty people if seated in portable chairs. Secretly, Matilda had the inkling to scream "I'm the queen of the world" while standing in these areas.

That would not be proper general manager behavior though.

"Why is that an issue? You can still see the stars even with the overgrowth."

"Well, currently that area might only fit two-thirds of the chairs allotted for that space, and tickets for vista point number two are halfway sold out."

"So…clear the overgrowth?" The tone of her voice tilted upward in hopes that the solution was that easy.

"It's the honeysuckle," Clark answered with gruff.

The news landed like a brick between them. "Shit." She wiped her fingers on her napkin, understanding what Clark needed of her. Matilda would somehow have to convince Eva to trim back the wildflowers.

So, not easy in the slightest.

Those bushes were special; Eva had planted them as a remembrance to her late husband, Louis.

"Will you speak to her?" he asked.

She peered at Clark. He was a decade older than Matilda, and had been working at the B & B for just as many years. He was like family; he was respected; he had his hands in everyone's front or backyard as a landscape consultant—it wasn't unusual for Peak folks to have one or two side hustles. "Surely you can handle Eva."

"With or Without You" by U2 sounded through the speakers, and the bar exploded in cheers. The microphone squelched as Lily grabbed it off the stand with both hands. Above the noise, Clark said, "Eva about bit my head off the last time I suggested trimming the bushes back. If I said I wanted to plant palm trees, Eva would go with it. But those flowers? I mean, they're weeds. But she loves them." He shrugged one shoulder. "Please…will you do it?"

"I don't know," Matilda said, then bit the inside of her cheek. A manager she might be, but the harbinger of bad news for something as personal as Eva's honeysuckle?

Feelings. They could be…uncomfortable.

While Matilda had never met Eva's late husband, Louis—he'd died in Iraq well before Eva purchased the B & B—she had witnessed Eva's quiet mourning. Stray tears at odd times, a sudden need to take off for a short hike. One time, she'd spied Eva sobbing on her balcony after polishing off a little too much wine.

"The overgrowth will be worse in a couple of weeks. You know how these weeds double, triple even, in the spring."

With an elbow leaned against the bar, Matilda pressed two fingers against her left temple. Honeysuckle plus the chef plus Noah. "Gah…"

"No gah. Say yes."

She grumbled through Lily's undulating, though not quite in tune, voice.

"Please?" Clark rested a hand on her shoulder gently and shook it. "I don't want to feel Eva's ire. And you seem to know how to talk to her. She trusts you more than anyone else at the B & B when it comes to running it."

Matilda's face warmed at the compliment, and she blinked back the rush of emotions. *She trusts you.*

To be trusted, to trust, had been all she'd ever wanted, from anyone.

Clark leaned in. "Promise me you'll talk to her."

She stuck her bottom lip out. "What is it with that word?"

"What word?"

"Never mind." She sighed. "Fine…fine. I'll do it."

He pointed at her phone, which was face down. "You gonna put it on your calendar?"

She cackled. "What are you, my mother?" Though she flipped the phone over and thumbed into her calendar.

"I know how you are. Calendar ruled, with an alarm. Once it's in there, I know it's done. Or will get done." He peered over as she added *honeysuckle* to her calendar a week from now.

"Happy?" she asked.

"You're the best." He stood and hooted at the bartender. He clapped loudly as heads turned their way. "Another round for this angel on earth."

"All right, all right." She urged Clark back to sitting, embarrassed, eyes darting around. Once more, she met Jared's gaze, and something inside her flared, like the glow of lightning during a rainstorm.

A moment's fun was all she'd wanted for tonight. And yet, as it went on, all that continued to mount was pressure.

Jared though—he was a stranger. He knew nothing about her, or her past. Spending a few minutes with him could take her mind off the reality of when she'd have to tell Eva about the honeysuckle, when she'd have to scour for another chef to interview. When she had to deal with knowing Noah had moved on.

Tonight, she could let loose—something she hadn't done in so long.

So, she turned to Jared and smiled—not stopping to think about whether this was a good idea, or perhaps the biggest mistake she could possibly make.

Chapter Three

Jared blinked.

Had Matilda really just smiled—at *him*? Or had it been an inadvertent gesture, or a trick of the dim light?

To be honest, her walking away earlier had kind of stung. He could admit to having a bit of an ego, but even then, he wasn't used to being so outright rejected by a woman. Then again, the last three months had been comprised of countless moments such as these, of minuscule paper cuts to his soul, starting with his watch party. That critic's comment had uncorked decades of emotion, which had since overwhelmed him.

His emotions had been, and were still, everywhere. Doubt had filled every fiber of his being. Wherever he went, he'd felt out of place. More than that—a fraud. Sure, he'd always felt a little different, sometimes othered as a biracial Asian American in the South, but since that night, a filter had been stripped from his perspective. He realized that he didn't really know who he was, or where he came from.

It then affected all parts of his life and his work.

Especially his work.

In all cases, he'd arrived at the same conclusion. It was as his sister had suggested: that to feel better, to feel at peace, he needed to know more about Louis. Since Louis was dead, he'd decided that it was time to find out about him through his family.

The thought became an itch he had to scratch. Aided by the good old internet, it wasn't hard to trace Louis's family. A simple search for "Louis Espiritu US Army" led him to the About page of Spirit of the Shenandoah B & B website, where an Evangeline Espiritu had mentioned the memory of her late husband as her inspiration. The same website revealed that there were two other Espiritus in the business, Francesca and Gabriella, who he had surmised were her daughters.

It had then led him to their social media, which he pored over.

With the blessing and probably relief from his boss—Jared had been unfocused—he'd packed up his car for Peak.

Jared thought he hit pay dirt in Mountain Rush, among Matilda's friends. He'd been ambushed upon his arrival. Their conversation engulfed him so that he'd allowed himself to relax and gather his thoughts for some initial "research" about what they knew about the Espiritu family. But they were surprisingly tight-lipped, intent instead on trying to hook him up with their friend.

Then he met Matilda, and his mission to find his father's family took a back seat. She was gorgeous, with dark wavy hair that landed just below her shoulders. She had alabaster skin, blue eyes and a heart-shaped face. But it was her overall demeanor that intrigued Jared. Like nothing could ruffle her feathers.

It compelled him. He wanted to be around her.

Matilda's rejection, however, had reminded him that he didn't belong at Peak.

But that look just now…that was an invitation, wasn't it?

One more time, he said to himself. *Look at me one more time.*

Then, finally, she lifted her gaze to him. Her head tilted minutely once more.

A green light.

Relief stirred inside him. Need. Want. They sent tingles to his fingertips, snagging him from his thoughts, pulling him to his feet.

Time would only tell if he'd made the right decision by risking his dream job for his impulsive decision to come to the Shenandoah Valley. And especially, keeping it a secret from everyone except Emma. He had no plans on what to do or say once he revealed himself.

But right this second, he was drawn to only one person—Matilda. For the chance to be the subject of her confidence—and, if he was lucky enough, a night in her arms—would give him much-needed courage for tomorrow's short trek up the hill.

But first he'd have to displace the man sitting next to her.

As he neared, the gray-haired man straightened on the stool, but Matilda laid a hand on his forearm. "It's fine, Clark."

"You sure?"

"Yes. And I'll take care of the tab."

"Great. I'll see you on Monday, Mat." Clark stood, towering over Jared's five-eleven frame, and with a final nod, sidestepped away.

Small towns. They were interesting. Louisville wasn't exactly a massive city, but it was large enough not to have to run into someone he knew every day. Peak, however, since his arrival this afternoon, had already shown some of its colors.

Like how invested those ladies were to set him and Matilda up, and Clark's protectiveness. Like this place was enclosed in its own dome, in which it was clear that he wasn't local.

"May I?" Jared gestured to the barstool.

"It's free, if that's what you're asking."

His lips quirked—she was specific.

Matilda continued to face away from him, toward the person on the stage finishing up her song. Applause rang through the crowd, and once more Jared clapped along. As the cheering simmered down, he asked if Matilda wanted another drink, waving the bartender down with a hand.

She lifted her glass. “I’m all set. Thanks.”

An awkward pause ensued where he took a pull of his beer. Where was his game? Apparently, he’d forgotten it when he crossed the Virginia state line.

He forced words out of his mouth before he could think twice. “So, you’re a local.”

She snorted; his cheeks heated at his pedestrian question. *Smooth, Sotheby. Smooth.* “Born and bred. Well, except for a few years of travel, I’m a proud local.”

There were layers in her tone, in her words. But one thing was certain. She knew this place, and people potentially, like the back of her hand. Which meant she could be a source of information about the Espiritu family. And yet, despite his logic trying to worm its way through his psyche, he couldn’t stop looking at her lips, at its well-traced Cupid’s bow—and wondering how sweet they tasted.

“So what does a local do around here?” Jared asked, mentally kicking himself for sounding like an amateur.

She laughed. “Do you mean like work and live and eat like any other town in any other state? Just because we’re in the valley doesn’t mean we’re completely provincial, you know.”

Her straightforwardness had him shifting in the stool, and her candidness relaxed him. She wasn’t easily impressed and it lessened the pressure. “Sorry. I swear I’m usually much better than this.”

“Oh? But your sentences are already so profound.” She took a sip. “Hopefully you don’t have to write up some of that research you’re going to be doing.”

Jared had the desire to excuse himself. He’d been initially attracted to her straightforwardness—these days it was all he wanted—but he’d obviously mistaken her gesture for welcome.

But then her lips curved into a grin, so he pushed on.

"Actually, my memory's a safe." He tapped on his head. "All I need is to listen or watch something once and it's all locked up. Directions, facts, recipes…"

An eyebrow rose. "Recipes?"

With that, Jared knew he was on better footing. Food facts for the win. "Yeah. Down to the teaspoon."

She breathed out. "If only that was a skill everyone had."

"What do you mean?"

She shook her head. "Nothing. Just thinking about work."

"But I bet you're a calendar person." He raised his eyebrows. "Instead of to-do lists, you track your tasks in time blocks and set alarms for everything."

An eyebrow plunged. "How did you…"

Jared gestured down to the bar top, where her calendar app was up. It was color coded and absolutely chock-full.

Her work was her life.

She grinned and flipped her phone over. "Someone's a little nosy."

"No, just observant."

"Intrusive. And obviously a little happy-go-lucky. With the way you cozied up to my friends, without a lick of fear."

"Fear?" Both turned toward the rowdy group, who were singing along to the music. "Of them?"

Her face softened then. "You're right. They are the best people. No need to fear, unless you cross them."

He raised his hands. "I'm harmless, I swear."

"We'll see about that," she said under her breath, a message that stirred something inside of him.

Then, she brought the glass to her lips. In an almost slow motion effect, he watched her tongue dart out for a small taste of her cocktail.

That stir? It turned into a yank at his libido.

He raised his eyes to hers—she was staring at him too.

After lifting her lips from the edge of the glass, a small dot of liquid remained perched on her lip.

On instinct, he reached forward. "You've got a drop right there." With a nod of consent from her, he padded a thumb against her lip, lightly smearing her lipstick.

His breath hitched at the contact, at how she scoured his face and at how the rest of the world seemed to quiet.

When he lowered his hand, she leaned forward. The scent of her perfume reached his nostrils, turning his insides to mush. "How old are you?" she asked.

The question jostled him out of his hazy thoughts, though he refused to move from her proximity. "Thirty."

Her gaze dropped, and she leaned back. "Ah. I'm…forty." She hesitated, then ran a hand through her hair. He could practically see a window closing in her mind. "And that is my cue to go."

"Why?"

She smiled at him. "Because I should really stay in my lane."

That confused him. "There are lanes?"

She sighed. "Definitely something a thirty-year-old would say."

Inwardly, Jared winced. He didn't want to be hustled into a box, to be grouped into a set of characteristics. But he relaxed into his seat. "Interesting. You don't think I can hang with you because of my age."

Her eyes flashed. "No. I don't think you can."

It was a dare. And he was never the kind of person to shy away from one. In this case, there wasn't much to lose, especially in his mission to find his father's family. "Wow. Hmm. That's too bad, because I might surprise you. Impress you, even."

She downed the rest of her drink, and as her throat worked, he couldn't take her eyes off her slender neck. Then, she swiped her mouth with the back of her hand. "All right, then, you. Impress me. Let's go." She hopped off the stool.

Surprised, he said, "Go?"

"Onstage."

He blew out a laugh. "And then what? Then you'll have a drink with me?"

One shoulder jutted upward. "Perhaps a duet with me will earn you more time. But only if you give it all you've got."

"So, let me get this straight." He was feeling warm from beer and the surge of bravado. "You may or may not have a drink with me if I go up there with you and sing in front of all of these strangers?"

"That's right. But if you don't do it, it's a definite goodbye."

Jared couldn't keep his smile from bursting forth. Among his friends, he was unbeatable at karaoke—and he planned to hustle her with the microphone. "Okay. Let's go."

Her eyes widened. "Yeah?"

"If that's what it'll take? Then hell yeah."

With the mic in his hand, Jared's insides unwound. Much like his favorite chef's knife, he was going to wield it with the same expertise, if anything but to rise to Matilda's challenge.

Staying in one's lane—what the hell did that mean anyway? People should be able to do what they want, and be who they want, right? Not to mention change, if the opportunity came up.

No, he'd have to agree to disagree with her about that one—

"I choose this." Matilda's voice interrupted his train of thought as she pointed at one title from a list of songs at a small table onstage. A classic: "(I've Had) The Time of My Life" from *Dirty Dancing.*

"Easy."

A smile grew on her lips. She leaned forward and mimed

the number to the DJ offstage, then gestured to a television. "The lyrics will come up on the screen right here."

"Now you're the one being sweet," he said. "I don't need the lyrics."

Her eyebrows lifted in surprise as the music started, and when he sang on cue, the smile on her face expanded to the size of the room.

It turned out that Matilda didn't need the lyrics either. She also knew some of the dance moves.

It could have been the lights, the beer, the people egging them on with their hooting, or Matilda putting her all into the performance, but as they sang, Jared's whiplash emotions settled.

His foundation, his whole sense of self had shifted the night of the watch party and since then he'd been living under a storm cloud. It was as if Matilda had ushered in the sun with this brief peek into her fun side.

Jared wanted this feeling to last, at least for the night.

He risked reaching out for Matilda's hand as the end of the song neared, and to his relief, she didn't keep him hanging, instead linking her fingers with his. She squeezed it, a sign for him to stick the crescendo, and they both raised their hands up, breathless, sweaty and spent.

The audience was on its feet, and after placing their microphones back into their holders, he faced her and took her other hand into his. He looked across to her dark eyes, her parted lips, reddened cheeks and her heaving chest.

Leaning his face closer to the microphone, he said, "Now will you have a drink with me?"

The audience screamed encouragement, for her to say yes.

Matilda's face stilled, lips pressed into a line. The wait lasted a few seconds, though just enough time for Jared to doubt being so public with his request.

Then, she nodded. "I suppose I can make room in my lane."

The audience cheered; Jared's knees almost gave out in relief.

"What's your poison?" he asked when they finally were off the stage, as he waved down the bartender.

He felt a squeeze against his fingers and met her eyes. "Do you really want to know?" she said, just loud enough for him to hear.

He tipped his head down. "I'm down for anything. Another song? Dinner? Or maybe tomorrow if that works better. I'm here a few days—" he began, his adrenaline flying high.

But he was stopped by the move of her hands up his chest, to his shoulders. Her fingers gently pressed against his lips. "Let's have this drink at your place."

His answer came as swift as his next heartbeat. "Let's go."

Chapter Four

Matilda padded through the dim bedroom while cocooned in a fleece blanket, one eye shut and the other adjusting to her surroundings. She cringed with each footstep as Kite Flyer's floors groaned beneath her. Her destination—the kitchen table, where her phone was buzzing.

She had been tempted to let the call go to voicemail in case it was Noah. But phone calls that came in at dawn were never good news. With the way her girlfriends had been partying at Mountain Rush when she and Jared had left, she couldn't be sure that one of them didn't find themselves in some kind of trouble.

Then again, Jared, asleep behind her, was proof that she herself was involved with her own shenanigans.

As if on cue, a swirl of need began in her belly, and Matilda wrapped the blanket around her even tighter. There were shenanigans all right; it had been a while since she'd laughed so much, on top of being made love to.

She inhaled a long breath to let the feeling pass, because her phone, now doing its own shimmy on the table, was a reminder that she had responsibilities, even if it was her day off. A quick look at the clock on the wall—five fifty-eight in the morning.

Thankfully, she crossed the room to the kitchen without impaling herself on anything along the way, where a lamp on the corner illuminated the mess Kite Flyer was in.

Their clothes were like breadcrumbs on the gray hardwood floors, from when they'd locked lips at the front door's threshold. On the kitchen counter was a fully demolished carton of ice cream, with two spoons in the sink. And on the stove was a pot and a pan, crusted with tomato sauce from the pasta marinara that Jared whipped up.

She had been satiated through and through in all the right ways.

A buzz knocked Matilda out of her thoughts, and she snatched the phone from the table as a text flew in. It was from Allie: I'm having contractions.

Matilda clicked to call. As the phone rang, she scooped up her clothing. One boot at the front door. The other under the couch. Her bra draped over a stool. *Shit.* Where was her underwear?

"I think it's time," Allie said without preamble. Her voice was shrill.

"Where are you?" She thought she saw a flash of white under the coffee table. But what she retrieved was a sock with printed chopsticks—one of Jared's. Drat.

"I'm already at the B & B. I was so uncomfortable that I couldn't sleep last night so I thought I'd get started on breakfast. Mat, it's too early. I'm only at thirty-two weeks…ohh."

"Wait—what do you mean, contractions? Why are you moaning?" Matilda decided she was going to go commando. She wiggled herself into her bra, though struggled with the straps.

"It means that I'm having a baby!" She grunted. "My goodness. I need to go to the ER. But Mat, I just slipped a quiche in the oven, and I started prepping the fruit. Do I put it all back in the fridge? I don't want the food to go bad." Allie's voice shook, her rising panic palpable through the phone.

Okay. This wasn't good. But above all else, she had to keep Allie calm, or at least within reason. She shut her eyes to clear her own thoughts and dug into what she was good at: organization. "Allie. Breathe. Forget about the food. Did you call Eugene?"

"That husband of mine is MIA!" she all but screamed into the phone, so loud that Matilda took it off her ear.

This *really* wasn't good. Allie's neurosurgeon husband was apparently once more in the doghouse.

"Babe," Matilda cajoled, "do you mean that you don't know where he is, or that he's at work?"

"It means the same thing, doesn't it? His calls are going to voicemail." Allie groaned and then…nothing.

"Oh God," Matilda murmured, running her hands through her hair. She'd had the experience of being a bridesmaid a dozen times, but Allie was the second of their friends to have a baby. Krista had teenagers and was pregnant so long ago and Matilda wasn't around for their birth.

Scratch that, Noah was going to have a baby too.

And like a zip of a needle on vinyl, the full truth lay clear before her.

She was behind once more. People were moving on. Doing big things while she couldn't seem to fulfill the promises she'd made.

Her eyes darted to the bedroom, to the dark shadow underneath the covers. The shadow that was thirty years old.

What was she doing messing around with someone so young? She wasn't ageist, per se. But at forty, she'd already been through her share of milestones, major and minor. She'd fallen in love. She'd had her heart broken. She'd gotten married and gotten divorced. After her failed marriage, she had started from scratch. Frankly, it was enough to try and shore up all the things she'd missed out on, not to have to worry about someone else who didn't know what they wanted in life.

Okay, so Jared wasn't a baby. He was anything but. In fact,

last night, she'd marveled time and again at how gentle he was and how keen he'd been to fulfill her physical needs.

But if she had been fooled in her twenties to have latched herself on to Noah like he had been her life preserver, certainly Jared was not in the same headspace as her. He couldn't understand what her priorities were at the moment.

Allie's groan woke Matilda from her thoughts and by the grace of everything good, her project management skills emerged. "Allie," she said now, "what I want you to do is go sit in the front room. I'll call Eva and the girls. You call your OB."

"But the quiche."

Matilda resumed looking for her clothes. "The quiche will be fine. Are you walking to the front room?"

"Yes."

"Okay. I'm hanging up right now."

"Okay."

Matilda thumbed the red button and stared at the screen while the consequences of Allie's early labor materialized.

She had no replacement chef. Matilda had thought she'd been able to count on another two weeks.

Where was she going to find one in the last minute? She'd exhausted her options.

"What's going on?" A gruff voice sounded from the other side of the house. The shadow that was under the covers was now sitting up.

"N-nothing." She lost track of what she was doing, thumbs hovering over her phone screen.

"That didn't sound like nothing."

Focus, Matilda. "Wait, let me think for a sec…"

Resetting herself, Matilda called Eva, and to her relief, her boss answered at the first ring. "Chef's in labor."

"What?" Rustling began in Eva's side of the world. "I'm putting on my robe."

"Are either of the girls awake? Allie needs a ride to the hospital."

"Headed to Frankie's now—she can drive. Liam's at his dad's for the night. I'll grab Gabby to man the kitchen." Seconds later, a knock sounded, followed by familiar voices in various levels of alto. Once more, Matilda was grateful that Eva's two daughters, Francesca and Gabriella, lived on the B & B grounds. "Where are you, Mat?"

"Still home." Sort of. "But I'm getting dressed now. I'll come in and help with breakfast."

"I can call in Drea. It's your day off."

"True." Drea was one of their all-purpose assistants, brought in for events and emergencies. A Jill-of-all-trades, Drea knew all the aspects of hotel management, and though couldn't commit to regular hours, could jump in on a second's notice.

The pad of footsteps brought Matilda's gaze to the doorway, which was now filled by Jared's frame. The band of his lounge pants hung low on his hips. Arms crossed, he had leaned against the doorway, all gorgeous and cozy.

He was pure temptation. She could feel the warmth of his skin from where she was standing, and her memory flashed to hours before when she was under him, sheltered and warmed by the heat of his body.

A delicious chill raced up her spine, but she halted it before it ignited her drool.

No. More important things were happening, and he was a distraction.

Which was exactly why she needed to go, right now.

She spoke into the phone. "By the time Drea's ready, I can be there. See you in a bit?"

"Bit," Eva said before hanging up.

"Sounds serious," Jared said, straightening, concern on his face.

"It is. I've got to get to work."

"I thought it was your day off." A shadow flitted across his eyes—disappointment.

All of which she couldn't deal with. Her priorities didn't include having to explain herself to a one-night stand. As memorable as it was going to be. "It's an emergency," she said anyway, and donned the next item of clothing she found.

"Can I help?"

"Not really," she added, eyes drifting to the ground, gathering her thoughts, her routine words. Might as well get it over and done with—because besides her theories on promises, she also had one about honesty too. Namely, that it was 100 percent necessary in any relationship. "Listen. About last night."

He stepped toward her and Matilda's skin warmed out of instinct. His demeanor, his vibe, was one she couldn't put her finger on. He was both serious and playful with how his eyes searched hers and with what seemed like a permanent grin on his lips. So drawn to him that when he placed a hand on her waist, she leaned forward, eyes shutting. And she was rewarded by a kiss on her cheek. "Last night was amazing," he whispered into her skin. "And I'd love to see you again."

Yet, despite how she felt otherwise, she shook her head. "No."

"No, it wasn't amazing?" An eyebrow rose, the action so cute that Matilda's heart squeezed.

"That's not what I mean." A giggle escaped her lips. An actual, honest to goodness giggle. Because it was more than amazing. It was honestly the best she'd had since…

She couldn't even remember, that's how sad it was. For a man his age, for him to be so generous, so sweet, and so… energetic.

"What *did* you mean?"

"That though you were amazing, and that while this was fun, there won't be a second time."

"Oh." He dropped his hand from her hip.

She steeled herself to keep going, though if she was being honest, she wished Jared hadn't let go. "It's nothing personal. It's me, not you." She internally winced. "I know that sounds cliché, but…"

A beat passed, and then two, after which he said, his smile turning tepid, "You're right. That's super cliché."

"There's so much going on." Her mouth seemed to have a life of its own. "I don't have—" the wherewithal, the brain space, the capacity "—the time. For feelings."

Looking away and leaving Matilda wishing that there was a better way to cut and run, he stepped back. "Can I help you grab your stuff? Or I can, I dunno, make you coffee?"

"I hate to ask, but I'll need a ride back to Mountain Rush. Could you give me one?" Kite Flyer was a mile away from the bar, and they'd taken his car.

His expression softened. "Of course."

Awkwardness rose, and Matilda wanted out more than ever. "Great. I'll—" she pointed to the bedroom "—just head in to change."

Matilda brushed past him without another word.

Because if there was one thing worse than promises broken, it was goodbyes.

"Thank heavens!"

The greeting and a hug from Evangeline Espiritu eased Matilda's brooding heart when she entered the double doors of Spirit of the Shenandoah B & B, along with the delicious smells of vanilla and cinnamon wafting from the kitchen.

"Eight months. Can she have a baby at eight months?" Matilda asked.

"Yes, she can. We'll have to wait and see what her doctor says. But Frankie's with her." Eva squeezed her tight.

Though Eva was shorter than Matilda by a couple of inches, her mama bear hug allowed for Matilda's thoughts to reset.

She pushed away the slight regret of leaving Jared without her phone number, and made room for the excitement that her best friend was, in fact, having a baby. It also clearly shone the spotlight on the fact that Matilda would need to come clean to Eva—that there was no chef in line to take Allie's place.

"Any updates from Frankie?" Matilda asked.

Eva stepped back, tucking in the strands of her gray-streaked brown hair. Had it not been for her hair and the way the sides of her mouth and eyes crinkled when she smiled, no one would be the wiser that Eva was fifty. "They're already checked into the ER. Allie's OB is on the way."

"And Eugene?"

A grimace appeared on Eva's face. "I have no idea."

"Oh dear." Looking over Eva's shoulder, figures passed by. "A guest just came down."

"First for breakfast." She heaved a breath. "Gabby isn't too happy that she's on kitchen duty. We should step in."

Matilda followed the clack of Eva's shoes against the multi-colored brown bamboo flooring deeper into the B & B, where the foyer transitioned to the expanse of the four communal areas. Dim bulbs from modern lamps lit seating areas, aided by soft sunlight streaming through the windows.

Unlike so many of the B & B's in the area, Spirit of the Shenandoah carried a special vibe, and that was what intrigued Matilda the most. There was not a single trinket or tchotchke around. The minimalist decor allowed the nature outside to be the star. Large wide curtainless windows in the entry and dining areas, clean lines, sustainable materials. Long, lean comfortable couches, soothing modern instrumental in the background. A bookshelf of classic novels with embossed covers lined up on one wall.

The B & B was cozy, comfortable and welcoming.

Then there was the kitchen, which showcased every bit of luxury. No expense was spared to provide the finest food service to guests, from the high-end appliances to custom tableware sculpted by a local potter. Allie had been allowed the freedom to source the best ingredients, from bread to meat products, and to start a vegetable garden out back.

But with the way Gabby, Eva's twenty-six-year-old daughter, was at cursing at the stove, it was as if she was being forced to work in a dungeon.

"I'll check on the guests," Eva whispered, gesturing toward the four-season space off the kitchen, where two guests were seated. The tables had been set for the morning.

"I'll—" Matilda worriedly looked over her shoulder "—help out here."

She nodded. "After, we need to talk about the next chef."

As Matilda watched Eva walk away, a glob of worry bunched itself at the base of her throat, though she nodded back.

Would she be fired? Worse, would Eva be disappointed with her? It wasn't as if Matilda hadn't tried. She'd listed the position on job boards and accessed her network of B & B folks. She'd interviewed a dozen chefs.

None had panned out. Either the chefs weren't of the caliber Eva was looking for, or they'd decided that the job description wasn't their cup of tea. A B & B chef wasn't a glamorous position. Every once in a while, the chef would need to placate their guests. Allie had done her share of fielding complaints, of being asked by guests to have their beds made, to take out the trash or bring room service.

"Dammit," Gabby squeaked from behind, snapping Matilda out of her thoughts.

"Hey, what's up?" Scanning the countertops, Matilda spotted the quiche under a clear dome. Thank goodness Allie had the foresight to get that into the oven. The woman was a rock star.

"Mr. Brighton mentioned he wanted a fruit compote. So—" she gestured to the simmering saucepan with her left hand "—I'm trying to get ahead of it."

Looking into the pan, it was clear that there was indeed fruit in there, but it was turning into a blackened mess. "Oh gosh, let's, um..." Matilda flipped the burner off and took a deep breath. "I think it's done."

It was more than done. The fruit might as well have been skewered and dangled over an open fire. Still, she offered Gabby a smile, nose wiggling at the burnt smell now invading the kitchen.

"I should have been the one to take Allie. Me and this?" She gestured at the behemoth of a cooking range. "Not compatible. Give me a timeline and a spreadsheet and I'm good. I like to eat food, but this is another thing."

"It's fine, Gabby." Though really, it wasn't, because there was no one to call on to take her place, but Matilda's goal was to keep everyone calm. "You're doing great."

"Really?" Her eyebrows furrowed.

"Really. But how about I take this from you before the fire alarm goes off?" She gently disarmed her off the ladle.

She burst out with a laugh. "Hey!"

"Look. No one is good at everything. I'd rather you focus on what you are excellent at. Namely Roland-Shim?"

Gabby was the B & B's wedding planner and also its social media presence, and the Roland-Shim wedding was the first of the season in three weeks.

"You don't have to tell me twice." She pursed her lips. "Though a photo of this might be good for a behind the scenes series."

"Please don't. We shouldn't scare off potential guests." Or chefs for that matter. They had a reputation to protect.

Eva walked in. "One each of orange juice and coffee. Both will take the quiche." Relief played across her features for a beat, followed by concern. "Is something burning?"

"Nope," Gabby said. "I think that's the new candle, called 'fireplace.'"

"Um, no, it's actually called 'burnt AF,'" Matilda whispered.

Eva lifted an eyebrow. "What?"

"Orange juice and coffee, coming up," Gabby choked out with a laugh.

Together, Matilda and Gabby readied the drinks under Eva's watchful and suspicious gaze, and despite the fact that she usually brightened at helping to prep breakfast—it was a nice change from making schedules and dealing with customer inquiries—she could read Eva's thoughts.

What were they going to do in the short-term, and especially in the long-term?

It wasn't ideal, but Matilda *could* call back one of the chefs that weren't quite up to snuff. In fact, one was within an hour's drive, and they weren't employed at the moment. But that chef wasn't very serious, almost a joker, and she wasn't sure if he would be a fit.

Thinking of the unserious… Matilda's mind wandered to last night, and scenes with Jared played in a quick clip. Jared was *not* a joker, but had a lightness about him. His easy laugh; his curiosity. That despite not knowing one another, how quickly he discovered how to please her in bed.

At the clang of a plate on the countertop, Matilda woke.

She really had to stop thinking about Jared.

This was her problem. Matilda had learned during therapy that her loyalty caused her to take relationships from zero to one hundred. She cared too much, and therefore, she had surmised, that caring not at all for the occasional fling and the average stranger was her best course of action.

Oh but his kisses…

The distinct ring of the bell on the check-in desk chimed and Matilda frowned. They weren't expecting any check-ins until this afternoon. "I'll grab that."

Wiping her hands on a kitchen towel, she darted to the foyer with her professional smile.

Only for her footsteps to slow when her vision tilted a smidge.

Because the person at the front desk was Jared, the man she had left behind at Mountain Rush's parking lot. The man who shouldn't be here.

She blinked. Every part of her tingled with the memory of last night. Yes, she'd told him that there would not be a repeat of their escapade, but seeing him now elicited a smile…

Except, he wasn't quite mirroring her expression. In fact, he was sporting a grimace.

"What are you doing here?" she asked at the same time he asked, "You…work here?"

"I do."

"Evangeline Espiritu." His voice was laced with urgency. "You know her? And Francesca and Gabriella?"

It was odd, hearing all of the Espiritus' names in full. Especially from him. Matilda hadn't called them by their full names in forever. "Um, yeah. Because I work here. This is their family business." Suspicion entered her tone. "Wait, do you know them too?"

"They…" His Adam's apple bobbed. "They're my family."

Chapter Five

"What are you talking about? What do you mean, family?" asked Matilda.

Jared's words were stuck in his throat as his mind attempted to piece together this scenario.

He'd admittedly felt dejected when he dropped off Matilda at her Bronco this morning. He'd thought…

He'd sworn that there had been a connection between them, beyond the spark of physical attraction. True, they hadn't gotten into deep conversation. There were no exchanges of last names or what they did for a living. They'd kept to safe topics, like favorite karaoke songs of all time, books and movies, and home improvement—which had stemmed from how Kite Flyer was a unique little place in need of a bit of upkeep. But it was how they'd spoken to one another, in soft voices, eyes locked. Like what they had was intimate on the cellular level.

It all had felt so real, and her rejection had been like sliding on black ice. Completely unexpected.

Jared had remained respectful despite his disappointment, resigned to the idea that what they'd had was a simple one-night stand. And he'd been grateful that it was she who brought the encounter back to reality. Especially since he still had his reason for being at Peak in the first place: meeting Louis Espiritu's family.

It had been, and continued to be, surreal.

"My father's family," he said, clarifying after gathering the fringe of his thoughts.

"Wait. I'm sorry." Matilda rested her hand on the bar top of the check-in desk, like she was bracing herself. She shook her head. "I think I'm hearing things. So, you're not here to see me?"

"No, I'm not." He frowned, because he was getting it all mixed up, his purpose for being here and his desire to see Matilda again. "Look, you don't have to worry about last night. I get it, no strings. But I'm here for a different reason. I'm here to see Evangeline and Fran—"

"Eva," she interrupted firmly. "Her name is Eva. And Frankie and Gabby. Those are their names."

It hearkened the moment when he cooked risotto just a hair too long and ended up with a sticky mess. Except at the moment, he wasn't sure what he'd done. "Why are you angry?"

She looked over her shoulder and lifted both palms as if to calm herself, lips pursing. "I'm not angry."

"If this isn't angry, then I wouldn't want to be around you when you are," he joked, though it didn't quite land by her expression. He cleared his throat, to reset the moment.

Two guests climbed down the stairway behind Matilda. They were in hiking gear, in slick cargo pants and windbreakers that swished as they walked. One was carrying a pair of walking sticks.

Jared waited until they were out the front door before he turned back to Mathilda. "So, um…are any of them here?"

"No." She seemed to turn to stone. "This has to be some kind of sick joke. I've known the Espiritus for five years. They've never mentioned you. In fact—" she fished her phone out of her pocket "—speak quickly because I'm a hair away from calling the sheriff."

"Wait." Confusion descended upon him. "This is a simple request. I want to speak to one of the Espiritus."

Her eyes narrowed. "I'm calling right this second if you don't leave. This is not funny."

"No. It's not at all." He reached out with a hand. "Please, put the phone away."

She stepped out of his reach.

This wasn't going well. He had hoped to keep his story to himself until he found the Espiritus, but it was clear that Matilda was their bouncer.

"My father was Louis Espiritu," he began. "He and my mother had a thing, and here I am."

"But...he's...dead..." Her hand flew to her mouth.

"I know he's dead. I've known about him for a while, since I was a kid. I thought I could sweep it under the rug, and I did for a while and now, well...now I feel different." He hiked his hands against his hips, the breath suddenly sucked from his lungs. He was almost woozy admitting it.

He'd spent late nights processing whether or not he'd wanted to meet his father's family, and coming to terms with the answer had been why he had waited so long.

It had been easier to deny the truth of their existence.

Easier to move through the world.

Easier to get the next thing done in his life.

It was easier just to turn his back to it.

And he had been right. Because facing it now caused him to be unsteady.

"No," Matilda said once more; her tone brought Jared to the present. "Nope. No way. Not even a chance." Matilda rounded the table and halfway spun him around. "Not on my watch."

"Your watch...what?" He was being pushed outside. "Hold on a sec, please..."

"Hello? Matilda, what's going on?" A woman's voice rose above both their chatter, properly silencing them. Jared focused on the figure walking toward them.

She was a woman of Asian descent with light brown skin and

light brown hair streaked with gray that landed just below her shoulders. She was wearing a striped apron with the B & B's logo. She was a few inches shorter than him, but with a strong, slim build. She looked to be his mother's age.

"Evangeline," he whispered. It dawned on him then that she wasn't just Asian, but Filipino, like Louis. Like him.

"Eva," Matilda said with emphasis, while slicing him with a glare. Then, she straightened, her face relaxing. "Eva, this is Jared."

"Sotheby. Jared Sotheby," he said.

"Why does that name sound familiar?" Eva's expression turned curious.

Jared's heart beat a steady drum. Did she know about him?

"You're that chef." She stuck out a hand, eyes rounded in glee. Dumbfounded, Jared took it. "That chef on CBN a few months ago, right?" she continued. "You made sisig." Then, her gaze bounced between him and Matilda. "This…is such a great surprise. Matilda, is he here to interview?"

Interview? He glanced back at Matilda, who looked frazzled for the first time since he'd met her.

"Oh, um…" Matilda stared, eyes meeting his. In her gaze was a message, and it told him to keep quiet.

"Gabby! Where are you going?" Eva broke the stalemate and brushed past him, to someone walking out a rear entrance.

Gabby. Gabriella.

His father's daughter.

His half sister.

As soon as the thought materialized, so did the woman. She reentered with a wary expression on her face. "Ma, I told you I was heading out. I'll be back in time to get lunch ready. Or to help, anyway." Her eyeballs rolled up, as if something was written on the ceiling. "But I have to double-check the flower shop order, and thought I should study since I've got my test…"

"Before you do, you should meet someone first." Eva scooped her up by the elbow and all but dragged her closer.

Jared couldn't take his eyes off of Gabby.

Pixie-cut dark hair with highlights. Brown doe-eyes. Prominent cheekbones.

His lungs halted.

"Oh wow! You're Jared Sotheby," she said, then tilted her head toward her mother. "And oh my God! Are you our new chef? Did Mom hire you?" For a beat, she covered her mouth with her hands and said, "Mom, are we going to be serving Filipino food? But even if we don't, can you cook our meals? Because I can't cook worth a damn, and Mom…well…"

Eva lifted both hands in exasperation. "Goodness."

The banter elicited a laugh from Jared, which he quickly disguised as a cough.

Next to him, Matilda was as still as a statue.

His goal had been to find the Espiritus. It had ruled his every action in the last three months. But his imagination never did go past this awkward moment, and now, he didn't quite know what his next step was.

"It's…nice to meet you." He offered his hand to Gabby, and when she shook it, he glanced down. Her hands looked like his, their fingers shaped similarly, with prominent knuckles. Sure, a million other people likely had the same shape of fingers, but this was something.

Because they shared some of the same DNA.

After she let go, Gabby said, "For what it's worth, I didn't agree with Will Gonzalez. No dish has to live up to anyone's criteria of identity."

"That…thank you." The truth of her words said so eloquently rendered him speechless. It continued to be hard for him to discern how Will's critique had affected him, and somehow, she'd summed it up in one small sentence.

"Is this why you've been so cagey the last couple of days?"

Gabby slid her eyes to Matilda. "To be honest, I was a little worried about your chef hire. You haven't really been forthcoming—"

"He's not our chef," Matilda interrupted, voice rising. "To tell you the truth, Eva..."

Jared recalled Matilda's phone call this morning, his thoughts processing the situation quickly: *chef's in labor...ride to the hospital...help with breakfast.*

The B & B needed a chef pronto, and he was there. Perfect timing.

"She's right," Jared cut in. "I'm not your chef *yet*. I'm here to interview."

Jared looked out toward the expanse of the land behind the B & B, though his brain spun with possibility. He had done it. He'd found the Espiritus.

"Are you listening to me?" Matilda said in between jagged breaths. "You can't work here."

She'd dragged him out the back door under the guise of a B & B tour, but since they stepped away from Eva and Gabby, all she'd done was snap at him.

"Why not? You need a chef. I'm a chef."

"No. No." Her cheeks had gone red. "You're not staying."

"*They* seem to want me to stay. So much that Eva wants to interview me herself." He gestured toward Eva's outline against the B & B's back windows.

"This isn't a game."

"I never said it was. It's never been." He caught her gaze. "This is very serious for me too."

Her head shook minutely. "This is like a soap opera unfolding and I'm not going to be a part of it. Do you know what Louis Espiritu means to this family? I've never met the man but he's like a ghost walking through these halls. You coming here would ruin things. It would ruin them. Eva... Eva shouldn't have to know about you, about this."

He frowned. "That's harsh. I'm a person, not just a fact."

"That's not what I meant." She was speaking swiftly, her voice softening. "But can you see what I'm trying to get at? How your dropping this bombshell could hurt them?"

Her words took his excitement down a few notches. Frankly, he hadn't stopped to consider how his appearance might affect the Espiritus. After all, it was he who had been left behind. It had been his mother who was the "other woman."

Did he really want to have a full-fledged reunion of sorts with the Espiritus, in which they had to rehash how they were all related? Did he really want the soap opera?

His answer came quickly.

No. He had a pretty good life. He had friends, a career that motivated him. He was loved. And that was enough, right?

And yet, every fiber of his being objected. He was here because of this mismatch between his brain and his heart. He was here because it had caused him so much confusion that the last good meal he'd cooked up was the night of the watch party. When his very identity, it seemed, had been questioned by a critic.

"What would *you* do?" he asked.

She turned away from him just as a gust of cool wind cut between them. "I don't know." Her face softened. "Eva hired me despite my lack of experience. She taught me everything about this business. Part of that was understanding how she thinks and how she works. That woman appears strong. She's got a shell of armor, but she's soft inside. If she finds out who you are, that the man she loved and trusted cheated on her, then her heart's going to break." She crossed her arms in a hug. "You either have to go, or stay and tell her who you are right this second. But you can't lie to her, Jared."

Her sincerity filled the space between and around them. It hearkened last night, though at the time it had been all about the fun.

"I cannot believe that you work here." He shook his head. "What are the odds?"

"High. The population of this town is less than ten thousand last I checked."

He cupped a hand behind his head. "Kind of wish I didn't have that kind of luck."

Her eyes darted away from him and it delivered another sting.

She was definitely no longer interested in him. Noted.

And yet, this care and loyalty to the Espiritus added another layer to her personality. It made her even more beautiful, more compelling, despite the accountability she seemed to demand from him.

Keep your lust in your pants. She hadn't wanted anything more from him, and he wasn't going to be that guy who pushed. Even if he was tempted by the memory of their night together.

"I came here to find out more about my father's family and that's what I intend to do," Jared said. From afar, Eva and Gabby were headed their way, eyes bright with excitement.

They knew him as Chef Jared Sotheby, and that was all. Did he really want to break apart everyone's life, including his own, by admitting who he was? Matilda was insisting he reveal the truth, but the more he thought about it, he knew he wasn't ready. He could barely get past having actually met them.

His chest grew heavy with indecision.

"I'm not going to stay long," he said finally, and when the words left his mouth, the tightness in his chest unfurled. "I have a life in Louisville. A whole goddamn life. But I need to do this, for me. I just need to know..."

"Know what?"

"It's hard to explain, Matilda. I just need to know what makes me *me*. I just need to observe. Not get close. I wouldn't know what to do with that, anyway. I'll hang out for a bit, then be on my merry way."

Her face softened, and her eyes cut to the right. "So, temporary."

"Absolutely. It's a win-win. You get a chef until you can find a proper replacement. I hang out in the kitchen and figure out a little bit of my father's DNA."

Matilda grumbled, though they both plastered on smiles as Eva and Gabby neared.

"So…what do you think?" Eva said, steps away. "Isn't it gorgeous? See that trail?" She pointed to a wooden post, with a painted white slash. "If you follow the blue blazes through the foliage, it will lead to our vista points, and then eventually, about four klicks out, you'll get to the white blazes."

"Klicks?"

"Kilometers."

"Ah. And white blazes?"

She grinned. "White blazes mark the Appalachian Trail. My husband, or my late husband, loved to hike. He used to drag me along and I fell in love with it too."

Late husband.

Jared swallowed the breath that had gotten stuck in his lungs. "That's interesting."

"Are you a hiker?"

He snorted at the question. Him and his stock of insect repellant. "Um…no. I'm a gym rat. Kitchen rat. Urban warrior if you will."

"Well, this is all we have here. The outdoors. And I hope you end up loving it." She clapped her hands. "But the big question. Are you ready for your interview?"

He couldn't help but smile—she was looking at him with so much pride. "I am. Though I was just telling Matilda, that I do have a caveat. I…have business back in Louisville."

"When do you have to return?"

"I'm open up to a few months. When I saw that this temporary position was available, I thought it was a great fit." He swallowed against his vague explanation. The truth was that he'd missed the mark in certain dishes and had buckled under the kitchen's pressure, and was told that a leave of absence was in order. Had he mentioned that he had been a mess?

A smidge of guilt ran up his spine that perhaps he wouldn't be able to turn on his culinary skills here, but surely the B & B's standards wouldn't crush him.

"Wow. It's serendipity, then." She placed a hand on Matilda's elbow. "Don't you think? Just in time to get through our season openers, and find another chef."

"I can probably find one even sooner," Matilda said, peering at him.

"Wonderful! Let's head to my cottage for your interview." Eva turned toward the B & B once more, this time waving. "But let me introduce you to my other daughter. She just got back from the hospital. Looks like she picked up Liam from his dad's."

The older Espiritu daughter, the one who was around his same age, Francesca, marched forward with a serious expression. She had long hair pulled up into a ponytail.

His jaw threatened to hit the floor. It was as if he was looking in the mirror. Though her coloring was a shade darker, the shape of her eyes, her chin and her lips were like his. They could have been twins.

In his research, he'd noted that he was only a few months older than Francesca was.

A little boy wearing a baseball hat appeared from behind her. He overtook his mother, stopping short upon seeing him.

Jared's eyes crossed for a half second. The boy looked like Jared as a kid.

"This is Frankie," Eva said. "And Liam."

"Nice to meet you. I'm Jared." He offered his hand; he was sure it was clammy.

"I know who you are. Wow." Her handshake was strong and no-nonsense.

"Jared's interviewing for the chef's position," Eva said.

She slid a glance over to Matilda. "You hadn't mentioned that he was coming. Or that you had a chance to interview him."

"I didn't want to have too high a hope. When he showed up, I was…pleasantly surprised."

"Do you ride bikes?" Liam said, drawing all eyes toward him.

Jared did a double take. "Who, me?"

"Yeah, you."

"I do."

"Climb trees?"

"Liam, sweetheart. Go ahead and run on home," Frankie said.

"But, Mom." He stomped his foot.

She turned him by the shoulders. "Go."

After a moment of hesitation, he whined, "Okay."

After he was several feet away, Frankie said, "You'll have to excuse him. Eight is a tricky age. Well, good luck with your interview." She crossed her arms and gestured toward her mother. "Though *she's* the softie. If she *does* hire you, you still have to deal with me for your probationary period."

Her expression could've cut glass, and Jared felt exposed. And a little frightened. He looked to Matilda for encouragement, but she shrugged.

"Anyway, Allie's all checked in. The contractions were still going on when I left, but her OB seemed to think she was going home." Frankie heaved a breath. "I left when Eugene got there."

"Who's Eugene?" Jared asked.

"Her good-for-nothing husband," she said sarcastically, though her expression had no trace of humor.

"That is our cue to go. We don't want to scare Chef with

small-town drama before he even interviews. Let's head up to the cottage." Eva stepped away from the group and gestured him forward.

"Yes, ma'am." He walked on with a smile. In truth, to be away from Frankie's glare and Matilda's insistence sounded good right about then.

And especially to spend a little bit of time with his late father's wife.

Chapter Six

"This isn't going to work," Matilda said, for the hundredth time in the short walk from the kitchen to her office in the northwest corner of the house.

Whatever initial giddiness she had felt at seeing Jared had dissolved and evaporated.

How did this happen? How did she get embroiled in this… lie?

The bigger question: how was she going to keep all of this a secret? Because the fact of the matter was that she needed Jared. She had no choice but to keep up this charade in the short-term.

"It will work. But whoa. It's like a maze in here," Jared said from behind her. He'd finished his interview with Eva, and apparently had passed with flying colors. "How many hallways does this place even have?"

Of course he had, because he was perfect for the job. He possessed a combination of traits that fit in their B & B crew: jovial, communicative and, from his culinary résumé, of which she had time to look up, capable.

Still. This all didn't sit well with her.

"There are a couple of interior hallways, one that leads to the offices, and another that leads into the break and storage rooms. The whole building has eight bedrooms with en suites.

Two guest bathrooms on this first floor. Two dining areas in the back."

They'd arrived at her office door, and she turned the knob, only for the door to stop halfway. She slunk in, grunting and silently cursing when her shirt caught on the doorknob. "Sorry, I've got stuff everywhere."

He followed her, stepping in sideways. "Your office is…"

"Don't say it's a closet. Because it's not even that big." She raised her gaze to him, grinning to herself as he tried to maneuver his way in, with how not in proportion he was to the rest of the office.

For a beat, she saw him half-naked as he had been this morning, leaning against the doorway, and her temperature ratcheted up a notch.

She cleared her throat and woke her computer. Her calendar popped up, and in seeing it, she calmed minutely. There was something about knowing what the future held that kept her steady. She guided the mouse to the hiring file folder and clicked to print the documents.

"This wins for the most organized office. Are all the drawers labeled?" He squinted at the floating shelves next to him, stacked with boxes.

"Jared, meet Laura." She nodded over to her most favorite tool in her office. It took the seat of honor next to her penholder. "The label maker."

"That's cute."

"Cute?" She grabbed the papers from the printer.

"Was that the wrong word?"

"Very much so. It isn't cute. It's…nostalgic. Cute is insulting." She groaned.

It really wasn't insulting. Cute *was* the right word. It was this whole situation that was throwing her.

She set the papers on the table. "I can't even pretend to go on with this conversation. I don't agree with any of this." She pressed her fingers against her temple.

"You don't have to agree for me to sign that paperwork." He picked up the stack from the desk. "It's straightforward. If I were you, I would be thanking my lucky stars."

She snorted. "Yeah?"

"Yeah. Without me, you would have had to DoorDash food for your guests for lunch."

It was infuriating how right he was. Matilda shut her eyes and took a cleansing breath. "We would have found a way."

He snorted. "Uh-huh. Also, I have my knives with me, but I'll need to check the rest of the tools in the kitchen. Maybe, by that time, you'll be a smidge more grateful." He scanned down the papers. "When do you need this packet?"

Matilda's opened her mouth but no words left it, mollified. "I…by the end of day is fine. Lunch is in about two hours, and we've got guests who've RSVP'd for the meal."

As he read, right cheek pinched in concentration, she took the moment to breath and watch him. He was wearing a thin long-sleeved fleece shirt, zippered halfway up, his muscles defined under the fabric.

Hours. It had only been hours since he was above her, arms bracketing her body while he rocked into her.

Heat rushed up her neck as she realized that they would need to discuss last night. Again. She couldn't have these lustful feelings in addition to the secrets they had to keep. Lines had to be drawn.

"Did you want to say something else to me?" Jared asked with a curl to his lip.

She startled to attention, heat clambering to her cheeks. "Yes. Actually." She steeled herself. "Eva is your boss as she is mine. And though *I* am not your boss, last night can't happen again."

"I figured. Especially with the whole the-Espiritus-are-my-dad's-family business. I don't want you to worry about it. I'm a professional. But more than that, I do have a conscience. I know I'm making you lie."

He said it so confidently that Matilda believed him. "Thank you," she said.

"It's me who has to thank *you*," he added, "for going through with this. Obviously you could very well tell them about me. I appreciate you giving me the chance to figure things out. It's all a little jumbled in my head."

His sincerity was disarming. It also brought back how she felt when her ex announced he was going to be a dad.

It didn't feel good; it was uncomfortable. It was pain that she couldn't quite target. "You're welcome. But, as soon as I can get someone in…"

"I fully understand I have to leave. To be honest, the faster I get back to Louisville, the better."

"For work?"

Half of his face crinkled down into a wince. "Yes, though getting back into my chef's good graces might take me a bit."

"What happened?"

"Might as well tell you, since you know everything else," he said under his breath. Shifting in his seat, he cleared his throat. "My cooking kind of took a nosedive. I was only in the sous chef job at Sizzling Platter for six months before that TV segment Eva and Gabby talked about. That critique…it affected my work and my concentration. I became a liability in the kitchen. I'm on a leave of absence. 'To figure out how to crack an egg' is what my chef said."

"Wow, that's harsh."

"Restaurant kitchens aren't for the weak."

"I don't understand. Isn't cooking just who you are?"

"Not when you think that what you're making isn't good enough."

"So I have a chef that can't cook?"

He showed her his palm. "It's not as bad as it sounds."

"It actually is." She heaved a breath. "I mean, that's your part of this deal."

"C'mon, I'm sure I can make anything on your menu."

She gauged his intention behind those words. He wasn't implying that the menu was basic was he?

Then again, if he could do the menu, basic or otherwise, it should all work out.

Her phone rang an alarm. Reaching over, she turned it off.

Jared's eyebrows lifted. "That just gave me bad memories. Those school bells were so annoying."

"It's distinct enough that I can't ignore it. I set alarms for everything. I hate being late. Which brings me to some house rules."

"No small talk has to be the first rule."

She rolled her eyes. "Here's the deal, Jared. You're expected at work each and every day you're scheduled. But the B & B is a seven day a week job, unofficially. On your days off, though, we have an assistant. You're to plan for those meals so it's easy for us to prepare for our guests. And you're to keep me informed of any changes. Even small changes in the menu."

"Eva did tell me of the time commitment, and I'm fine with that, I guess." He rolled out his shoulders, as if uncomfortable. "But what do you mean by small?"

She peered at him. Already, she could tell that this was going to be a bigger challenge for him than he had expected. "I mean all changes."

He snorted. "So, I guess it's not just your things that you like to keep organized."

"No," she huffed out a laugh. "We run like an well-oiled machine here."

The door opened with a squeak to reveal Eva in the doorway. Her eyebrows were raised. "Sounds like Matilda's setting the ground rules."

Worry skittered across Matilda's skin. How much had Eva heard of their conversation? "Yeah, we were just covering… communication."

Eva's gaze slid between the two of them. "Perfect, exactly the reason why I'm here. Because I think the two of you have kept something from me."

Matilda whipped her head to Jared, who's eyes had grown to saucers. "I…"

"What do you…" Jared added.

"Peak is a small town, and well—" she spun the watch on her wrist and looked at the time "—I'm impressed that it took till almost noon for this news to get here. Then again, Clark *did* just start his shift." She hiked that same hand on her hip. "He told me that the two of you met last night. And perhaps that explains why Matilda, who is never quiet, seemed to clam up when you arrived Jared."

Matilda exhaled. Oh, thank goodness. It was, of all the secrets in this room, the least detrimental. "Yes, yes we did meet last night. And your summation is correct."

"And why you were practically pushing him out the door this morning."

Both Matilda and Jared nodded.

"It isn't any of my business, of course. I respect your privacy. I value my own. But we've got a very busy few weeks coming up, and I want to make sure that whatever happened between the both of you doesn't affect business."

"Oh, of course not Eva," Matilda jumped in to say. "You can trust me on that."

"It is absolutely clear on my end, too." Jared nodded.

Eva's shoulders relaxed as she exhaled. "Good, then. We're all set. Jared, why don't I show you the rest of the B & B?"

Jared lifted the papers in his hand.

"Leave them here," Matilda said, with a smile this time, holding out a hand. Relief coursed through her, that they had somehow passed the first test. "You can pick it up after your shift."

"All right then," he said, also visibly relaxed, placing the papers in her hand.

"Later, Jared. And um. Welcome to Spirit of the Shenandoah B & B."

"Thank you."

Eva beamed. "Talk about luck, right?"

Was it luck? Or maybe it was trouble waiting to happen. No matter the word, Matilda was now caught in its web.

The only way out was to get another chef in, pronto.

"So, you're really not available? Not even on a temporary basis?" Matilda asked through gritted teeth. On the computer screen was Chef Luke Farley, one of her previous interviewees who lived an hour away. He was the fourth and last on her list of chefs to follow up with. In the past hour, she'd been turned down by the other three.

This was it. He had to say yes.

"Please?" she added with a squeak.

"Dude, I can't," Chef said, with an incredulous impression.

Did he just call me dude?

"I don't think it's a fit." He leaned back and linked his fingers behind his head. "You-all are stressed AF over there."

Matilda's eyes threatened to shut in exasperation. This attitude was the very reason why he hadn't been hired after their first meeting, though his résumé was impressive.

She inhaled a cleansing breath. "It's not stress—it's passion that you see. Determination. Drive."

"You can call it all you want but it's stress. I don't know if I can work in a place like that. And anyway, when you said I had to deal with guests? I'm not meant for that. I'm an artist," he said, the *i* sounding like the double *e*. "Guest relations are not my thing." He shrugged. "Sorry, dude."

"I'm the one that's sorry," Matilda said under her breath, before they ended the call. With a pen, she drew a red line across the name Luke Farley with force.

Now, looking at each of the four names in front of her with a red line drawn across, reality set in. She was once more starting from scratch. These four had been her best callbacks.

Matilda linked her fingers under her chin.

How had she lost control of this situation? Where had she faltered? She thought back to when Allie had announced her pregnancy, when she was four months along. Still, Matilda had thought she had more than enough time to find a replacement. She'd conducted her first interview two weeks after placing her first ad. But the B & B's location, the job description or maybe the pay…something had given her most valuable chef prospects pause.

Ultimately, it was her responsibility to get someone in. Jared bought her some time at a high cost, and she couldn't give up now.

When her phone rang, Matilda had never been so grateful to press the green button, knowing exactly who was on the other line. "Hello, Mother."

Water ran in the background; Linda Matthews was doing dishes. "Darling. Are you okay? You don't feel bad about Noah do you?" Her voice was breathy and curious.

"Boy, did news travel fast. And far."

"His mother called me first thing. I hung up on her."

Pride swelled in her chest. "You did?"

"I never did like her. She can take that announcement of hers and shove it where the sun doesn't shine."

Matilda laughed; she would never get used to her mother not acting like her mother, which was someone who had seemed so perfect.

"I thought that since you weren't home last night—"

Matilda gasped. "Mother. Did you check my location?"

"Maybe." Linda all but mewed.

"You promised."

"You said I could check your location during emergencies and I had one of my worry spells. It was either that or having your father drive us back to Peak. I'm sure you wouldn't have wanted for us to show up without notice. Though, your father has missed you. He got into a new thriller series and he can't stop talking about it."

Matilda groaned, though it wasn't because of Phil Matthews's book choices. Her parents had retired in the Alabama Gulf Shores, though still tried to exert control as if they were still living in town.

"Now, now, I don't need to know what you were doing. I get blowing off a little steam."

Matilda sighed, audibly.

"Really, Matilda, it's as if I was never your age. Though, when I was forty, I was married to your father and the last thing on my mind was blowing off things. Now, a decade before I met him, it was a different story—"

"Mother, please don't say another word."

Matilda was tempted. So tempted to hang up. At sixty-eight, her proper mother had lost her filter.

The last thing Matilda wanted to hear about was her mother's sexual escapades.

But Linda would come through with her threat of a road trip if Matilda hung up.

Linda sighed. "I hope you know that you are better off without Noah. That you've made this completely amazing life. That you barely missed that train wreck—you were literally on the tracks, dear. You saved yourself."

A memory flew in of Matilda jamming her clothes into a duffel bag when Noah had been at work. They'd gotten into another fight, and this time, it was because he didn't want Matilda to visit Linda on her birthday.

It was as if she'd proposed that they break up. Noah had leveraged their whole relationship on one visit home. It hadn't been the first time they'd fought or yelled. But at that moment, full clarity had descended that she had been under Noah's thumb. That for fourteen years, eight married, she had minimized herself to fit into whatever shack he decided to move them into.

As soon as he'd left for work that next morning, Matilda had taken the next Greyhound out, and that evening, she was at her parents' doorstep.

"That bastard moved on. And so should you," Linda said.

"I don't need anyone."

"I'm not talking about needing someone. I'm talking about you holding that time over your head and still beating yourself up about it. It hasn't gotten past me that in five years, you haven't been with anyone long-term. Or that you're a workaholic."

Matilda's heart squeezed at the sincerity in her mother's tone. She seemed to always get to the bottom of the well of Matilda's thoughts.

"Thanks, Mom. I appreciate that, but I am fine." Because she was, right? She was doing her thing. She'd recovered from living under doubt, and she had a great job in one of the most beautiful places in the country. She'd made it through by the skin of her teeth and her self-esteem.

Except you're stuck.

She stood to jostle that random thought and looked out the window. Jared and Eva were chatting.

No, she wasn't stuck. Her temporary answer was right there looking as fine as he could be. Her eyes wandered to his bottom, encased in his jeans. It was criminal how perfect the fit was.

Then, as if sensing her lustful thoughts, he turned.

She spun away from the window. Argh.

"Fine is a spectrum," Linda said, adding insult to injury.

"Well, I'm in the range of 'I'm going to hang up now and I love you.'"

Her mother sighed. "All right. Check in with me later?"

"Yes, Mother."

"Promise!" she added as Matilda took the phone off her ear.

A groan rose out of her. That *P* word again.

Still, things were in order for now. Their kitchen would function, and the guests would never know the difference—hopefully. It wasn't an ideal situation, but Jared would have to do.

It would have to be better than "do."

She just hoped he could pull it off without blowing up the Espiritus' entire world.

Chapter Seven

Sweat dripped from Jared's temple as he lifted a round baking pan in the air. "Got you!"

At that moment, three guests wearing hiking gear entered the kitchen, and his momentary glee came crashing down. Still he kept his smile on his face. He nodded. "Afternoon."

One approached the bar island while her friends milled about the dining room. The travertine slab was massive, and while the woman, who wore her brown hair in a ponytail and threaded through her visor, was a good five feet away, it was too close for comfort.

"Ooo, whatcha making?" she asked.

"Chocolate cake, our dessert for tonight."

"What else is on the lineup?"

"Tonight's menu is beef bourguignon. Alternatively, we have a pepper-and-garlic-encrusted tofu, then a warm kale salad with citrus and roasted root vegetables."

"Yum. But tofu? I'm not a fan of the texture. It's too…weird. Are those my only options? I'm the vegan of the bunch."

"What do you have in mind?" His thoughts were on the cake, which he was in the middle of constructing. Time was of the essence, since dinner was in a couple of hours.

"Oh, I don't know. What can you make me?"

He grinned, though inside, he was more impatient and a little insulted.

There should be a rule against guests coming through the kitchen while he cooked. Two days had passed since his arrival and he couldn't get used to it, the freedom in which folks just passed through where he worked, suddenly needing something as banal as a glass of water. Or to discuss their personal preferences. Yes, he often spoke to diners at the restaurants he'd worked in, but it was under his terms. His choice as to when he was ready, with a clean chef's jacket on, and prepared for any kind of critique.

How was a chef supposed to work under these conditions? And especially with some hesitance still coursing through him.

Admittedly, while he'd succeeded in creating meals the last couple of days, it didn't come without some trouble. He'd needed every bit of his brain power to focus and not assign too much meaning to his cooking.

He'd reminded himself that he was simply cooking according to the recipes passed down to him, classic favorites of the B & B that kept guests returning year after year. Nothing more, nothing less.

Still, he wasn't on his game.

"How about pasta?" he asked. "I can cook up a batch of egg-free noodles?"

She looked at the ceiling and Jared prayed that the answer for her was there. "I'm fine with pasta, with Alfredo sauce. You can do that, right? I saw you on TV that one day, and I know you like to put a little spin on things." With a pointer finger, she drew a circle in the air. "But I want mine basic. American style with all of the thick cream. Okay?"

"Thick cream. As in, dairy. That's not—" he tiptoed around the words so not to offend, because she seemed to be the kind of person who would be "—really vegan."

She waved a hand in the air. "Oh, I'm eighty-twenty vegan. You know, on plan eighty percent of the time. It works for me!"

"All right then," he answered with as little sarcasm as he could manage, and with a smile.

To his relief, the woman left, and he returned to his task at hand, which was to fish out the second round baking pan. Reaching in, he hooked it with his fingers, though as he stood, he hit his head on the island countertop.

"Shit!"

"Hey. This is a G-rated establishment." Frankie strode in with a basket of flowers. From the other hand dangled a wide-brimmed hat. "You're lucky my son wasn't here to hear you."

Jared watched her place the flowers on the countertop. He cataloged her posture, and how her shoulders were broad as compared to her waist. Like him. It had been advantageous. Jared appeared to be bigger and stronger than he really was.

"What? Why are you looking at me like that? Do I have something on my face?" She pulled her phone out of her back pocket and turned on the camera to inspect her image.

He tore his eyes away, caught red-handed, though assessment confirmed. They were so much alike.

How could she not notice?

And her attitude was sharp, protective. So much like his sister Emma.

Frankie is technically your sister.

"No, um, you're fine. Where's the little guy?" He shook himself out of his last thought; he couldn't mull over that connection. He was here to find out more about Louis, and not get snagged on this family tree where he didn't belong.

"He went round the back, straight to his lola's cabin."

Lola, as in grandmother. He'd heard it a few times in the last forty-eight hours, but it continued to nab his attention. At how Filipino words were thrown around like it was nothing.

"Oh good. How was the garden?"

She peered at herself on her phone, looking up quickly. "Fine. The herbs are so happy in this weather."

"Eva mentioned there's even a chef's garden and a wildflower garden out there."

She leveled him with perplexed expression, and his excitement at the possibility of working a farm to table arrangement was hampered by Frankie's obvious disapproval.

"Haven't you been back there?"

"No, not yet. I'm still getting to know the layout of the kitchen and the run of the place. Eva pointed out all the outdoor spots, and I jumped in to work the kitchen straightaway. I haven't really had the time."

"That's a poor excuse."

"It's a real one," he countered. It was a lie, though. He was fledgling. In this kitchen, in this new chef's role and his half-baked plan that had placed him in his biological father's family. He wasn't in a hurry to explore everything. A sponge could only absorb so much liquid.

"I know you're here temporarily, but as the chef, you need to know everything about this place all the same." Her statement was a challenge, and just as he would with Emma, he half wanted to roll his eyes at it, and half wanted to reassure.

"I understand." He opted for neutral. "I'll be sure to walk the grounds today."

"Good. Because our guests always have a lot of questions for us."

"Um, yeah I got that for sure," he mumbled.

She raised a finger. "They have expectations. We might not be a fancy city hotel with all the bells and whistles, but we are unparalleled in our customer service and hospitality. Which means there's no such thing as 'not my job.'" She neared. "You know what I find interesting?"

He picked up his jaw. "What?"

"Out of the entire staff, Matilda and I work the closest together. And up to right before she finished her shift on Friday night, she hadn't yet recommended a chef for Mom to hire. When did the two of you speak to set up the interview?"

He meandered to the mixer to set up the stainless-steel bowl. It was easier to lie when he didn't look at her straight on. "It was a while ago. At first, I was noncommittal about coming in to interview. My arrival was…a last-minute decision."

He grabbed the flour jar from the cupboard. In his periphery, he saw that her hip was cocked against the island. Pressure in the kitchen wasn't a new thing, but this felt like fire against his skin.

"So what changed your mind?"

He swallowed and opted for truth. It had sat on his shoulders all the way on his drive on I-64 east. "I guess I wanted a change, and to get to know a little more about myself."

"And working here will do that?"

"Yes." He peeled softened butter from its packaging and dumped it to the bowl along with the sugar. "New challenges, new people, new environment." Seeing her raised eyebrows, signaling that she was waiting for more. "You know, the trees, the air, just being outside."

"Which you haven't even really experienced."

"No… I'm kind of a city kid." He turned on the mixer, prepping ingredients to add according to the recipe.

"So we've come full circle, of you needing to know everything about this place. You've had two days. You're avoiding it, though I don't know why."

He shook his head and a grin burst out of him. She wasn't backing down, even with this mundane point.

"I'll take that tour today, I promise," he said.

"What? Who's making promises?" Matilda blew in, and her appearance was like a cool gust of wind, changing the temperature of the room. He couldn't help but light up—and he noticed Frankie did too. It wasn't that Matilda was cheerful, because at that moment, she certainly wasn't.

It was how she possessed a room. She was in charge, undoubtedly, and nothing was going to get past her.

The contrast between the woman he'd spent the night with and this person in front of him was stark. Never at work had he seen her express an emotion besides sternness.

"Chef Jared needs a tour of the entire property," Frankie said. "Apparently Mom told him about the garden but he hasn't even stepped inside its fence. He needs the full shebang."

Matilda shot him a quick look. "I'll take care of it. Pretty soon you'll be plucking the tomatoes off the vine yourself."

"This'll be my first time managing a garden. Should be a fun experience."

Frankie threw her head back and laughed, the first Jared had witnessed. It was more sharp than joyful though. "Wait. Are we trusting Chef Allie's plant babies to you?"

"I..." His face burned with embarrassment. "I've always worked in kitchens that had ingredients brought in."

"I think that Chef has realized that the B & B is a lot more intense than he thought it would be." Matilda's lips turned up in a grin. Like an *I told you so.*

"That's right, honey. Here, we do it all." Frankie fanned her hat so her hair lifted, and she gathered the flowers and walked away. "Matilda, you have your training cut out for you."

Neither one of them said a word until Frankie was outside.

"I don't know what I did," Jared said, eyeing the batter as he added sifted flour.

"With Frankie, you don't have to do anything for her to pick up on your vibe." She lowered her voice. "If there's anyone we have to watch out for, it's her, and not Eva. But have no fear. I've got another chef coming in tomorrow for an interview."

His body jostled to full awareness and he shut the mixer. "Oh? Who is it?"

"Angeles is her last name. Do you know her?"

"From New Jersey? Karla?"

"That's her." She smiled. "She seems to be a good fit. She's coming from a boutique hotel and says she's ready for a change." She neared, peeking into the bowl. Her proximity caused Jared's skin to tingle with need; their night together continued to be a memory he reached for since his arrival.

"You want a taste?"

She bit her lip. "No, I shouldn't. What if I get salmonella?"

He cackled. Jared's mind flipped away from the topic at hand and his pervasive self-talk, enamored with her expression. "Have you never eaten uncooked cake batter?"

"I have, but I don't make a habit of it."

"You take the same risk eating from a salad bar. Go ahead."

With a giddy smile, she plucked a spoon from the drawer and scooped batter and tasted it. Her eyes shut, moaning.

It sent heat straight to Jared's core. He licked his lips, wishing he was the spoon. "Like it?"

"I do. Make sure you save me a piece." She straightened. "But about this new chef."

The whiplash was dizzying; Jared swallowed away his growing lust. "What about her?"

Footsteps sounded from the hallway, and a couple appeared, laughing. The Petersons, if Jared remembered. They signaled for Matilda's attention.

She waved back. "I'll be right with you." Then, she leaned in. "Meet me at the gazebo after lunch for a tour, and then we can talk."

Jared nodded, the whole encounter leaving him slightly breathless and with greater motivation to make the best chocolate cake Matilda had ever tasted.

"I'm lost," Jared said into his phone hours later. His eyes scanned the narrow trail, banked by foliage and not much else.

"What do you mean, lost? Aren't you in their backyard?" Emma said on the other line. In her part of the world, someone strummed on a guitar, the notes interspersed by an occasional drumbeat. Band practice.

"It's not a backyard. It's literally the wilderness back here, Em."

"Well, aren't you glad I called then? Just in case you got lost, or eaten by a bear."

He halted. Did they have bears in the valley? He shook his head to clear the distraction.

Of course he'd lost his way to the gazebo. There were no directions to the structure, just paint on stumps and rocks and trees, and he'd been distracted at how lush the trees were, at his sister prattling in his ear and from the stress that had built up this morning.

"How are things going over there?" she asked. "Besides being Goldilocks."

"It's…interesting."

"Do you mean the job or the people?"

"Everything. All of it."

She sighed. "I still don't know what you're trying to accomplish. You don't want to tell them who you are, and yet, you've subjected yourself to getting to know them."

"I can't just barge into their lives and not get to know them, even if it's Louis who I'm trying to figure out." Though, it was a tangled mess in his head. "It's complicated."

"It's only complicated because we humans make it that way. And though I supported you heading out there, I'm worried that you're going to get hurt."

Her words pressed around him despite being solo on this trail. Then again, these were the roles they played. Jared was trusting and an idealist, while Emma was a realist and a devil's advocate. "I'm not going to get hurt. I'm grown, remember."

"Grown and yet, lost in the woods." She snickered. "Mom's not going to be happy about this."

"That's why you're going to continue to not tell her."

Emma growled. "Our mother is a smart woman, Jared. She's starting to wonder why you're not on any of Sizzling Platter's socials."

He mumbled to stave off an actual agreement when the path narrowed, darkening. Then steps later, the path opened up so that all he could see was sky. Like he was at the edge of a cliff. With the way the foliage and the hills had rolled and settled, with how the trees had nestled among themselves, his entire view was his and his alone.

Beyond, he heard music and a woman singing to the song with emotion.

His lips curved into a smile. He only knew of one woman who sang like that.

"Hello?" Emma prodded in his ear.

"Yeah, I'm here. I've got to go."

"Tell me you're okay, and not just fine."

"Yep. No bears."

"I'm not talking about bears."

He halted then, heaving a breath. "Things are good. I'm going to take things a step at a time. I'll come home if it starts to get weird."

Finally, Emma let him go. Jared followed both the music and the path to the left, and a white gazebo came into view. With her phone sitting on the railing playing music, Matilda was holding a can of paint with one hand and a brush in the other. As she touched up the columns, she sang, swaying side to side.

Cute was the least of it. It was adorable.

Their karaoke night flew back into the forefront of his memory. At the warmth of her proximity. At how the spotlights dimmed the rest of the bar, and it had been just the two of them, singing to one another.

He remembered both the wholesome and sinful memories from that night. Then, his mind slid to the absolute neutrality of her current attitude.

Matilda had such a good poker face. If she had felt anything for him at all, the last two days hadn't shown it.

Or maybe it wasn't a poker face? Maybe, he truly was just a person in her life that fit the moment. Just because he hadn't been able to fully get her out of his system didn't mean that she hadn't already done so.

He couldn't think about it; he wasn't here for her anyway.

He knocked on one of the pillars of the gazebo, taking a step up. She stiffened and turned surreptitiously. Her eyes narrowed.

That was cute, too, if he was being honest.

"How long have you been standing there?" she asked.

He tapped his chin. "Part of that second stanza and the full refrain."

A flush creeped up her neck. Against his better judgment, he reveled in it. He'd noticed he could get the tiniest bit of rise out of her when he engaged in banter, and he'd taken the opportunity when he could.

"Funny. Anyway, took you long enough to get here." She spied her watch.

Apparently it was back to business. "The Petersons held me up. Something about heading into Charlottesville to visit their kid while they're here. He has a new girlfriend, apparently."

"We're rooting for this one." She nodded sincerely, then set down the can of paint and replaced the cover. "Not like the other one, who just wasn't a nice person."

"How long have you known them?"

"Years. They reserve with us whenever they visit their son. Which is almost every month." She grinned.

"It feels so personal, to know about our guests' business."

"Don't you have regulars at your restaurant?"

"We do. But as a sous chef, I don't do the rounds in the dining room often."

"It's not the same here."

"You mean Peak, because it's a small town?"

"Peak and the B & B," she said.

"Feels a little too close for comfort."

"I find that funny coming from you—I thought you would like being around people all the time."

"It's hard to explain. Sounds as though you actually like the interaction."

"I do, because it's personal." She peered at him. "Are you saying I'm cold?"

"No, that's not it." Jared felt the conversation turn. Weren't they just bantering? "I just meant that since you're so professional and I don't know, um…serious."

"You ready for your tour?" She turned off the music and stuffed the phone in her pocket.

Jared lifted both hands in surrender; Matilda was simply unreadable. Just when he thought he could make conversation, she yanked him back to the professional zone. "Yeah. Sure."

He stepped aside and she came down the three steps. If professional was what she wanted, then she was going to get it. "So, not only are you the manager but you're doing the maintenance too?"

"Sometimes. Being the manager means I know everything about what's going on. I find resources and jump in wherever I can. And I don't mind the painting or any outside work. Clark's got a whole list to tackle for the SE—that's the solar eclipse event—and the paint touch-up's nothing. Which reminds me, we'll need to talk about the event in depth. I wanted to give you a couple of days to see if you were going to work out." She stepped out ahead of him. "Let's go down this trail. It'll take you to the very edge of the property."

He caught up to her so they were side by side. The path was just wide enough for two and descended a short hill.

"Stop right here, and turn around," she said.

He spun and inhaled a sharp breath at the view. At the wide

windows of the B & B, the gazebo, the wildflowers, then the view of the mountains behind it. "Wow."

"This is why people stay with us." She left his side. "C'mon, and get those quads ready."

They climbed a steep hill. By the time he reached the top, his lungs struggled and he was out of breath. When he caught up to Matilda, they glanced at each other and both laughed.

"Damn, I'm out of shape," he said.

"I don't know about that. I live here. I walk the property every day and that hill still gets me every time. But, it's worth it." She gestured to the land in front of him. "Welcome to vista point two. Take all that in."

"This is cool." The sky was limitless. He felt truly solitary and on top of the world.

"There you go and your perfectly crafted sentences."

He recalled their first night. "Ha. Is it me, or does the air smell different up here? It's subtle."

"It's the honeysuckle." She gestured to the bush. Or, rather, bushes. "They're Eva's favorites." Except he noticed that her expression had fallen.

"And…that makes you sad?"

"Contemplative." She gave him a brief side-eye. "I suppose you should know about this, given why you're really here. Eva planted these bushes for what would have been her and Louis's twenty-eighth wedding anniversary."

"And that would have been?"

"Three years ago."

He nodded, allowing her words to settle into his system. His late father and Eva had married about thirty-two years ago, and shortly after that Louis slept with his mother.

And yet, to his relief, he found that he wasn't hurt by it. The idea felt too distant. "Is there something wrong with these flowers?"

"We have to trim them back. This is one of the ticketed

areas during the SE. But we can talk about that more when we get back to my office."

"Before we head back," Jared was still mulling over the timeline of Louis and Eva's marriage, "I wanted to say thanks again. For giving me this chance to find out more about the Espiritus."

She faced him, and a strand of her dark hair swept across her face. "You're welcome. Though you're helping me out, too."

"Yeah, but I'm helping you out in a practical way. You needed a body, and I'm a body. But this, for me, is different."

Beats passed in which they simply stared at one another, though there was no discomfort.

Matilda looked away first. "I have to be honest, though. It's been…uncomfortable…being around Eva while keeping this secret. I feel like it's her right to know."

"Not telling her is *my* right, too. You were spot on the other day, that this is not just about me, that it's about the Espiritus too. But it's also about my mother. She doesn't know I'm here, and exposing myself to the Espiritus will somehow involve her. I don't even know how to approach that dynamic. So telling Eva is out of the question."

"That makes sense." She nodded. "I thought about what you said while I was painting. That you just need to know what makes you, *you*. It took me a long time to come back home to find myself, and though it was hard, it was worth it. I don't like lying to Eva, but I understand how that feels, to search for yourself."

To be acknowledged, to be understood, and especially by Matilda rendered him silent. In the two days at the B & B, he had started to become lost in the new job, in his thoughts, in trying to fit in once more.

A buzzing noise broke through the mood, and Matilda lifted the phone against her ear. "This is Matilda."

He swallowed down the growing emotion in his chest as she spoke, and instead of allowing it to bloom, he smiled. Because what else was there to say without going down a rabbit hole of feelings he couldn't even describe?

She ended the call swiftly, pocketing her phone. "We've got to head back. Frankie needs me. Let's reconvene soon." She hesitated. "About Frankie earlier…she's suspicious of everyone new, so don't take it personal. Then again—" she pursed her lips in a wry smile "—with you, she has every reason to be worried. But hey, um… I just wanted you to know…you're not just a body. Okay?" Then, she stepped away as if they hadn't just had a heart-to-heart.

She looked back seconds later, "Are you coming?"

Jared nodded, still processing her words. "Coming."

Chapter Eight

Matilda winced as Krista cackled with a hand clutching her belly. They were in Matilda's Bronco, parked in front of Chef Allie Lang's house. After hearing that Allie was back home—and now on bed rest—after a two day stay in the hospital for monitoring, Matilda stepped away during her lunch hour to make a short visit.

If Krista ever decided to gather her composure.

"I should have never told you." Matilda rolled her eyes.

"Nope. You should always tell me everything." Krista snorted. "You said he wasn't a body. That is pretty…Freudian."

"Ugh. I can't believe I said that."

"According to the doctor himself, it was within you to say it. Your id is a powerful thing, you know. So, might as well embrace it. From what I remember, you mentioned that his body wasn't so bad."

Matilda raised her arms in exasperation. "You and your elephant memory."

"These are important details."

"Well, nothing can happen between me and Jared."

"But it doesn't erase what you-all did."

"Why do you have a comeback for everything?"

"Because!" She spun to look at her. "I love this for you. Finally, Matilda Matthews is unraveling."

"I am not unraveling."

"Yes, you are. I have never seen you fuss like this over a fling. Usually they don't matter. They're forgotten the next day."

"It's quite hard to forget since the guy has been working with me for—" she looked at her phone "—five days."

There was also that whole issue of Jared being Louis's son—except this wasn't something she could say to Krista, or to anyone, even if every cell in her body wanted to unload this news.

Her chest was heavy with secrets and responsibility.

It had been hard enough to reveal the bare bones of Jared's arrival at the B & B, that he happened in for a job and lo and behold, they had already known each other quite intimately.

"Not true." Krista tsked. "You are perfectly capable of icing someone out. There was that guy who hung around for three months working at one of the resorts. That didn't bother you an iota, and he spent all summer trying to get your attention for a second night together."

Matilda shrugged. "It's proximity. And it's temporary."

Though Jared's situation continued to linger in Matilda's psyche, so small was her friend circle that it felt deceitful not to say anything about it. Sure, they would have been able to keep his secret, but it was not hers to tell.

Most of all, Matilda was starting to think that Freud was right. She didn't mind seeing him on the property. Her body had been magnetized to his.

Since that short walk to the vista point, she *might* have strolled through the kitchen on purpose more than once. And when she'd forgotten her purse at work, she'd given Jared her address so that he could drop it off. Sure, it was under the guise of other reasons, but it was to see Jared, to watch him work and to feel his presence.

"Better temporary and fun than long-term and frustrating," Krista said, raising an eyebrow.

Matilda knew where this conversation was going. Noah's

news had proliferated through their friend group. Apparently he'd also announced it on social media.

Thank goodness Matilda didn't frequent her socials much since the divorce—it hadn't been comfortable to sit and watch everyone's highlight reels while her own life had begun to crumble—and it was another reason to keep avoiding them.

"I don't want to talk about Noah."

"But I know you have thoughts."

Matilda sighed. "I do, but I just don't feel like hashing it out. And I definitely don't want to bring it up around Allie. Last thing she needs is to get riled up."

She pouted. "Fine."

A ding sounded through the Bronco, and Krista looked at her phone. "It's Allie. She said, 'look up.'"

Matilda peered through the windshield to the window above the garage, to their friend, who had plastered a piece of paper that read Help.

"Shoot, we better go," Matilda said, jumping out.

An eighties ballad spilled out when the front door was opened by Allie's mom. A German American woman in her sixties, she was formidable, lean and strong. Her bright blue eyes lit up when she saw them.

"Hi, Ms. Greta!" she and Krista said in unison, like they were still in junior high coming over after school to drag Allie out to hang.

"Girls! I was wondering when you were going to come in."

Matilda's heart squeezed at the term "girls." She and her girlfriends had known each other for decades and the familiarity gave her comfort. That despite all the things going on at work, much remained the same, to include being looked after by a mother figure like Greta.

Matilda kissed the woman's cheek. "It's Krista's fault."

"Hey!" Krista objected as she was being bear-hugged by Greta.

"Whatever it is, you'll need to bring that excitement upstairs." Her gaze strayed to the ceiling.

"Is she okay?"

"She needs her best friends. Being on bed rest is tough. She's impatient for the baby to come," said Greta, channeling a message through her eyes. She patted Matilda on the arm. "I hope you brought your appetite. I'm making pfannkuchen. Breakfast for lunch."

The scent of melting butter on the griddle was already tantalizing. Matilda sighed. "Have I said how much I love it when you visit?"

"Good. I'll make extra and you can bring some back to Eva." Greta gestured with a head toward the staircase. "Go."

Matilda took the stairs by two with Krista at her heels, and entered the door at the end of the hallway, the bedroom. Inside was dimly lit, with Allie lying on her side, her hand gently cradling her belly. The television was on, to a baking show. Her favorite scented candle was lit. But her face was wrinkled into a frown.

Allie was not a frowner. She smiled through everything.

It reminded her of Jared, who traipsed around the property charming every person and flora and fauna. She swore that a butterfly had landed on his shoulder the other day.

Knowing that Allie was showing her discontent so easily meant that things were not great. She rushed toward her friend and wrapped her arms around her. From behind, Krista did the same.

"You look—" Matilda searched for the word "—miserable."

"Matilda!" Krista reached over and pinched her in the upper arm.

"What? It's the truth. Not that it's your fault, Allie. Or the baby's. It's the look you're giving us. And you wrote us a Help sign." Her sentences were running away from her.

Sometimes she wished she had the capability to be less frank than she was.

"What she means is that you're beautiful, Allie," Krista said.

"I'm not beautiful." Allie sniffed. "I don't think I've slept for more than a couple of hours at a time. And I'm dying to get up and walk around, but I'm not allowed to. Thank goodness for Mom, because at least I'm being fed the best food in the whole world."

"It doesn't help that you're in a cave. We should open these windows, don't you think?" Krista jumped up, the ever-optimist. With a swoop of her hand, the curtains flew open, bringing in much needed light.

"I'm melting," Allie whined, with a hand blocking the sun. "Besides, opening the curtains, or the windows, or even me getting up and walking around won't change the fact that…" Allie's voice trailed.

"What is it sweetie?" Matilda coaxed her on, though she could predict her words. Flashes of the last year, when Allie's husband started his surgical residency and her increased unhappiness, came to the forefront.

She started again. "It won't change the fact that Eugene and I aren't doing well, and now I'm scared. I'm scared that I'm in over my head. Raising a baby, it feels so overwhelming, and Eugene is so checked out. He barely had time to visit me when I was admitted for observation."

Matilda glanced at Krista, the look in her eyes begging her friend to intervene. Dealing with all these feelings, and especially about commitment and pregnancy, was out of her comfort zone. Who was she to give advice when her only real relationship had failed miserably?

Krista understood the assignment—she was adept at being a mother and happily married—and took Allie's side. "Let's take it a day at a time, Allie. Eugene—you know Eugene.

He'll come through. Just as you're adjusting, he is too. And that damn residency, it's so stressful."

"He said that about med school, and even during undergrad. Hell, high school, even. Everything is hard for him, and I always end up last. I don't want this baby ending up last."

Krista's eyebrows furrowed and so did Matilda's. Allie didn't speak like this.

"I just wonder…if Eugene can't step up to the plate, can I even return to work?" A tear trickled down Allie's cheek.

Krista leaned in to hug their friend once more, and a second later, Matilda followed suit. She was in her own state of shock. This announcement had more implications. Allie had planned to take four months off, but she was supposed to return to the B & B.

Matilda bit her lip as she decided how to tackle her next questions. It would be better for her to wait, but with hiring the next chef, she needed clarification. Hiring a temporary chef was entirely different than a permanent staff member.

"What that means for work?" Allie said, reading Matilda's mind. "Is that I'm not sure yet, and I don't know what my plans are. I'm just…venting. Is that okay?"

"Yeah. Of course. Totally. Fine." Matilda nodded vigorously, even if oh my goodness, her chef might be leaving. For good.

Allie laughed. "Thou doth protest too much, Matilda. You look like someone rearranged your books. I will give you enough notice, okay?"

Matilda heaved a breath. "Okay."

"Until then there's Chef Jared," Krista said with a smirk on her lips.

Allie's face lit up, the change of subject like cold water on a fire. "How is he adjusting? Hopefully all right."

"Better than all right," Krista added, her voice light and mischievous.

Allie looked from Krista to Matilda. "Oh? What did I miss?"

"Absolutely nothing." Matilda shot Krista a look.

"One of you better spill. C'mon, give me the goods. It sucks being on bed rest."

"Okay…fine." Matilda rolled her eyes, though inside, she was thrilled at the smile on her friend's face. She would do anything for her, and anything for the people she loved.

It was both a gift and a curse.

While Matilda would do anything for the people she loved, everyone else was fair game. Fair game for fair treatment, and certainly without her deep emotions involved.

Yet, somehow, dealing with Jared brought out another side to her. At Mountain Rush: intrigue. At Kite Flyer: playfulness. At their tour: empathy.

Currently, he made her want to scream.

"So you're telling me there's no room for change in this." Jared waved the menu. "No seasonal rotations."

He'd asked the same question three times in different ways. She stood her ground. "Not true. If you look closely, so much of our seasonal vegetables from our gardens are incorporated."

"Right, but the themes, the flavors. How about introducing Filipino food?"

"Until we find a more sustainable and reliable way to manage inventory, this is it." She was getting a headache. "There's nothing wrong with this menu."

It was the day after her visit with Allie, and now Matilda was in her office with Jared. For the umpteenth time, Matilda wished that she had more space. Because the room was getting hot. It didn't help that for all the arguing they were doing, Jared looked tempting in his apron and his ballcap turned backward.

Another three feet in the room would also help in avoiding inhaling his body wash, which reminded her of her lips on his body.

Matilda went to the window and opened it, breathing in the cool air. Hopefully it would work like a cold shower.

He was still talking. "There isn't anything wrong with the menu, but it feels…basic. Instead of the roasted lemon and herb chicken, for example, I could use the same ingredients to—"

Matilda put up a hand before the guy could go further. "You're only going to be here temporarily. Surely you can follow what we've been doing all this time."

"Fair. That's fair." He heaved a breath. "But the dessert. If I have to make another chocolate cake—"

"It's a favorite."

"After a while though? Can I add hazelnuts?"

"No."

"Peanut butter?"

"No."

"How about a different dessert, like leche flan or—"

"The entire menu will remain the same for the time you're here. Look, why don't we talk about something you *might* be here for. In case my interview with Chef Angeles tomorrow doesn't work out." She went to her office door. The fabric of her jeans brushed past his knees—innocent enough—and yet, her body sparked to life. She shut the door, albeit a little louder than she anticipated to wake herself up from her thoughts.

"Whoa. Now that is a good use of space."

From inside came a beam of pride. "You like it?" She faced her closed door, where she'd mounted white boards, filled with her handwriting.

"I do. I thought you were organized with your calendar. This is next level."

"Thanks." She cleared her throat to keep herself from basking in his compliment. "The top white board covers the general tasks of the solar eclipse, which is in a week, and then our first wedding of the season a week after that.

"We're completely booked in the lead up to and in between these events. And while there's specific catering ordered for the wedding, of which you will help assist—Gabby is in charge of that since she is our wedding planner—the solar eclipse will be a public event."

"I still cannot believe this event is going to be public. It's going to be packed."

"Yep." Her heart sped up. She had the same reaction when Eva had pitched the event to the whole team six months ago. The appeal of the flow of extra income and exposure won out, but for that night, the B & B was going like an amusement park.

It was going to be chaos.

"Both events will require all hands on deck, but with the solar eclipse, you'll be provided with a menu of foods to make for purchase."

Half of his face wrinkled into a wince. "What kind of a menu are we talking about? Because if I have to cook for an army, I need qualified kitchen help."

Matilda felt his hesitancy, but she was loyal to the mission. "The menu's straightforward. Mediterranean-inspired rice or salad bowls. Slices of our house desserts, like the chocolate cake and tiramisu, which you're familiar with. And you'll have a couple of assistants, as I mentioned."

"Right. But if I'm cooking on the spot, I need actual cooks so they're sure to know their way around the kitchen." He pursed his lips and shook his head. Then, he peered at the board. "I have some ideas, fan favorites that cost little to make but will sell quickly."

"The menu's set. The ingredients have been ordered."

"Okay..." His voice carried a layer of doubt, causing Matilda to turn around.

"You know, I don't remember you being this stubborn."

"You mean six days ago? At Kite Flyer. When we were decidedly not discussing work." His expression smoldered, expression turning dark. "There's a lot more of me and how I do business to know."

A slight shiver ran through her, and she headed back to her computer to put her desk between them. "Anyway, I can send you the current information I have regarding the event."

She fiddled with her fussy mouse through the awkward silence, then finally sent the document through email. To her relief, her phone rang.

The caller was Chef Angeles.

"I have to take this. Let me know if you have any questions or concerns." She pressed the green button.

He backed out of the room. "I'll catch you later."

Matilda steadied her breathing and spoke into her phone. "Hey, Chef! How can I help you?"

"Matilda, I hate to say this."

No. She leaned back in her chair and shut her eyes. "Then don't say it, Chef."

"I have another opportunity that's going to be a better fit. It's a permanent position."

"But—" she thought of Allie's conversation "—there might be the opportunity here for a permanent position."

"Is it available today?"

"No," she admitted. "No, it's not."

The rest of the phone call was a blur, and after saying goodbye, Matilda set her phone down on the table. Chef Angeles had been her last lead.

Her eyes meandered to the back of her door, with all of her intricate plans. For all the timelines she had created, there were cracks and flaws in it.

Jared was her only option. Jared, who could very well be the thing that destroyed the Espiritus. And if that happened, Matilda would have to live with the knowledge that she'd been an accomplice.

Chapter Nine

Jared trudged the second floor hallway of the B & B, weighed down with a garbage can, two pillows and a plastic bag of a guest's dirty laundry. This was his third time up on this floor today, and it was well past the end of his shift, and once more, he told himself that he hadn't signed up for this.

He was a chef. He worked in food service, not in housekeeping or guest services. There was nothing wrong with those jobs, but he belonged in the kitchen and just in the kitchen. While he still thought the menus were basic, each and every meal he had cooked since arriving brought back a little of the confidence he'd lost after that critic's review. He would have rather spent his time researching recipes to present to Matilda.

As he neared the staircase, Eva emerged from it with a smile. "Just the person I wanted to see."

His smile, however, froze on his face. Another reason why he kept to the kitchen—in there, he was comfortable, and no one really bothered him. Also, he could avoid interactions with Eva, whose presence stirred up an odd mixture of bitterness and curiosity in his belly.

Seven days. He'd been at the B & B for seven days, and things hadn't gone as planned thus far. He didn't know any more about his father than he had when he'd arrived. And it *was* for the lack of trying.

Eva could be his primary source of information about his father. And yet, he couldn't muster the strength to be around her.

"Evening," he said now.

"Let me help you. My gosh." She was using her customer service voice as she said this. Her gaze darted over his shoulder, and Jared turned. A guest had exited from the hallway restroom. She waved. "Have a great night, Mr. Kline." Then to Jared, she said, "Let's get rid of this stuff and head outside to chat."

They descended the stairs, to the cleaning and storage area first to set down their things. "Everything okay?" he asked.

"Let's wait till we're alone." Eva gestured him out the back door. After a brief glance of their surroundings, she said, "Normally, we would be having this conversation in my or Matilda's office, but I thought it was better to get it over with."

The air had a bite to it and Jared shivered. Or perhaps it was Eva's tone, which had taken on a stern quality. She surely sounded like a boss at that moment.

"Have I done something wrong?"

Her expression softened. "It's not that. It's your smile. It's a little…fake."

"Wh-what?" The idea made him laugh. "I'm confused."

"I'm just going to come out and say it, and risk the fact that we all love that you're here. Not only have you been making delicious food, but you've jumped into the team dynamic. But you're doing all of it with a grimace. It's like you're sad, uncomfortable. It's not a good look, especially to guests."

"I'm not…" He let his words trail off because he couldn't lie. He *was* sad, and mostly uncomfortable. Not only with how the scope of his duties varied at any given hour during the day, but because he felt adrift in his purpose.

"I just want to make sure that you're settling into the B & B atmosphere. That we—me and Matilda and the whole team—are a fit for you."

"Thank you. I appreciate that," was the first thing that came to mind, and he reached for the next available feeling. "I guess

I didn't realize I was going to be making beds and emptying the garbage."

"Do these things bother you?"

"No." His answer came quickly, because it wasn't the work. It was everything else, or the nothing else. "I like helping out. I think I'm still in a transition phase, you know?"

Her shoulder dropped. "Good. Good. Transition is completely fair. In addition to your obvious talent as a chef, you break up all of the type A personalities here. I know that my girls are usually out and about, but when we're all together? It's a scene."

Jared half laughed, but doubt coursed through him. Did he really belong? He couldn't relax, couldn't settle in. He had no one here. Matilda could be the closest thing to a friend, but their shared secret had built a wall between them. The only real thing working for him was his cooking, and even with that he felt restricted. "There is something..."

"What is it?"

"Honestly, I'd love to be a little more creative...in menu planning. I understand I'm only here for a short time, but if I could bring in new flavors, that would be great."

To his surprise, saying it eased some of the tension in his body.

"I think we can make that happen. You let me take care of it." She beamed. "I'm glad we chatted, then. I'm here for you if you need anything, Jared, even while you transition. We're lucky to have you. I want you to be happy here."

"Thank you."

"Well, I'm off to bed. I'm a text away." She held up her phone, then turned to head up the path to her cottage.

Once she was out of sight, Jared was bowled over by the rising tide of emotions. She'd said all the right things: *I'm here... lucky to have you... I want you to be happy...*

How he wanted that too.

Sweet. He needed something sweet. Something to take him out of his funk, even for the next hour. That would make him happy.

He headed to the industrial refrigerator, pushing leftovers aside.

Thank goodness there was a sliver of tiramisu left from dinner today.

He uncovered the dish, exposing the decadent dessert. And after grabbing a fork, he took a bite while standing at the kitchen island.

The first taste of the light, espresso dessert was like a balm to his senses, allowing him to process his thoughts.

"Knock knock," a woman said from behind him.

Jared turned, the fork still in his mouth. It was Gabby, the younger of the two Espiritu sisters. She was wearing sweats, and her short hair was tucked into a beanie. "Oh, hi," he said weakly.

She laughed. "Looks like you had the same idea as me. Except usually I'm here alone." Her eyebrows plunged. "Which means that you're here super late."

"I was actually almost done." He wiped a napkin against his lips. "Thought I'd grab a snack before I left."

"Hope you saved me a bite." A smile grew on her face.

He pushed the covered dish to her, an honest to goodness smile emerging from his lips. Gabby, of the two sisters, was the easier one to be around. "It's all yours."

She hopped up on a stool and skipped grabbing a plate, digging a fork right into the cake. A moan escaped her lips when she took the first bite. "I have been craving this all day long. School knocked me on my butt today."

This was his first time alone with Gabby. She was the wedding planner, and as with the rest of the staff, picked up the slack where it was needed. But this announcement surprised him. "School?"

"Technically an online accounting certificate. Do you know

how many numbers we have to crunch in this business? I've been doing my best to help my mom out, but I thought I would get a proper education on it, so eventually I can do more around here instead of just eating the dessert. Which I'm very good at doing."

Her personality was easy, her speech relaxed. So open was she that Jared sat down next to her. "I hate numbers."

"Oh my God." She spoke through a full mouth of tiramisu. "I love numbers." She dramatically swallowed. "But how can you be a cook without liking numbers? Isn't everything measured?"

"Let me tell you a secret, Gabby. All those measurements? All suggestions. In fact, you don't need to follow them at all. Just peep at the ingredients and the general process and jump right in."

She gasped. "That sounds like blasphemy."

He laughed. "Let me scandalize you even more. Sometimes, you can even switch out ingredients and make them better."

"See." She pointed at him with the tines of her fork. "You sound like just like my sister."

"Frankie? Really? She seems more… I dunno…"

"Inflexible? A hard-ass?"

"I was going to say accurate."

"Eh, she's all bluster. She wings everything. Sort of like you. And oh, my dad."

Jared was halfway through an inhale, almost choking out at "my dad."

"Yeah. I remember being little, maybe five? Six? He was trying to put together a bookshelf. Even at that age, I wanted to read the directions, and he literally picked the instructions and—" she demonstrated by flicking the napkin in her hand "—tossed it aside."

"That's funny."

"Funny and stressful. I felt it even back then, how he and I were different. Anyway, if there's one thing that'll bring down a business, it's money, and not under my watch."

"Is this place in trouble?"

"Nope, and we definitely want to keep it that way." Her eyes widened. "Oh no, did I just finish all of the dessert?"

Sure enough, she had. "No worries, I was full anyway. I'm glad you liked it."

"Jared. Come on. Everything you make is delicious." She set down the fork, then clasped her hands in her lap. "And to be honest? I'm glad you're here."

"Yeah?" His face warmed.

"Yeah. Not only can you make a great dessert, but it's nice to have another Filipino around. There's not a lot here in Peak. That doesn't make me sound rude, does it? Not that I don't value anyone else..."

"No, I understand what you mean by that. Being biracial is different though. It's in its own box. Though not really in a box." The sugar was getting to him and his thoughts were ping-ponging everywhere. Because it was something to be sitting here with Gabby.

"I get it. Sometimes..." Her voice trailed off.

"What?"

"Sometimes I miss my dad more than other days. Because I think... I think if I could see him on the daily, then I would understand me better." She shook her head. "Sorry, I'm waxing all kinds of inner thoughts. Frankie says I'm always in my head. Are your parents still together?"

The question startled him; he was still hung up on Gabby's admission. "Technically, yes. I grew up with my stepdad, and he and my mom have been constant in my life. It was my biological dad who was Filipino."

He wasn't sure what more to say. Would she connect the dots as to who he was? Would it be a good thing for her to find out?

No, it's not, his conscience warned. He wasn't here to mess things up.

The mood had gotten awkward, so he smiled to alleviate the silence. "Well, it's late. I've got to be back here early tomorrow." He made to stand, eager for space. To think. To breathe.

"Oh, of course. Sorry, I didn't mean to hold you up." She tugged on her beanie. "Gotta face those numbers. But I'll see you soon." She took one step backward and after a haphazard wave, left the kitchen, heading toward the back door.

When the door closed behind her, Jared brought the dishes to the sink and rinsed them, heaving breaths through the steam of the hot water.

This was getting hard.

Jared drove his car down the long driveway from the B & B to the main road, and the dim lights cast a yellow glow in front of him. Up above was a half moon, though there were no other streetlights to provide additional illumination.

This was hard too, this driving to and from work after a long day, along these two lane roads from which a deer could jump out at any moment. It didn't make sense for the chef to live off property, with how his job lasted from dawn to dark.

He would need to add that to his list of suggestions on how to make the B & B processes better. A list of reasons why he wasn't feeling comfortable.

He flipped on his bright lights with force, rewarding him with a better view. Still, there was an inordinate amount of energy pulsing through him. It had been a lot, talking to Eva who he couldn't look in the eyes, and then to Gabby and feeling a connection.

How was it possible for a stranger to affect him so much? Sure, he and Gabby shared the same DNA, but they hadn't shared moments. They hadn't spent time together.

Furthermore, should a DNA connection make a relationship, or was it commitment, love and time that truly mattered? If the latter, then why weren't his family and friends in Kentucky enough? Why had he subjected himself to this experience if commitment trumped blood relation?

What the hell was he trying to accomplish?

Jared hadn't realized that he'd stopped the car until he heard a knock on his window. He jostled to Matilda's concerned expression, her face close to the glass. She pointed a finger downward.

He pressed the button to lower the window, to the full view of her front porch, to the proximity of her skin and the scent of her perfume. His adrenaline eased.

Then, he realized: he had driven to her house. The only other time he'd been here had been when Matilda had forgotten her purse at work and asked Jared to drive it to her.

"Jared?"

He was speechless at first. "I didn't know I was coming here. I was cleaning up, and Eva wanted to have a talk, and I had some tiramisu and Gabby came in late and ate the rest of it." Apparently, his mouth decided to take over and he was rambling. He shook his head. "I'm sorry. Coming here was inappropriate. This can wait until tomorrow."

She raised an eyebrow. "Are you sure?"

No. "Yes."

"Did an issue come up at work?"

"No." Because all the issues were within him, and he wanted to do something about it.

She was the only one around who currently understood the situation.

"Then what are you doing here?"

Her voice was comfort. "I guess I wanted to commiserate."

"We can commiserate. Except." She looked over her shoulder. "Not here. Let's go to Tin Cup Café. They're open until midnight."

"Okay." He nodded, and watched Matilda walk back into her house. Her outline was visible through the curtained window, and as the seconds passed, he felt more and more foolish. Why had he come here? For all he knew, she had other plans.

Not that it was any of his business. He'd promised to keep it professional.

He wasn't the needy one. He was the person people went to for encouragement. And yet, here he was, asking for her attention well past work hours.

He'd picked up his phone to text Matilda that he'd changed his mind, when he heard the rough clap of her front door closing. She emerged from her dimly lit doorway wearing a long coat and had a purse in her hand.

"C'mon." She gestured him toward her SUV.

"I can drive."

"You look like you need a breather."

He jumped out of his driver's seat and came around to her SUV. The passenger door whined when he tugged it open, and though the interior had seen better days with its push button radio and stick shift, it was immaculately clean. New car smell emanated from a hanging tree on the front mirror.

"Jared, this is Misty. Misty, this is Jared."

He shut the door. "You named your car too?"

"Of course I did. But…your door's not shut all the way."

"Oh." This time, Jared pulled the door with one swift yank, rocking the truck.

She turned the key in the ignition, and the engine sputtered to a growl. "I had to name her to let her know that she belongs to me."

"It's an inanimate object."

She gasped. "That has feelings."

He snorted. "If you say so."

"I do say so." She glanced at him. "So, what are we going to commiserate about?"

"The SE." Again, he opted for easiest thing, the most neutral topic, though not a necessarily stress-free topic. "It's going to be hectic."

"Yep." She nodded, biting her bottom lip. The line between Matilda's eyes deepened. "We've never had this kind of a crowd. Not even our weddings are this big. Do you have concerns about handling it?"

"Yes." His chest loosened a smidge with that admission, despite the fact that there was more to his anxiety. "Even as you described it a couple of days ago, I didn't process it all the way through."

"There will be a huge number of bodies on the property, though not necessarily in the B & B," she said, putting on her blinker. Then, she parked next to the brick building before cutting the lights. "But we'll also have more staff available. Security, parking attendants, extra help with grounds maintenance and cleanup."

"I just don't know if I can do this," he whispered, following her through the glass door, which jingled their arrival.

The truth of his own words hit him in the chest, so much that entering the café felt like he'd been shoved into a new reality. He was starring in a silly movie where everything could have been easily solved by all the characters talking to one another or doing the right thing.

The right thing was him not coming here in the first place.

Tin Cup Café was tiny, with a total of eight small tables. A bar counter lined the back wall. A woman with dark hair hiked up in a high ponytail greeted them with a wave, and in the air was the smell of sugar and something being fried.

Something sweet. Thank goodness.

"Sit wherever you'd like, darlin'. What beverage can I grab for you?"

"Decaf." Matilda led the way to a corner table with two chairs. "How about you Jared?"

"Diet Coke. What dessert do you have?"

"Apple streusel."

"I'll take that." He sat opposite of Matilda.

She clasped her hands on the table. "Didn't you just say you had tiramisu?"

"One can't have enough sweets. Dessert therapy."

She frowned. "You're going to do great at the SE, Jared. The menus are set and many of the baked goods can be done a few days before. It will be a whirlwind of course, but we're all going to help one another."

"It's not just the eclipse, Matilda."

"It's personal?" Her face tilted. "Do you want to tell me about it?"

He sat back. It wasn't her role to take on his insecurities, and she had been clear in her position. "I thought you didn't do feelings."

"Look, I *do* do feelings, obviously I have to, with managing the B & B. You and I have had our discussions."

"Arguments."

"Banter." She smiled. "And that's par for the course. It's that I don't like to deal with emotions. My own emotions I guess." Her cheeks reddened. "But this conversation is about you, and it's about work, and also about the Espiritus who are my second family. So, talk to me."

He cupped the back of his neck, discomfort rushing through him. "It's also about you, because of our arrangement."

"Just come out with it, Jared." Her expression was stoic but sincere. It was enough for Jared, because he desperately needed to get whatever he was feeling off his chest.

"I'm in over my head."

"In what way?"

He sighed. "With being around Frankie and Gabby and Eva. Today, I couldn't stop looking at Gabby, and at noticing the things we have in common. Sometimes I'm angry around

Eva, which is completely irrational. I don't even know these people. None of this is their fault. They're not responsible for anything that happened to me. They were just as wronged by what Louis did, weren't they?" He shook his head. "You were right, Matilda. I didn't really think this through, not in the way that mattered. What was I supposed to get from it? So far, it's been just more confusion."

He couldn't tell what was going on in Matilda's head, except that her poker face was on point. "And?"

"Not that I'm planning on leaving overnight." But as he said it, he realized it wasn't true. He recanted. "I take it back. I don't think I'm cut out for this. I might have made a mistake, like you said when I first showed up. Lying every day. This is too much. And leaving sooner than later is ideal."

"Yes, I did. I did say that." She went quiet once more, though her fingers wrung themselves in earnest. "I understand. I appreciate you telling me. But I hope that you can stay until I can get the next chef in."

"Absolutely. Of course. I wouldn't do that to you or the B & B. But I hope that it will happen sooner rather than later." Jared exhaled as some of the burden lifted from his shoulders. "Thank you for listening. I know the plan was always for me to leave when the new chef comes in. I'm just saying that when Chef Angeles is onboard, you won't get a single objection from me. I'll be on I-64 on my way back to Kentucky."

Jared expected for Matilda to be satisfied. His acceptance in leaving was what she had wanted. Instead, her expression fell. "Okay."

Like a child, seeing her disappointment was intriguing. Had she wanted him to stay?

"Decaf and a Diet Coke. Apple streusel." The server set a mug, a glass, the dessert and two spoons on the table.

They both thanked her and once she left, they each picked up a spoon. After coaxing Matilda to take the first bite, she scooped the dessert into her mouth and rotated the spoon so she could savor every morsel. Her face seemed to soften; her body sank even deeper in the chair and a quiet groan escaped her lips.

Jared couldn't help but smile, enamored by these tiny glimmers of vulnerability that she didn't reveal often.

Soon, he wouldn't be around to witness them at all.

The thought brought him back down to the moment. "You don't seem thrilled by my news. I thought that you would happy to hear that I'm raring to get out of here." Jared wanted clarification.

"Chef Angeles declined the interview."

He could've kicked himself. Of course this had nothing to do with him. "Wow."

"She wanted a permanent position and I couldn't promise it."

"That's fair." He racked his brain, knowing he still couldn't stay, especially with seemingly no one on his side, and no one to turn to. "I might know someone who could be interested in the job."

Matilda brightened. "Really?"

"Yes. I'll reach out to them soon." Then, without anything else to say with his thoughts in a mush, he enjoyed a generous helping of apple streusel.

Chapter Ten

Not even fully caffeinated coffee with extra sugar could stop Matilda's yawning this morning. With two days until the solar eclipse event, she was running on fumes, so she took her work outside. She set up on the eastern patio under the bright sun and among the sounds of the rustling trees and the myriad of workers transporting chairs to the vista points.

But she didn't fully wake until Jared strode across the back patio with his disarming grin, radiating cheer.

It was a one-eighty from a couple of nights ago, when they'd shared a late-night snack at Tin Cup Café, when he'd announced that he wanted to leave.

It was what Matilda had wished for, but right then, she was hit with an emotion she couldn't pin down. Was it disappointment? Regret?

"There you are," Jared said. His adorable factor continued to bump up by increments of ten every time she saw him, especially now that he was in his kitchen gear. "I have a question—whoa. You look…perturbed."

"Not even close. Maybe…confused." She refocused on the work on the screen.

"Ah." He frowned. "So, not good."

"I'm combing through chef hopefuls." In truth, it was the list of chefs who'd applied that didn't meet the required criteria to even interview.

She was that desperate, but he didn't need to know about it.

"That bad?"

"It's fine." She nudged the chair next to her. "Sit. What's up?"

He swept into the seat, and as if Jared had stirred the wind with him, Matilda breathed in the scent of his bar soap. It was the same scent she'd caught on his skin when they'd tumbled under his sheets.

The word hit her then: *regret.*

Regret that she'd spent almost two weeks with him and not gotten to know him more.

Regret that she continued to push down her attraction, when he'd been the perfect person to have had a temporary fling with.

Was that her libido speaking? Yes, it was.

Jared held out both hands. "Isn't it great?"

"Oh, um, what?" Her cheeks burned at her delayed reaction.

"That chef candidate for you coming from Norfolk. He's just left the army, where he worked in every part of food service, cooking for large groups. Award-winning too. He's not looking for anything permanent, just a gig while he settles into what he wants to do next. He said that he was open to whatever time frame."

Matilda sat up. "That…was fast."

He rested a hand behind his head. "I made a few calls this morning."

"But it's only nine." Matilda apparently had misjudged how much Jared wanted to leave.

He shrugged. "He answered right away. I left his number on a Post-it at your desk. But the gist of it is that he can come a couple of days after the SE, which is great. I can be around to show him the ropes, and it gives me time to let my property manager know about leaving Kite Flyer and…again with the weird look."

"I'm…processing. But this news is great. I mean, more than

great." She infused enthusiasm into her voice even if her body felt heavy. "Thank you. I appreciate it."

"You're welcome." He was beaming, even more than usual.

"What else is up? It's like you had a double dose of caffeine." She didn't yet want him to leave.

"Okay. Get this." His hands took a life of their own. "Jameson's called regarding our food delivery for the eclipse and there are last minute changes to what's being delivered. Supply chain issues."

"Oh no." Jameson's was a local grocer but also the B & B's supplier for wholesale ingredients.

"But I already have a solution. Eva and I got to talking and we decided that instead of serving food platters, we can switch to sandwiches and wraps. Then, we pivot toward desserts that need zero silverware. Jameson's has baking materials in bulk that they can off-load, so there's no issue with ingredients, and less waste overall because everything will be single served and separately wrapped or contained. This also solves the assistant situation— I won't need actual cooks to help me."

"Wait." Her mind had yet to catch up. "You talked to Eva about this, before me?"

"She was there when the phone call came in. Was I not supposed to discuss it with her?"

"That's not it." Discomfort ran up her spine. "Eva already has a lot on her mind. I'm here to make things easier for her." Matilda had yet to tell her about the honeysuckle, as her calendar notification continued to remind her. "For next time, please take all of your thoughts to me first."

He frowned. "Next time. As in, sometime in the next couple of days until I'm replaced."

"Yes, because all rules still apply. I thought we talked about it."

"This was a different situation. Eva was *right there*."

"Jared." She was heating up, and this time from irritation. No one at the B & B questioned her to such lengths.

"Fine." He stood. "You know, even as a sous chef, I'm usually entrusted with making important decisions, and one of those things is determining when I can speak to the boss. Maybe it's good I'm leaving."

He was looking at her so intently that she shied away, placing her fingers on her laptop's keyboard as if she was in the middle of typing. "You said it, and for once, I agree."

"Noted."

The temperature dipped, and Matilda knew that she'd said the wrong thing. And yet, she couldn't take it back. Moreover, she wouldn't. Did it matter anyway?

"Hey, you two." Eva's singsong voice cut into the icy tension. Matilda looked up to her boss just as Jared turned around. To her relief, he had plastered on a smile as she had. "Small meeting?"

"Yes, actually." Matilda might as well pop the can of worms open. "We might be doing a chef transition here, soon."

Eva frowned. "Already? It hasn't been two weeks. I thought for sure we had at least a couple of months."

Jared hesitated before responding. "I've got business back in Louisville, but the chef coming in is great, maybe even better than me. In fact, I look like a novice next to him."

The act wasn't working—Matilda herself cringed at his poor explanation.

"When does this person come in for their interview? Because they still need to interview with me." Eva's gaze darted to Matilda.

"A couple of days after the SE."

Eva's chest rose and fell and she emanated a deep sigh. "Matilda, can I see you in my office? Ten minutes?"

Her heart thudded in worry. "Yes, of course."

Silence descended after Eva's footsteps faded away, leaving Matilda staring off into the distance, to the path to Eva's cottage.

Matilda gathered her things haphazardly. "I'd better go."

"Yeah, okay. I've got to meet Frankie at the garden anyway."

"What for?"

"She wants to talk to me about something gardening related. She seems to be warming up." He stepped closer to Matilda so that she could feel the heat radiating from his body. "How about you and me? Are we good?"

And despite the contentious conversation they'd had, her body began to melt in his proximity.

It was wrong how attracted she was to Jared, and especially when their situation was soon to end.

Her resolve was fragile, but she hung on to its edges. "You still have to run things by me, Jared. I understand how you feel, but it's just the way things work around here. But yes, we're good. I'll catch up with you later." With her laptop across her chest, she headed toward Eva's cottage.

She was being summoned to the boss's office.

Now she was really awake.

Matilda was halfway up the eighth of a mile trail to Eva's cottage when she was startled by a noise. It resembled the hoot of an owl, which was interesting since it was midmorning.

She turned. At the start of the trail was Clark, gesturing to her with his hand.

She shook her head. She didn't have time for this.

He pressed his hands together in prayer, and she swore that he was sticking out his bottom lip. And did he just mouth the word *please*?

Her shoulders sagged. She gestured him forward, and for seconds they stood at an impasse, until Matilda stomped back down to the beginning of the trail.

"Are you going up to talk to her? About the honeysuckle?" he whispered.

Inhale. Exhale. For the moment, she had forgotten all about those darn flowers.

"We're two days out," he added, "and I've got the guys here today with the right equipment. We can get most of the trimming today and touch-up tomorrow once I get Eva's approval."

"All right," she whispered.

"Fantastic. I'll get everything set up. Once you get the thumbs-up send me a text and we can whack those suckers away. Easy peasy."

"Easy peasy," she repeated, nervousness rising up.

Matilda hurried up the trail after they bid goodbye, and she was out of breath by the time she spotted the cottage's wraparound porch. The dwelling was on higher ground, and from the front door, one could see the gazebo and the trail that she and Jared walked on a little over a week ago.

Time had passed by in a flash. Jared could be gone next week, and the idea of not seeing him…

The front door of the cottage opened as she climbed up the two stairs to the porch, refocusing Matilda.

"Come in. Want something? Coffee?" Eva beckoned her with a hand.

"Coffee is always good." As per usual, in Eva's home, Matilda kicked off her shoes and followed her into the kitchen and the family room.

There, she was hit with a yearning.

The front part of Eva's cottage was sparse. It was her office, furnished by one large desk, where two computer screens sat. In front of the desk was a tufted leather couch; to the side was a meeting desk. The vibe resembled the B & Bs.

The back of the cottage was a different story. Meandering into the family room, she was greeted by framed photos covering one wall, with the center of it a canvas family photograph of a young Eva with her girls. With Louis.

Matilda had passed by these photos countless times in the five years she'd been an employee.

But this was the first time that she was drawn to that center photograph.

Matilda approached it, eyes on Louis's face and the arc of his strong dark eyebrows. His posture, with a slight round of his shoulders. And that smile. That same smile that Jared spared without expense. It was Jared, except with a darker shade to his skin.

It was so striking that Matilda's heart thumped.

This was what Jared needed to see. This photo. All of Louis's photos. A peek into snippets of what had been his life.

"Mat?" Eva called from the kitchen island.

Matilda tore herself away from the gallery wall and met Eva at the island. Java had been poured from the coffeepot, and the smell was just enough to remind Matilda why she was there.

Eva handed her the cup and the heat warmed the tips of Matilda's fingers. She hadn't realized how cold her hands had been. "Thank you. It smells so good." She breathed it in, deciding then that she couldn't avoid this conversation about those flowers.

"So, I called you here because I wanted to discuss Jared," Eva started. "I feel like there's some tension going on."

"Is it that obvious?" She took a sip.

"Very." Her tone was flat.

Matilda set down her cup and braced herself.

"And," she continued, "a little birdie let me know that you and he had dessert late the other night."

Matilda shut her eyes. "Maggie."

"I didn't say Maggie. I said a little bird."

She smiled. "Jared and I *did* meet up, but it was to discuss work. You asked us to be professional, and we are."

"I'm glad." She took a sip of her coffee. "But."

"But what?"

"Now he's planning to leave, and earlier than expected. I'm concerned, Mat. I asked you to be professional, but I hope." She paused. "Let's put it this way. You have a tendency to be… territorial."

"Territorial?" An image came to her: a video posted on social media of a lioness going toe-to-toe with a lion twice her size to protect her cubs. Was she that? "I might be protective."

"No, I mean territorial." A smile grew on her face. "You're like our bouncer."

"A bouncer. Really, Eva?" Matilda giggled, inwardly relieved that the tension had eased, despite being described as territorial.

"Yes. Up on your little stool and patting everyone down, and throwing those unworthy out on their ass." Her expression softened. "I appreciate that, you know? You love this place and my family almost the same way I do."

Matilda heard the rest of Eva's thought, and in the pause, jumped in. "And you like Jared."

"I do. And while I'm sure the chef coming in to interview will be just fine, I feel like Jared fits. Even Frankie likes him, in her Frankie way."

Matilda's mind raced, understanding what she was asking. "You want me to try to convince him to stay."

"Will you?"

"If that's really what you want, Eva, then—" *God help me* "—yes. I will." She heaved a breath.

"Thank you. It's worth a try. Okay, now that that's out of the way, is there anything to update? There are overlapping meetings today with Gabby and the Roland-Shim wedding teams that I need to be present for. And I've got Liam for the night. Frankie's got a date."

"How exciting."

"It's her first since the divorce, so yes." She went to the back windows and paused, staring out.

Seconds passed, and Matilda waited for her cue to answer. This was Eva at times; her thoughts wandered. Matilda imagined that she was thinking of Louis. Maybe she was even speaking to him.

She spun around, eyes bright. "But anyway. Any updates?"

Matilda inhaled a lung full of air. "Actually, yes. It's about the honeysuckle."

"Aren't they beautiful this year? The scent—sometimes I think I can smell them all the way from the B & B's patio."

"They've definitely proliferated."

"It's so hopeful, seeing those blooms, especially in the spring. They seem to be the first flowers to wake up from the winter."

Matilda swallowed her hesitation. "Eva, where they've been planted—they're starting to encroach into the space. We won't be able to fit as many people into the vista point."

She frowned. "But can't the eclipse be seen from everywhere on the property?"

"Technically, yes. But we'd anticipated selling up to thirty tickets—"

"Then sell less." Her voice was steady, though Matilda could detect an edge to her words.

Matilda met her eyes and inhaled a sharp breath at the strength in them. Eva didn't pull rank—it just wasn't in her personality. She led with cooperation, with feedback always under tow. For all the decisions Matilda had helped her make, like building the gazebo and upgrading the appliances five years back, expenses so large that had knocked her socks off time and again, Eva had never demanded her way.

And yet, this was why Matilda was paid the bigger bucks. She was paid to manage this B & B and the grounds fell under her supervision. "Clark thought, and I agreed, that the honeysuckle..."

"No." Eva set her cup down. "You agreed that the eclipse could be seen anywhere on the property. We have the prerogative to decide how many people to allow on our vista points. And it isn't as if our guests won't be moving around."

"Vista point two is a favorite."

"Our guests will find another favorite spot. But the honeysuckle stays, at least for this season. I know it doesn't mean much to you. But I've started to forget the little things about him—pictures are never enough—and the honeysuckle... I just need it." She shook her head. "At most, it can only be trimmed." She took a sip. "Is there anything else?"

Apparently, no, so Matilda shook her head. "That was all."

"Okay. Well, thank you for coming up." She straightened.

It was her signal to go, so Matilda set her cup in the sink.

At the front door, Eva said, "And, please tell Clark that if he has a suggestion, or needs something, he should come to me directly. The honeysuckle and the grounds are under his supervision."

Down the porch stairs, Matilda heaved a breath. This wouldn't be good news for Clark at all.

She didn't understand how things were slipping from her fingers.

Chapter Eleven

Jared popped the straw hat over his head as directed by Frankie.

"You look silly." Liam looked up at him, squinting, shaded by his bucket hat.

"Don't listen to him. It's not so bad," Frankie said from under the shadow of her own wide-brimmed monster. "Just because you're brown doesn't mean you shouldn't protect your skin."

"Fifty SPF, minimum," Liam parroted.

He peered at the boy. "Is that right?"

"Yep, especially because you aren't just Filipino but white too. Just like me."

"Honey, *all* people should wear sunscreen," Frankie said.

Jared met Liam's eyes, and only then did he notice that they weren't brown but hazel. Like him, indeed.

Jared stomach flipped in over itself.

"Can you fly kites?" Liam asked.

The sudden change in topic brought Jared to laughter. "Yes, I can definitely fly kites."

"Liam," Frankie said. "Chef Jared is here to work, not to play."

"Chef Jared sounds so…formal. You can call me Jared."

Frankie straightened and shook her head in objection.

"Chef Jared will do," Jared corrected himself, but with that concession added, "Maybe after the eclipse we can do something, bud."

"Really?" Liam produced a toothy grin.

"Yeah. If that's okay with you, Frankie."

He swore her lips had turned up at the corners. "Yeah, I guess that's fine. But back to business. I've been watching you the last couple of weeks."

"Oh?"

"Yes, and you have got a green thumb."

"I do?" He thought back to his daily trips to the garden to harvest. Not once had he watered the plants—Frankie had been specific about what he could and couldn't do. "I haven't really done anything green-thumb worthy."

"I can just tell. You're comfortable in here."

"I guess it's because I am." He *did* find peace within the garden's gates. There was also something so pure about looking out for the plants. Sometimes he'd found himself just touching the leaves or the soil.

"I admit, I'm a mama bear over this space. It's my baby. I started most of it from seeds. Once I got to know Chef Allie, I extended the garden for her." She opened the gate to the garden. "You're new, but I could use your help. I'm in the process of designing our new website, and with the PTA running me ragged—"

"Excuse me. Did you say PTA?"

"Yes, I'm the president."

He snorted. "Of course you are."

"I hope it's because you think I'm so capable of the job."

"I absolutely think you're capable of the job. I just didn't think the PTA would be your scene. You seem more like you'd fit in at the head of a boardroom or courtroom instead of a schoolroom."

"Ignorant words that people who have never been on a PTA say." They came upon a planter box where lettuce leaves sprouted from the soil. "We're like the gardeners, the harvesters. These are jobs thought of after the fact. The PTA raised enough money to pay off lunchroom student debt, and to add new playground equipment. The PTA supports our teachers and our students, who are the future. My investment is with Liam and the good he's going to do."

"Hold up. Lunchroom student debt?"

"I know, right?" Frankie shook her head. "Anyway, next week is crunch week. I need for you to come out here every day and water and watch and speak to these plants. This should be a no-brainer. Can you do that for me, please?"

"Yes, I can, but…" he began, now thinking of his departure.

"Don't say you don't have time, Jared, because I know your schedule. If I have time to garden in addition to being a mom and running the marketing for this place—"

"And as the PTA president."

"Exactly, then you have time to come out here between breakfast and lunch."

He couldn't resist saluting at her directives. Frankie was utterly convincing. "Yes, ma'am."

She half laughed. "My dad used to do that."

"Oh?" Caught off guard, he didn't know what to do with his hands. So he wrapped his arms around himself to contain both the curiosity and the similar discomfort he'd felt chatting with Gabby the other night.

"He was a soldier. Not sure if you knew."

"I… I think someone had mentioned it," he lied.

She picked up the hose and pressed the trigger, sweeping water evenly over the planter boxes, her gaze trained away from him. "He was a tough guy except to my mother. Hence the salute and the 'yes ma'am.'"

"Eva *is* pretty strong."

"More than strong. She's a beast. To run this place and to keep it going for a decade? And while guiding us on her own?"

Though not sure where the conversation was going, Jared

absorbed it, a word at a time. "Is Virginia your mom's home state?"

"No. Both my parents are from a small town in Oregon. My dad was on leave after some army training, and she was working at the local grocery store. He came in for something sweet and she was there stocking up the packaged cookies and voilà. Me and Gabby were both born in North Carolina, and we moved back to Oregon after he died."

Something sweet. "I'm sorry for your family's loss."

"Yeah, well." She sighed. "Thanks." Her tone encouraged Jared to go on.

"How did you all end up here in Virginia?"

"This was her and dad's dream. As Gabby got close to her high school graduation, Mom went on a massive search for her B & B. There was no stopping her. By then we had moved into a little house near Lola and Lolo's. She calls this whole thing her second life." She let pressure off the hose. "So can I count on you to water? I really don't want to come back and find my babies parched."

"Actually." He gently took the hose from her and looped it around his arm. "I'm leaving. Soon."

"What do you mean?"

"There's a new chef coming in. I'm going to train him and then head on out of here."

"Oh." She stepped away and halted at the gate. Liam rushed past and headed toward the B & B. As he exited, she locked it. "Do you not like it here?"

"No, that's not it. It was always going to be temporary."

"This feels fast though. Have you talked to my mom about it?"

"She knows." He thought of the encounter this morning. "She'll still have to interview the chef, and I'll be training him and—"

"So wait, you're already telling us you're leaving when

the chef's not even hired. It sounds to me that you're the one jumping the gun."

They had made it up to the B & B, where the landscaping staff had invaded the grounds. The buzz was palpable. He caught sight of Matilda, speaking with Clark.

He wasn't 100 percent sure, but had Matilda seemed disappointed that Jared had found a replacement so quickly? He'd expected her to be ecstatic that there wouldn't be a gap in transitioning the position.

And now, with Frankie's reaction, he wondered if he was truly "jumping the gun."

"I've got to get Liam to his playdate." Frankie glanced at her watch. "This is all such a disappointment."

"What is?"

"You."

Her words were an uppercut to his solar plexus. "What do you mean?"

"You let us get used to you. And there won't even be two weeks' notice." She shook her head. "Forget about the garden. I'll check on it myself. And please don't make any promises to my son that you can't keep."

He didn't know how the conversation went sideways. "I'm still here a few days. I can still help with the garden, and do something with Liam."

"No. I don't let random people take care of the garden, Jared. Or get close with Liam, if I can help it. I want people who'll stay." She raised a hand, sighing. "I'll see you later, I guess."

She hiked down the path to the other side of the house instead of going through, and Jared was left with a feeling of disappointment too, except that it was at himself.

Jared busied himself by making lunch, all the while peering out the back windows to see if he could catch Matilda alone. He wanted to have a conversation with her, to get a feel of what she really thought about his departure. But she was a woman with a to-do list that was endless apparently, and it seemed that there was no break in sight.

After lunch, he headed to Peak's grocery store, Jameson's, for some odds and ends. After a short chat with Eva, they'd nailed the SE event menu: chocolate chip cookies, gluten-free blueberry muffins, dairy-free lemon bars, cinnamon bread, chicken salad sandwiches, Nutella and jelly on gluten-free bread, with some substitutions for guests with allergies. Roast beef with Swiss on French bread. A quinoa salad with roasted vegetables, which would be the only item on the menu needing utensils. Filipino favorites like bibingka—sweet rice cakes—ube crinkle cookies and savory meatballs called bola-bola. Eva had been eager to see how the Filipino menu would fare.

Jared, to his surprise, felt no hesitation. When it came to his cooking, his confidence was on an upward trajectory.

Simple dishes meant a simple grocery list, and during Jared's drive into town, he allowed himself to think about his exit from the B & B and the sick feeling that came with it.

Staying won't change anything, his conscience reminded him.

Seconds later, the foliage fell away and he passed the sign for downtown. The rumble of the tires against the cobblestone jostled him from his thoughts.

Peak continued to surprise him. It was quaint with its traditional town square, and streets that jutted like spokes from the center with older brick buildings and sidewalks lined with faux gas lampposts. Yet it wasn't quite as sleepy as he'd initially assumed. People filed in and out of shops, pedestrians strolled along the sidewalks and the parking lot of the grocery store, which was a street down from the town square, was full.

It was a burgeoning little town, but the people he'd met thus far in his errands had remained kind toward him, despite him being a stranger.

He entered Jameson's, and the bright lights illuminating the rainbow colors of fruit and vegetables flipped his mood. He'd known from the third grade that he'd wanted to be a chef. So enthralled was he in the produce section that he'd considered it a treat to grocery shop with his mother.

Third grade. Eight years old.

As old as Liam.

He grabbed a cart and moved that thought along as he cruised the aisles. He'd only been to Jameson's three times, but he'd already figured out the layout of the place. Soon, his cart was half-full, his list almost complete, except he'd forgotten Meyer lemons for the lemon bars.

At the produce section, he took his time and picked the very best lemons, filling up a plastic bag. But he soon noticed that the guy across from him picking his own vegetables did a double take. He had floppy, curly hair and wore a wide grin.

"Um, hey," the guy said, raising an onion in greeting.

"Afternoon," Jared answered.

"I'm Chip. I was the bartender at Mountain Rush a couple of weeks ago?"

Jared thought back but couldn't place his face, though the name rang a bell. "Oh, nice."

"Yeah. I hear you're up at Spirit of the Shenandoah. You're the chef there, right?"

Apparently word got around. "Uh, you heard right. Couple of weeks, now, though it's a temporary position. I'm moving on soon."

"Aw, that's a bummer." He placed an onion in his bag.

"Why? Is there anything I can help you with?"

"I, um, own Kite Flyer."

"Oh! Well, hey, nice to meet you." Jared crossed over to

Chip's aisle with his cart, and Chip met him halfway. He shook Chip's hand. "I've loved the place. It's perfect."

"That's good to hear. Can I ask why you're leaving?"

"It's just time for me to head back to Louisville. I was going to send in my notice as soon as things were solidified. But hey, I can try to connect the new chef once he's in town. He might need a place to stay, too." He gripped his cart tightly.

"That would be awesome. Though I'm sorry to lose you." He looked down for a beat. "But while you're still here, would you want to go on a hike?"

"Hiking?" This conversation was taking a turn he hadn't anticipated.

"I'm a trail guide for Cross-Trails Hiking. It's a shop here in town. We lead trail hikes and teach some wilderness survival, but we also do conservancy, like maintaining trails. We're really trying to get the community involved, get folks outdoors, especially now in the springtime."

"You bartend, own a short-term rental and are a trail guide?"

"Yeah. Keeps me on my toes." He grinned. "You in?"

Chip's expression was sincere, and to be honest, Jared was touched. In Louisville, he lived in a walkable neighborhood, and any trace of loneliness could be snuffed out by heading to the closest restaurant. Work stress could be relieved by knocking on a buddy's door and having a quick beer.

And yet, he was leaving. Would this become a promise he couldn't keep?

He grimaced at what Frankie had said.

Jared couldn't stand one more person to be disappointed with him today. "Sure, why not. So long as I'm still here."

His face lit. "How about I send a text with some dates? If you're still in town, you can join us." He handed Jared his phone, to which Jared typed in his number.

As he did, Jared said, "Warning, though, I'm not much of a hiker. I have some low pro hiking boots but nothing else."

"No worries." Chip walked backward. "We'll get you set up. I've got extra equipment that I can drop off."

Jared laughed. "Okay. Should I come by the shop?"

"Nah, I know where you live and work. I'll call or drop by at Kite Flyer." He lifted his chin. "See you soon."

Jared said "see you soon" belatedly, shaking his head at the interaction. This place continued to surprise him, and this time, it was for the better.

Chapter Twelve

"We're going to have to be creative." Matilda avoided Clark's eyes. They were at vista point two, staring at the offending honeysuckle. Hours had passed since her meeting with Eva, and she and Clark were at an impasse.

"There is no being creative about dealing with this chaos. It's about removal."

"I know, but trim judiciously."

"How was Eva when you asked?"

"She was…directive." She offered him a small smile. Truth be told, now that the shock over Eva's reaction had settled, Matilda was quite disappointed. Did she feel empathy for Eva? Yes, but Eva had always been open to conversation.

Matilda's phone buzzed in her pocket. It was her mother. "I've got to take this."

He nodded. "I'll map out some extra seating areas in the backyard, and I'll trim this section myself." Then, with a wave, he walked down the hill, shoulders rounded in what Matilda knew was frustration.

While she shared the sentiment, Matilda would need to follow up that Clark understood Eva's decision.

She pressed the phone against her ear. "Yes, Mother."

"I've got more news."

The lack of a greeting meant that this had everything to do with Noah.

"Okay?" Matilda braced herself and looked to the right,

where the full back side of the house was in view. The sky was gray, and the lights inside glowed dimly. Then, a person walked out the back door: Jared, wearing his apron. He was followed shortly by two guests, and by the way he was gesturing, he must have been giving them a small tour.

A smile creeped onto her lips. Two weeks ago, he hadn't been keen about helping guests, and now, here he was, making conversation with them. How he'd changed, and how she'd grown to like seeing him around.

Should she have told him that she didn't want him to go? Would it have mattered?

"Are you sitting?" Linda said, interrupting her thoughts.

"Mom. I'm really busy right now. Can you just—"

"Noah has proposed."

Matilda's view tilted ever so minutely. "Proposed what?"

"Marriage, to the woman who's carrying his child."

Matilda swallowed down the hurt and regret that boiled up from somewhere deep.

Noah had moved on, when she was still grappling the effect he'd had on her life. "Well, I'm happy for him," she said now to her mother.

"That's generous. I feel sorry for his fiancée."

"Clearly he's no longer my problem."

"Certainly it isn't, but as your mother, I can still be suspicious of him and fearful for her. I don't understand why you aren't affected at all."

"He's in the past, Ma."

And yet, just like the night she found out about his girlfriend's—nay, his fiancée's pregnancy—she felt unmoored.

Her mother snorted, disbelieving.

Which meant Matilda had to hang up before Linda asked leading questions about how she felt. "I've got to go. Thank you for telling me."

"Okay, honey. Just remember that I've got your back. For when you're ready to share your real thoughts."

"Mom, those were my real thoughts. I love you, but I really have to go now."

She scrambled to hang up after another set of reassurances. Ready to get on with the rest of the night, she hiked back into the B & B. Entering the kitchen, the scent of sugar and cinnamon engulfed her. Breathing in, she willed away the ill thoughts threatening to invade her system.

Jared was drizzling icing on bread loaves that lined the kitchen counter. She was drawn forward, mesmerized by his smooth movements and the gentle drape of icing over bread. She didn't realized she was within proximity of Jared until his eyes darted up to meet hers. She was close enough to see the glints of gold in the brown of his irises.

"Want a piece?" he asked.

"No." She sighed. "It's for the event."

"Um, I think I get a say as to who can have a piece. Besides you have a tiny little drop of drool…" He gestured to the corner of her mouth, then grinned when she actually raised her hand to wipe it off.

"Brat," she said.

He set the piping bag down and sliced up one of the loaves, sectioning a piece and handing it to her on a napkin. "A basic cinnamon bread."

She slipped a piece into her mouth, and the bread melted on her tongue. "Yum. It's delicious."

"Good. I wasn't sure about adding the icing, but thought—why not give those sun gazers more sugar? But the best part is that it's very easy to make, with basic ingredients. Max profit." He waggled his eyebrows. "See, not a bad decision, made by Eva, and me of course."

Matilda had to give it to him—he was right.

And perhaps she had been wrong all along, her whole life.

Maybe her judgment continued to be flawed even five years down the line, and micromanaging had simply been her attempt at control.

She inhaled against her spiraling thoughts. "Did you make enough for me to have another slice?"

"More than enough. I made a couple of extra loaves for the staff. It's important everyone knows what the food tastes like, you know? According to the boss, everyone should know everything around here." At Matilda's questioning look, he added, "Frankie."

She laughed. "I mean, she *is* right."

She stuffed the rest of the slice into her mouth and was glad for the rush of sugar and Jared's easy attitude to dampen the rising gloom.

God, she didn't like being in this space where it was all doom and gray and the fuzzy past. There were more urgent things for her to contend with, including the chef in front of her, who was a few days from leaving.

"Matilda?"

She looked up at him, though her mind followed a beat later. She swallowed the last of the bread. "Yes?"

"Are you okay? You kind of faded there."

"It's nothing." But, she shook her head, suddenly tired of her usual *I'm fine* response. "I take that back. It's the stress of the SE. The honeysuckle Eva doesn't want to cut, the seating at the vista points and the food, but at least you're taking care of that."

"Hmm, sure that's just it?" He sliced loaves with precision, transferring them to precut wax paper. "Logistics excite you. You like to discuss. Delegate. This is different. You've gone quiet."

She carefully formed the words at the tip of her tongue. When she had been at the height of her issues with Noah, that question—are you okay?—came up often. But she'd found out that people were only equipped to hear "I'm fine." Only her real friends and her parents had the capacity to take in the real answer.

Sometimes, she wished that these false offers were never placed on the table.

"You don't really want to know. And besides, it isn't professional." The words that left her mouth had more bite than she had intended, but she wasn't going to take it back.

Jared was silent for a beat; he'd ceased his work. "I wouldn't have asked if I didn't want to know. Look, I showed up at your house the other night, and that's on top of me asking you to keep my secret. I think we crossed that professional line a long time ago."

She blew out a breath, only hearing that she was a hypocrite and failing at everything. "Maybe that's the problem. I haven't been on it lately," she started, then bit her lip. It was all rolled up: Noah, the logistics and Jared himself.

"You're being hard on yourself. You're one of the most capable people I've ever met."

She hadn't been ready for a compliment, and she didn't know what to do with it. "Okay, out with the favor. What do you need?"

"I mean it." He wiped his hands against his apron. "I was upset that night we went to Tin Cup Café, and you didn't turn me away. You heard me out. That meant a lot. You have a heart for people, which is sometimes more important than doing everything perfectly."

Matilda's heart squeezed at his honesty, and with it came bravado to share her thoughts.

But voices sounded from the living room, so she rounded the corner so they wouldn't have to speak across the island. She slipped on a pair of disposable gloves and picked up from where Jared left off, wrapping each slice of bread. "I appreciate that. To be honest, Jared, the last couple of weeks haven't been so bad. You're a part of us already. You're an amazing chef, and you and I work well together despite your insisting on going rogue." She looked up and smiled just as he shot her a grin. "I did want to mention that Eva wants you to stay. She asked me to try to convince you to change your mind, If only..." She swallowed.

"Damn family history." His voice was a whisper.

Still, she heard the regret in it.

She felt that regret within herself; she was attracted and attached to him despite her best efforts. Working with him had, plank by plank, dismantled her usual barrier.

Still, she tried to infuse lightness in her voice. "But connecting us with the new chef—that alone is huge. Thank you for that."

Her response didn't feel right. It was a sanitized answer to a man who had shown her vulnerability. Jared was leaving anyway, right? She could share more of herself. "I'm also stewing over something my mother said."

"What did she say?"

"That I'm not reacting properly to something."

He grabbed a large rectangular plastic tub from the pantry. He set the wrapped slices of bread within it. "Is it a thing that requires a reaction?"

She held out a wrapped slice to him, which he took gently. Their fingers touched, and with the contact she found a little more courage. "I suppose it should. It would have before. But what's the point of emotion when I can't do anything about it?"

As he fit in the last loaf, he laughed.

"What?"

"You almost sound like me."

"How's that?"

"My sister constantly tells me that I'm in denial. That my superpower is looking on the bright side."

"That's exactly what my mother says. Except she says that I simply ignore it. But it works for me." She met his eyes.

There was no judgment in them, to her relief.

"If it works for you, then it works for you," he said. "You certainly are doing fine."

"I'm not sure about that."

"What are you talking about? This place runs like a well-oiled machine and it's because of you. Somehow, you can take all the moving parts and puzzle it all together." He snapped the cover shut. "And I don't want to hear any words of humility. Because of you, I think I might have some of my cooking mojo back."

A smile snaked across her lips; she was unable to contain herself. Matilda had received praise—Eva didn't hold back in that aspect—but she hadn't realized how much she needed it at that moment.

"I would never want to take credit for your cooking. But, thank you."

"No problem. Now it's my turn to be honest. I'm…going to miss this place."

Miss you, was what Matilda read in his eyes.

Again with the stomach giving way. Matilda peeled off her gloves. That was enough feelings for the moment.

"I need to check back in with Clark." She waved him and the moment away with a hand. "Too many things to do, too little time."

"Yes, ma'am." He lifted the plastic tub, and she turned, eager to get herself out of there. Thank goodness, he didn't object. Perhaps he was right: that she was just like him when it came to emotions.

And maybe, they had more in common that she'd given him credit for.

Apparently, it didn't matter whether or not Matilda wanted to feel, because her heart overrode her brain. Once in her car after her shift, she dictated a novel-length text to her friends into her phone, letting them know she needed to meet up, then headed toward downtown. By the time she arrived at K Salon, Krista's shop, the cars of her other friends were already there.

The salon was lit brightly despite it being well past closing time. Krista was sweeping while Bess and Helen sat in the salon chairs. Their cackles resounded through the front windows as Matilda walked up, hands tucked into her fleece jacket.

The warmth of the shop and her friends' arms enveloped her when she stepped in. She melted into their hugs, shutting her eyes.

These were the same hugs she'd returned to after she'd left Noah five years ago.

She'd needed these hugs. She'd needed *them*. Especially today.

"We saw that damn engagement announcement," Helen jumped in.

Bess added, "How are you feeling?"

"Wait. Hold up. Don't forget Allie."

They pushed Matilda into a salon chair and took their own spots around the salon. Krista walked into the back room briefly, returned with a water bottle and pressed it into Matilda's hand. Meanwhile, Bess called up Allie on video chat.

On the screen was the whole crew, and for the first time in a couple of weeks, Matilda could breathe.

"Did you all know before I texted?" Matilda tested the waters. With Peak's interwoven and proliferate grapevine, she needed to know what she was up against. She wanted to be ready for the looks, for the whispers.

Bess winced. "Noah's sister and I are friends on social media, since we were in the Junior League and all. She reposted it everywhere."

"It showed up on my feed, too," Helen said.

Krista nodded. "Same. I was just about to call when we got your text."

"How about you, Allie?"

"Eugene mentioned it. How did you find out, Mat?"

"Mom."

All four hummed.

"Tell us really. How are you holding up?" Krista asked.

Seeing the concern on her friends' faces made Matilda feel foolish. Was she making a big deal over someone who had been voided from her life? "You know what? I'm fine. I don't know why I called you all here. It isn't a big deal. I guess I was just…surprised."

"Don't do that, Mat. Don't minimize it," Helen said. "Because it affects you. Because he was your last real relationship."

"A relationship that lasted over a decade," Krista added.

"And because he's gone out of his way to tell everyone," Bess said.

"He's the same old person. Narcissistic," Allie said. "And somehow you're going to have to try to ignore it."

Too late, Matilda thought. Since that night at Mountain Rush, as much as she'd tried, Noah would enter her subconscious. Not him, per se, but the feeling of uncertainty. The same feeling she had lived under long ago, a feeling that she'd mistaken for excitement, but had permeated to all parts of her life.

Krista began to pace, and tapped her chin. "I bet he's going to try and contact you, Mat."

"He already has."

A collective groan rippled through the room.

"He left a message that night at Mountain Rush, saying that he needed to speak to me. I haven't called him back."

"Oh thank goodness," Krista said.

Helen shook her head. "That jerk. Good for you, for not calling him back."

Bess's head tilted to the side, as intuitive as she was. "Hold on. What's that I see on your face? Do you…want to call him back?"

Matilda bristled under their scrutiny, knowing they would be displeased by her answer. She stood by the window. "I *did* think about it."

Various versions of why were lobbed at her, laced with disappointment, anger or curiosity.

"I don't know why." She shook her head. "Honestly I thought I had moved on all the way. But when he left that message—"

"Yes, I know that feeling. It's called toxicity," Krista said, arms crossed. "You know what I mean—the pull. You must resist the pull."

The rest agreed.

"The pull?"

"Yes. They're like slivers of the old feelings beckoning you. That can still mess with your head, Mat."

"But I don't want to be with him."

"It's all a trick." Bess tapped her brain. "It's not romance, it's dependency, you know?"

Helen nodded. "So it's even more crucial that you don't speak to him. Okay?"

"Promise you won't call him back, Mat," Allie said on video chat.

In that salon, among her friends, Matilda was swept up in their convictions, in their strength. With them, it was easy to agree. "I promise."

Chapter Thirteen

Jared was surrounded by eager individuals waiting for the eclipse event to begin. They vied for his attention like he was a bartender of sugar-filled desserts. But while he served and made small talk, Matilda's words continued to cycle in his head: *You're a part of us already.*

A couple of days had passed since that heart-to-heart, but his body still tingled the same way it did the first time he heard it.

He had wanted something, a sign, that he was there for a reason. That he belonged in a way. That he was doing the right thing.

Matilda's words became that sign. She'd reminded him that despite it all, he was important.

He'd woken up the morning of the SE feeling more positive. Those words buoyed him as he managed event guests. He doled orders out with pride, knowing how hard he'd worked making the menu.

An hour before the eclipse, Jared's throat was dry from laughing. The guests had doubled, and most had found their way outdoors to claim their seating areas. Through the windows, he took in the vast colors of the sky. It was an ombre of white, blue and orange, and along with the twinkle lights that had been draped along the bushes at the perimeter of the patio, it gave that feeling of Christmas. That magical moment when anything could happen—except that it was the middle of spring.

His phone buzzed in his pocket, and it was Emma. do you have a date when you're coming home?

His momentary joy dipped at the reminder of his departure. Not yet. Newest chef comes in a couple of days to interview.

Great!

???

Suspicion flew in.

Spill it baby sister

I kind of moved in. Just for a few days.

What had Emma gotten herself into now?

"Whoa Nelly!" A voice dragged him out of his thoughts and he turned to Matilda walking in, an empty bottle of water in her hand. Cheeks red, she rested two hands on the kitchen island.

His conversation with Emma would have to wait.

Do not mess with my record player. Talk later.

Yeah yeah

Jared set his phone down. "I'm afraid to ask what's up out front."

At the start of the event, Matilda had taken her spot at the entrance and managed tickets and admission. Except it looked like she was the one being dominated. Her hair was windswept, and she had a defeated expression on her face.

"Let's see. There was an almost-fight that security had to step in and squash. Then a fender bender, but thank goodness those folks were calm when they dealt with it. And my phone won't stop buzzing."

To accentuate her point, a buzz sounded.

He hadn't seen Matilda this frazzled before, so he pulled up a stool from the dining room and brought it to the kitchen island. "Take a load off."

She seemed to think twice, then hopped into the seat, burying her face in her hands.

A buzz sounded once more, and she fished her phone out of her pocket, laying it screen side up. Peeking, she groaned.

"More drama outside?"

"No."

"Care to share?"

"No." Then, she looked up at him and peered. "The problem is the sharing. People overshare. They share without thinking."

This was more than frazzled. Matilda was bothered, and every part of him wanted to make her feel better. He hadn't forgotten their previous conversations, about pushing away emotions.

He waggled a finger at her, and turned to the stash of desserts he'd kept back for the staff. "I know exactly what you need."

"Look, not everything can be fixed with—" Her eyes widened when he presented her with a hefty square of bibingka on a dessert plate. As expected, she pulled the plate toward her.

Or tried to.

He kept a finger on plate. "Uh-uh. Not until you spill what's up." At her incredulous expression, he added, "And yes, I really *do* want to know."

She sat up in the stool, her gaze over his shoulder. "I don't have time to talk about it. The place is filling up."

"And you could have told me a couple of seconds ago and taken this bibingka to go. Instead, we're still sitting here."

She heaved a breath and mumbled, though he picked up the words *husband* and *pregnant*.

"Hold on." He leaned closer. "Did you say husband? And who's pregnant?"

Her face screwed into frown. "Oh my gosh, sorry! Ex-husband. And no, I'm not the one who's pregnant."

Jared pressed a hand against his chest and willed his heart to slow. Though, as the seconds passed, he realized that the shock was more about the word *husband* rather than *pregnant*.

Which was curious.

"I've been divorced for five years. But now my ex is going to be a father and about to get married and the whole town knows. Except, apparently, you."

A sliver of jealousy crept up his throat, but he swallowed it down. He had no right to feel that way, since they were never a thing. He, too, had a couple of serious relationships in his past, none of which he'd discussed with her either.

He cleared his throat and tried to piece together her apparent stress over the situation. "Was it a surprise to find out?"

"Yes. That's the least of it. It's complicated, and made worse by everyone calling me and expecting me to fall apart. Which I am *not*." She pointed at him. "Don't you dare object. It's just…he symbolizes a part of my life that I've worked hard to leave behind. And when he's even mentioned, it forces me to think about who I was then, and whether I'm a better person now." She picked up the bibingka and took a bite. "See? Complicated."

He watched her, mulling over her words, words that were valid in his own life despite their drastically different circumstances. He leaned down and rested on his elbows, compelled to be at the same eye level. As she swallowed, she met his gaze.

"Who you are now is great," he said.

"Really?"

Her vulnerability made him want to scoop her into his arms. "One hundred percent. And who you were before was a hundred percent, too."

"I don't know about that. Heck, you don't know that."

"The fact that you think so confirms that it's your ex with the problem. And having been around you, I can confidently say so."

Her eyes darted away, to the plate.

Her hand was resting on the counter next to it.

What the hell, he thought, so he linked a finger around her pointer finger. To his relief, she didn't pull away, and instead threaded all of her fingers into his, so they were holding hands.

Jared held his breath as a newfound energy surged within him, as if she were the source of it. All that he'd tried to deny—his attraction and admiration for her—welled up inside of him.

"There you are. Matilda, they ran out of change out front—" Frankie charged in.

Jared dropped Matilda's hand and stepped back while she straightened, expression nonplussed.

"—not to mention, garbage bags," Frankie continued.

"On it." Matilda stood, gesturing to the plate. "Keep that safe for me, Jared?"

"Will do." Jared nodded, willing his body chill out.

What was that moment? Did that mean something? Could it mean something?

"Earth to Jared."

He tore his eyes from the back door to Frankie in front of him, and his mind reset. "Yes. Hi."

She crossed her arms. "Hi. So I'm actually glad that I got you alone. About our talk in the garden. I might have been a little too rash."

"No, it's fine." His mind was on Matilda.

"It's just that sometimes my filter's nowhere to be found…

okay fine, it's mostly missing, but I know what I said was over the line. I didn't mean to say that you were a disappointment. The real truth is that I'm the disappointed one. I…get attached. I've gotten used to you."

Attention caught, he said, "Really?"

"Yeah. We all have. And I'm sorry about what I said about you and Liam. I was riled up about something completely unrelated to you but all about my son, and I'm a little bit of a mama bear. You just happened to be there."

The sound of quick footsteps softened Frankie's face, and they turned to the doorway. Liam bounced through. His cheeks were ruddy and his eyes were alight, and he was going to town on a blueberry muffin.

For a beat, Jared thought he was looking at one of his baby pictures. His heart pounded, and he dragged his eyes away from him and toward the counter, littered with napkins.

He didn't know what to do with these feelings, for Matilda and for the Espiritus. It was connection, but completely misplaced. He didn't belong here; his home wasn't among these people.

"Hey, bud. Did you find your lola?" Frankie asked.

"Yep. She told me to come in here to get you. But…" He eyed Jared. "Mom, can't Chef Jared teach you how to cook for the festival?"

"No, he doesn't have time to do that," Frankie said.

Jared's ears perked. "Festival?"

"It's really nothing."

Except, a blush had crept onto her cheeks.

"I heard you talking to Tita Gabby about it." Muffin crumbs had formed on Liam's lips and the corners of his mouth. To Jared, he said, "Mom needs help."

"Where's the loyalty, son?" Frankie glanced at Jared. "The PTA is planning an international festival. Parents from the district are encouraged to showcase something from their culture.

Apparently it's not enough that I help plan it. I don't seem to have a backbone when it comes to my best friend so—"

"You don't have a backbone? I object," Jared said.

"I'm softer than you think. Anyway," she rolled her eyes. "I was volunteered. To cook. Filipino food."

"Okay."

"And I'm not much of a cook."

"I like your food, Mom," Liam added, wiping his mouth with the back of the hand.

She ruffled her son's hair. "I love you, kiddo."

The entirety of Jared's heart melted in its cage. This kid was sweet. This kid. His nephew.

My nephew.

"But you can help her, right?" Liam asked, tugging Jared to the moment.

He shrugged. "I'm pretty good at cooking."

Though you don't have much time, his conscience added.

But a part of him wanted to be entrenched in this moment. And again, he didn't want to disappoint either person in front of him.

"You know what?" Jared said, throwing caution to the wind. "You name the time, and so long as I'm off, then I'm game."

Frankie's face lit up in expectation. "Really? How about tomorrow sometime?"

Her smile quelled any hesitation to dig himself deeper into this family's roots. "Tomorrow is perfect."

By the time Jared made it outside, after sales of food ended, the crowd had settled in chairs or on blankets on the ground waiting for the main event.

He, on the other hand, only looked forward to one thing—person. Matilda.

Something had transpired between them earlier, and he couldn't allow it to be swept under the rug. For all the confusion he felt around the Espiritus, with Matilda, he had been honest; he had been himself.

A hand landed on his arm. "There you are."

He turned to Matilda, now carrying a basket of disposable solar eclipse glasses. His heart betrayed him at the sight of her; his entire body relaxed. "Hi. Mind if I have one?"

"Help yourself." She lifted the basket for him to take his pick. "Everything go well inside with Frankie?"

"Yeah. We're getting together tomorrow," he said, though that wasn't what was pressing. He tried to read her expression. Was she happy to see him?

"That's good, Jared." A buzz sounded, and she looked at her phone. Her face lit up as she read. "Oh thank goodness."

"What's up?"

"A couple of grandmas were in some kind of scuffle up at vista point three. But they're all good now."

A laugh bubbled out of him, eyes cutting to her face. "Grandmas?"

"You can't make this stuff up." She giggled. "Speaking of, will you come with me to vista point two to make sure everyone's got glasses?"

"Absolutely. Hold on a second." He texted one of the part-time kitchen assistants as to his whereabouts and followed her up the hill.

The area was packed, with very little room to walk in between chairs and people. "Wow."

"Talk about close quarters," she whispered. "But as long as no one leaves their spaces, it should be just fine. Right?"

"Nope." He breathed out. "You should text security to get up here pronto. Once the eclipse starts people are bound to move around."

"Good idea."

They passed out glasses, and as people shuffled, Jared guided her by the elbow to a free area under the overgrowth of the honeysuckle. The smell was intoxicating, or maybe it was because Matilda was stood only inches away. He was taken back to that first night, when they stumbled down the hallway to his bedroom, peeling their clothes along the way.

A buzz sounded between them, pulling Jared from the heat of his thoughts. His phone lit up with the notification that the eclipse was happening soon.

"It's funny how we need a notification for the eclipse, when it's literally right above us." Matilda set down the basket and turned her face to the sky.

He lifted a hand to block her gaze. "We should be putting our glasses on."

"Thank you. That was close."

They slapped the flimsy glasses over their eyes and faced the sun, where a sliver of the moon had inched in front of the sun's glare.

Jared was overcome. By the eclipse. From witnessing the eclipse with Matilda. "Wow. This is…"

"Amazing," she whispered back. "It's a reminder that we're really just a tiny piece of the puzzle."

"And yet, still necessary to complete the puzzle."

She heaved a breath and there was a brief pause in which all he heard were the hushed conversations around them. "Yeah, but sometimes I wonder if I've made myself into the right shape. Most of the time, I fit. But sometimes there's a remembrance of what my shape had been, and I wonder, was that really me? And shouldn't I try to move on from who that was? I don't know. I can't explain it."

"Surely there's a word in that vocabulary bank of yours."

"Ha." She drew in her bottom lip for a beat. "No, I can't think of a word right now."

Jared frowned to himself; this was unlike her. "I don't think it's a bad thing to remember who we were."

"No?"

"I mean, our past is a part of who we are, right? Not remembering would be saying that we're willing to forget that part of ourselves. But I also think it's okay to change and continue to change. It's how we survive our environments."

He'd said it for Matilda's benefit. She'd been vulnerable today, and he'd wanted to be in the moment with her. But when the words left his mouth, he realized he'd needed the message, too.

In the puzzle of his life, he knew there was always a piece missing. He even knew what this piece was. He could even name it.

He'd tried to fill that space with all of his ambitions, with his denial. With his love for the family that raised him. But none of it perfectly fit.

Now, at Spirit of the Shenandoah B & B, he had some of the components of this missing piece. There was also Matilda, a woman who he wanted to get to know. A woman who he knew he would miss. A woman, while not part of the puzzle, was currently the only person he could trust.

And now he was trying to run away from them?

"What the hell am I doing?" he whispered to the sun, now half-covered. It was alright for him to change, too. Just because it had been a challenge for him to be with the Espiritus and with Matilda didn't mean that they couldn't have a future together.

"What's that?" Matilda whispered, face tilting his way. Though he couldn't see her eyes, worry showed in her raised eyebrows.

He took a deep breath, the honeysuckle invading his nostrils, and to his surprise its scent bolstered him. "I don't want to leave."

"You don't?"

"No. I was, am, overwhelmed. I'm really out of my league. But Frankie asked for a cooking lesson, and Liam wanted to fly kites. And Chip, from the bar in town, he asked me to join a hiking club. I mean, I don't like being out in the dirt, but I couldn't say no." The words were just spilling out of him. "And then there's you. I look forward to seeing you every single day. And I don't want to keep myself from you."

She took off her glasses, which prompted Jared to pull his off his face. With a hand, she guided him deeper into the brush. "What are you saying?"

"That I can't leave now, even if it scares the living daylights out of me to stay. But I'll only do it if it's okay with you. I can't stop pretending that that first night didn't matter. I…" He took her hands into his. "If you tell me that it's no good, that it's not all right, I'll respect it. I'll go."

Silence stretched between them, and though there were too many bodies up at that vista point, all he could hear were Matilda's breaths. Then, she let go of his hands and rested them on his hips, just above the band of his jeans; she gripped the sides of his shirt. "I…"

He swallowed with anticipation. This entire experience was wrapped up in Matilda, and he couldn't stay if none of it jibed.

The touch of her fingers against the nape of his neck snapped him out of his doubts. She pulled him down so their lips were inches apart. "I want you to stay, too."

"Really?"

"Really. I can't pretend that first night didn't matter, either." With gentle pressure from her fingertips, he dipped down lower, until their lips touched. The warmth of her skin zapped the chill from the occasional gust of wind and brushed away the oohs and aahs of the observers.

It was just the two of them, surrounded by honeysuckle.

"I wish we could get out of here." His complaint came out as a groan. "I want to be alone with you."

She giggled. "Later, after everyone leaves. Okay?"

"Okay."

"But it doesn't mean that we have to stop kissing right this second."

Chapter Fourteen

Just after two in the morning, Matilda raced down the road toward Peak, anticipation roaring through her. With her window rolled down, she savored the cold wind against her face. She had been counting the hours—the seconds—since her kiss with Jared at the vista point, and the memory played in a continuous loop in her head. As she'd herded observers off the grounds after the eclipse, ensured that the B & B property had been clear of stragglers, took care of the needs of the B & B guests and then, of course, touched base with Eva one last time before she turned in, all she had wanted was to leave, to meet Jared.

Who was staying.

Matilda smiled to herself, and beside all the potential repercussions of his decision. Right now was not the time to think about it; she wouldn't allow it to dampen her current mood.

Our past is a part of who we are, right? Not remembering would be saying that we're willing to forget that part of ourselves.

She hadn't realized how much she had needed for him to say those words. At a time when she had craved encouragement, he had been there. She had been vulnerable with him, and he didn't minimize her worries.

Even better, logistically, she no longer needed to rush hiring a chef, and the first wedding of the season would go off without a hitch.

And then there was the kiss. One that she yearned to replicate and deepen.

Two turns from the main highway and Matilda was on Kite Flyer's narrow, winding road. She slowed, anticipation growing as the house's signpost came into view. She turned right into the driveway of the bungalow.

Parking, her lights shone on the figure on the porch.

Jared.

He stood when she hopped out of the car. He was still in his jeans and work shirt, cozy-looking and sexy, and she yearned to be cocooned in him, under him, swallowed by him.

But before she headed toward the front porch, she looked over her shoulder. Allie's house was the next street over but built on a hill. From where Matilda stood, Allie's back bedroom windows were in view. Currently, all of her lights were off.

She and Jared would need to talk about this…them…and the implications—small towns and all that. While Allie would keep their secret, and with his—their—secret of who he was still in the balance, the less people knew, the better.

But all that would have to wait. She and Jared had two weeks of catching up to do, though very little of it required talking.

Jared popped the front door open and gestured her inside without a word. Two steps into the dimly lit house, Matilda turned, throwing her hands around his neck and crashing her lips to his.

"You don't know how much I've wanted this," he said in between kisses, words vibrating through her. The sensation traveled all the way down to her toes.

"Me, too." Words escaped her, caught up in all of her synapses firing. "I forgot how good you kiss."

Laughing, he swept her into his arms.

The click of his front door dead bolt was like the pop of a racing gun. But instead of running, she surrendered, her body melting into him. She allowed her senses to take it all in, and as she moaned into his mouth when they kissed, she savored the hints of cinnamon, sugar and the scent of honeysuckle that engulfed her.

He tugged his shirt over his head with a grin. The brief break in his kiss was torturous and she pulled him back down. She walked backward to where his bedroom was, peeling off her clothes. Jared matched her state of nakedness, one article of clothing at a time.

Much like their first night together, her usual inhibitions were out the window, even in the lit room. But this time, she found no need for hesitation. She might have led him into the bedroom, but he steered the mood with his playful attitude, that contagious smile, and that expression that said he liked what he saw.

Fully naked now, she climbed onto the bed, pulling him toward her. It was as if weeks had not passed, during which time they tried to keep their needs under wraps. With him, Matilda felt a kind of freedom. She felt no judgment. In the gentle way he touched her, she felt cherished, and in the way his lips moved against hers, it was as if he'd studied and committed to memory all of the little things that had set her on fire.

He laid her on her back and kissed her deftly, hands taking a more confident role. Like how he managed the tools in the kitchen, with expertise.

She was coming undone by the second.

Then, he pulled away, and her eyes flew open. Jared was looking down upon her with his dark eyes. His shoulders rose and fell with his deep breaths, and a lock of hair fell over his forehead. He was painfully beautiful, but the suddenness of his withdrawal caused her to be slightly panicked.

"What's wrong?" She burst out after finding her words, heart pounding.

"Nothing's wrong. Not a single thing." His lips curled into

a grin. "I wanted to take this in, I guess. I didn't think it would happen again."

She exhaled in relief, and her heart softened at how honest he was in so many ways. That he could say exactly how he felt. Just like that. "Well, consider yourself a lucky man."

"Oh believe me, I do." He scooted her so she was fully under him, so their bodies were flushed. From her toes to her upper chest, every part of her was touching Jared, and it felt just as intimate as making love. The intensity of the moment surged through her and she shut her eyes briefly to reset herself, and then focused her gaze on Jared's nose.

"Hey. Why do you do that?"

"Do what?"

"Look away."

She forced her eyes to meet his, cheeks blazing. The attention made her self-conscious, like he could see right through her. "I'm not allowed to look around?"

"That's not it. As long as you're looking in my direction I'll take it, especially when we're out there. But in here, when you do look away, I worry. I want to make sure that what we're doing is all good with you."

This is more than good. You are exactly what I need.

The words were at the tip of her tongue. Working with him the last couple of weeks had been a tease in every way, not just for her body, but for her heart.

It was silly that she could be this attracted to him in a short amount of time. Maybe it was all the tension between them. Maybe she was just really lonely; of all her friends, she was the only one who was still on her own.

But did it really matter? He was here. That had to count for something.

Still, she had said enough earlier at the vista point. That alone had been…a lot.

She grabbed his butt with both hands. The mood had gotten heavy. "Do you know what's good? *This* is good."

His eyes lit up in mischief.

So predictable, she thought. But she was glad for it, because the moment moved forward. She tilted up and opened her mouth, her legs and herself to Jared, in the best way she knew how.

Unlike the first night together, their second night was unhurried, even up to the moment that Matilda opened her eyes to the slow rise of the sun that beamed through the bedroom's uncovered windows.

As if tuned into her, Jared, spooning from behind, wrapped an arm tightly around her waist. His warm lips pressed against the back of her neck, sending a thrill through her for the umpteenth time.

"Morning." His voice was hoarse, and it rumbled between them.

"Morning." Matilda shifted so she was on her back. He nuzzled his nose against her temple. He wasn't quite all the way awake; his breaths were heavy and threatened to lure her back into slumber. Especially with how his arm grounded her to the bed, and how she was perfectly warm though it was chilly outside. But work called. "I don't want to leave this bed."

"Then don't."

She felt him smile against her temple.

"Yeah, right. And the B & B will run itself."

"Yep. It'll cook breakfast and clean up and make beds, greet and check in people, give them a tour." He punctuated each point with a kiss, trailing down so his lips made it behind her ear, making her giggle.

"God, if only. Then we could take our time and have our own breakfast."

"Even better, we could have breakfast in bed."

"No, we can't eat in bed," Matilda said. "We should make the bed and eat in your kitchen."

"Or we don't need to make the bed at all." He caressed her belly, making her insides shiver with lust.

"A made bed's overrated anyway."

He tilted her chin up toward him. "I'm glad we're on the same page."

Her heart soared with glee. It wasn't about the sex, though that didn't disappoint at the very least, but all these small moments and bits of conversation. They were so wholesome and innocent and exciting that she was tempted to skip work and frolic and find out if the energy this man continued to display could go on through the morning.

But as he softly planted a kiss on her lips, something inside her stomped on the brakes of her desire and imagination. Skipping out on work and setting her priorities aside were the kinds of things she'd done so long ago with her ex. She'd let her emotions and people-pleasing tendencies dictate her actions.

When Noah had said "jump," she hadn't asked how high. She'd just done it.

Everything had been about Noah. Everything had been about pleasing him. She'd found happiness by doing everything he had wanted; that had been her barometer.

She'd discover later on that these small sacrifices had been at her expense, in every facet. Slowly, as time passed, her desires and dreams had been blurred out, smudged like an eraser over pencil marks.

The funny part was that for a long time, Matilda had thought that it had been her choice. That all of it was her choice. But the truth was, she'd simply considered Noah's choices more important than hers.

Was she doing the same thing now? Was she doing it already, even considering skipping work, when she hadn't done so since moving back to Peak?

She couldn't go back to being that person.

"I have to head home and shower," she said after Jared lifted his lips from hers. A day had not gone by when she hadn't shown up early. Even on her most tired days, she'd tried not to show it.

He eased himself from her. "Oh, okay."

Matilda sat up, glancing at the clock. Though she had a full couple of hours before her shift, she slipped on her clothes, refusing to meet his eyes. "Shouldn't you get ready also?"

As if answering her, Jared's bedside alarm rang. A smile curled on his lips. "Yep. I'm actually meeting Frankie this morning before work."

"Frankie?"

"Our cooking lesson."

"That's right." She turned to look at him. "That should be fun."

"Yeah. But hey… Matilda."

Matilda slipped on her socks; she could feel a discussion coming, and she'd had enough of her own internal conversation. The light, fun night was officially over. "Mmm?"

"Hold up a sec."

She felt a hand on her elbow, and she turned to Jared, now leaning up against the headboard. He was bare chested, and he radiated heat and cuddles, and the temptation…it was overwhelming. "What is it?"

"Was last night okay?"

He spoke softly, and his demeanor stomped on Matilda's brakes. It slowed her actions. "Yes, it was."

"Good. I don't want this…for you to think…that this was a mistake. Because last night was great, and I hope, that maybe, we can do this again?"

The relief that coursed through her was surprising. Her heart rate spiked; she hadn't realized that she needed to hear it.

"Matilda? You look like you want to say something."

She sifted through her mixed-up thoughts, because it wasn't just her head thinking, but her body too. And allowing her body to do the talking was bad news. "Last night changes things."

"I know." He linked his fingers on his lap. "I was thinking about all of that. About me staying and what to do with Eva and the others."

She nodded, now feeling the full weight of his secret.

"I'm going to tell them who I am."

"You are."

He nodded, running a hand through his hair. "I don't know when. I need to get all my thoughts together."

The wind left Matilda's lungs and she was speechless. This was truly happening, and she wasn't sure if she was relieved or worried.

"What are you thinking about?" hc asked.

"That this was what I wanted." And yet, especially after their night together, there was more. There was the chaos of the upcoming week. "But we have a wedding in a week and the news might be a lot to process. I don't want to throw a monkey wrench into all the work that's coming up."

"It's *me* that has to process seeing your fine self every day knowing I can't touch you."

Her cheeks heated as a smile wormed its way to her lips. She tapped him lightly on his blanket-covered leg. "You know what I mean."

His expression turned somber. "I do. How about this—I won't tell them until after the wedding. Which is probably better for me too because I may need to wind myself up for the reveal."

"Okay. But there's another thing. I don't think *this*—" she gestured to the both of them "—is something we should be parading at work."

"You mean I can't take you on one of the dining room tables whenever?"

She laughed. "No."

"The butler's pantry?"

The image sent the butterflies in her belly on full throttle. "You're so bad, I swear."

"I try, just so I can get a rise out of you." He reached over and linked hands with her. "But I promise to keep my hands off of you out there."

Matilda still harbored a final worry. *The* worry that ruled above all. "Jared?"

"What's up?"

"Could you keep me out of the secret…if that's okay."

He looked surprised that she would ask. "Of course I won't tell them that you knew. I don't want to be the person that gets in between your relationship with the family."

It was a sign for Matilda to go, before they delved even deeper into their entire conundrum, into what their status was. How long would they truly last? How long was he really going to stay? She still had a job to do, which included finding another chef, and a permanent one, if Allie decided not to return.

Matilda simply wanted to pocket last night and this moment. And, for once, not to overthink it.

She stood. "I should go. We still have more cleanup after last night, and my to-do list is full. See you soon?"

"I'll be there, apron on. Are you sure you don't want breakfast? I can whip something up."

"Rain check?" She needed some space, a moment's breath. This was so much to take in.

"Rain check. For next time?" He held out a hand.

She linked her fingers with his, and just like last night in the kitchen, it filled her with warmth. "We'll need to be careful. Keep it discreet."

He nodded. "I can do that."

"And, no promises." She pressed her lips together; the words tasted bitter on her tongue. "What I mean is, I don't want any pressure on this, on us."

There was already so much riding on who he was. But she didn't have to say so; he knew the stakes.

"Agreed. No pressure."

"Next time, then."

"Tonight?"

She was amazed how forthcoming he was, at how easy he answered, without thought. Was that a product of him, or his age? Of the fact that he had ten fewer years of challenge and hurt?

At the moment, she didn't care. "Sure, why not."

He clutched his chest. "You're killing me with how excited you are."

"I am excited."

He leaned forward and kissed her on the lips, and a thrill traveled throughout her whole body. She climbed onto the bed, drawn to him, and straddled him once more. He buried his hands in her hair, and she reveled in his hold, in his command of her body.

She *did* love this. He was so different from her. With him, she could let go of what she had been, even for a moment. It was an escape from what she had known of herself.

Jared's snooze alarm rang, eliciting a groan from him.

"Reality calls," she said.

His eyes lit up. "What are you talking about? This is reality. We just get to extend it at work."

"You say that so easily." And yet, Matilda then realized he was right.

Chapter Fifteen

"Is this right, Chef?" Frankie steadied the onion with her left hand, fingers curled in, with the knife of the blade at the ready.

"That's perfect. It's the best way to keep your fingers safe. Now, a sure but swift push down on the blade."

Jared watched Frankie slice down on the onion, heart leaping at how well she had taken to chopping. At how natural she was in the kitchen, despite saying that she wasn't much of cook.

They were in Frankie's cottage on the B & B property, an hour before his shift. But despite strong coffee and a high from his night with Matilda, his mood was heavy.

He'd decided to stay. He would soon need to tell the Espiritus who he was.

He had almost hoped that Frankie would cancel their cooking lesson.

"Nice." Jared stood back as Frankie methodically dice onions. She had wanted to learn how to cook sisig using his recipe.

The same one he'd used on the television segment months back.

It was a full-circle moment of pride that Jared never could have predicted.

A loud thump from the living room caught his attention.

"I'm okay! No blood!" Liam stood from behind the couch, hands up like he'd done a triple backflip.

Jared laughed.

Frankie looked up from her slicing. "It drives me batty when he does that. At this rate, he'll have ten broken bones before I send him off to college."

"I actually did have a couple of broken bones by the time I went off to college. I was a little bit of a daredevil on Roller-blades." Then, it struck him. Was it hereditary? Had Louis also been a little bit of a daredevil? He *did* join the army, though Jared didn't quite know how he had lived, or how he'd died.

Did he want to know how he died?

What else about Liam was like him and Louis?

"I don't really mind the energy more than that it's all happening indoors. I'd rather he be rowdy outside. But his father doesn't do any kind of limiting, so I've got my work cut out for me on setting rules for indoor play." She set the knife down with a flourish and raised both hands up. "Done!"

Jared corrected himself: *this* was where Liam got some of his mannerisms.

He held back a smile. "Great. Now the garlic."

As she tackled mincing the garlic, Jared's thoughts flew to Frankie's ex. It was her first mention of him, and Jared couldn't tell from her focused expression if it was overstepping to ask more about Liam's father.

If Matilda was closed, Frankie was Fort Knox.

Frankie sifted through the garlic pieces and lifted up two pieces that were not minced more than they were smooshed. "Dammit."

"Eh, variety is the spice of life, right?"

"I just want to do it right."

"It *is* right."

"Thank you. Even if it's evident that it's not." She sidled to the sink and turned on the faucet.

"You remind me so much of my sister, Emma."

"Is she a horrible cook like me?"

"No," he laughed. "She tends to get caught up in the process, in whatever she's doing. But cooking is all about enjoying the process."

"For me, it's about eating the end product." She wiped her hands on a kitchen towel. "And if you can't help me, I'm not sure what can."

"You're already talking about failing and we've yet to get started. But it's okay, because I'll fix you yet." He called her over to the stove.

She pouted. "Fine."

He guided Frankie with step-by-step directions; Frankie listened carefully, asking an inordinate number of questions. And after twenty minutes, they ended up with a kitchen full of smoke and sisig that didn't look half-bad.

She scooped a spoonful of dish and took the first bite. Jared stood back and watched her. To his surprise, he found that his heart was beating a steady drum. That critic who lambasted his sisig still weighed heavy in his mind.

Frankie shut her eyes for a long moment—a good sign.

Then, she moaned.

Jared could have fainted on the spot. "You like it."

"Not only do I like it… I love it." The right side of her lip curled up. "My uncle on my dad's side supposedly makes the best sisig in the family. Apparently it was my dad's recipe." She cleared her throat. "Look at me. Going down memory lane. Anyway your recipe blows it out of the water. Do you think that's disrespectful?"

He was still stuck at the fact that she compared his sisig to, essentially, Louis's.

Also, an uncle of *hers* would be an uncle of *his*, wouldn't it?

He started to stiffen, resisting against the thought, but breathed through the discomfort. He was staying now, and soon, Frankie would know who he was. Which meant that it was all right to think of these relationships more deeply, right?

"I don't think it's disrespectful at all. I'm pretty honored."

"I hope I can re-create it for the festival." She frowned. "Did I say something wrong?"

"No. Nothing at all. I like it…family stories, that is." Curiosity burgeoned in his chest. "Tell me more about your dad."

Frankie looked at him a little funny. "Why do you want to know about my dad?"

Smooth, real smooth, Sotheby. "Nothing, just that you mentioned him a couple of times. What else did he like to cook? Um, maybe I can teach you how to make those dishes, too."

"Heh, like you'll have time before you leave the B & B." She looked down and wiped her hands on the apron.

"Actually." He picked up the ladle and placed it in the sink. "I'm staying."

"You're what?"

"Yeah. You were right. I was…rushing my stay a little." He bit his bottom lip.

"What made you change your mind?"

"The eclipse, I guess. Matilda—"

"Matilda?" Her eyebrows rose and her tone took a teasing quality. This was new, and Jared wasn't sure how to react.

He would need to be careful about revealing anything about their relationship.

"She and I got to talking, and I realized I can't leave until—" he cleared his throat "—my work here is done."

She scoured his face for several seconds, so long that Jared felt like his mind was being read. He started to sweat.

"I'm glad you're staying." She gave him a playful punch on the arms.

"Oh. Good."

"And I'll take you up on that offer to help me with other dishes. I know Mom has a notebook of my father's recipes somewhere, though I haven't seen it lately."

The whiplash of the conversation was sudden. "He had recipes."

"My mom didn't really dig into cooking until after he died, and even now, she's a basic cook. Dad made the best meals though. He enjoyed the process like you do, I guess." She half laughed, gazed in the middle distance. "I have very few vivid memories since he died when I was twelve. Getting older sucks in general, but especially because it's getting harder to hold on to tangible memories. Anyway, much of it was me sitting at our kitchen table watching him cook, sometimes even in his uniform." Her eyes twinkled as she looked off to Liam. "Sorry, that's probably TMI. I sound super cheerful right now. Tell me more about you? Who of your family is Filipino?"

Jared took care in his explanation. "My birth father was Filipino. My mother's white—her parents were Greek. She and my birth father were kind of a one-night stand. Her best friend stepped up to help her out after she got pregnant. They fell in love and married. So I've never known any other father figure but him."

"Is your stepfather Filipino too?"

He rested a hand behind his head. "No. His family's English. I'm the only Filipino person in my family and extended blood relative family, though I'm only half."

She frowned. "I hate that term."

"What term?"

"Half. You're not half. You *are*. I'm Filipino, and I may have Spanish blood in me, Chinese even. And depending on how you were raised, and your associations…what makes you less Filipino than me?"

Jared was stunned silent, mouth agape, at the depth of what Frankie said.

"Mom, look at what I did over here!" Liam yelled, lifting his game controller over his head. "I got to the Ice Realm!"

"Okay, I'll be right there." With a gritted smile, she said, "Sorry, but I actually like this game. I'll be right back."

Frankie walked away, and it was only when she reached the living room that Jared began to process what she had said.

That so much nuance existed in everyone's lives. That even in one family, in his, in Frankie's, so many intersections made up an identity. That he could exist in this intersection; that he had been even if he had tried to deny his association with Louis.

That by refusing to face his relationship with Louis, he'd refused to accept a part of himself.

Belatedly, he said, "I'll clean up."

She yelled from the couch. "Don't do that! I will."

"Chef's rules. If you cook, someone else cleans." Jared turned away to face the window. Thank goodness for the distraction, because his heart had grown heavy, and tears had sprung to his eyes.

Cleanup at the B & B eclipsed the labor of the actual SE itself, but Jared was glad for the time outside by himself on one of the trails, armed with a garbage bag and a heavy duty pickup tool.

Garbage was everywhere: utensils, balled-up napkins and the occasional cigarette butt, despite the B & B's standing rule that there would be no smoking on Spirit of the Shenandoah property. He picked up trash and took the moment to breath the clean air.

This morning with Frankie had rocked him to his core. What Frankie had said about his identity felt like a boot against his back, grounding him to exactly what his problem was.

Half or whole Filipino? Half or whole Espiritu? Half or whole of the truth of who he was?

He was nudged from behind and he jumped in surprise. "Whoa."

"Hey." Matilda was breathless, cheeks pink. Her hair was up in an intricate braid, and like him, she was wearing fleece and worn jeans. She had an added puffer vest, which made her look that much more comfortable. When she threw her arms around him, he lifted her up by the waist.

He breathed her in with his eyes closed. She came at the perfect time. "Damn, you feel so good."

"I was yelling for you from all the way up there. I thought that maybe we could do a trail together, you know?" She waggled her eyebrows.

He pressed his lips together to keep his libido in check. This was new, this flirtation, and he liked it. "I don't see you with a garbage bag or gloves."

"I have other tools." She dipped her head and gazed at him through her lashes.

He set down his things and took off his gloves. He cupped the side of her neck, bringing her closer so their lips hovered. The last time he had kissed her was earlier this morning, but he couldn't have enough. "Don't tempt me."

She tugged him down by his shirt and her kiss dashed away some of his thoughts. Then, she eased herself away. "I've got news. Allie just had her baby."

"Wow. That's great."

"It was quick, apparently. But she doesn't want any visitors until she gets home."

"Please give her my congrats when you see her. I know we haven't met, but a new baby is something to celebrate. Hey, maybe I can bake her something. Or I can cook up a nice hearty vegetable soup?"

"I'll definitely tell her. And a soup would be so nice. She's allergic to nuts, but anything else goes." Her smile narrowed. "Anyway, I wanted to get you alone, to find out what's up."

"What do you mean?"

Her head tilted to one side. "We've known each other less

than a month but this is a fact—you wear all your emotions on your sleeve. And something's going on. I could tell from the moment you clocked in. Did it go okay, cooking with Frankie?"

A sigh escaped his lips, and he felt his body go slack. He had no idea that he was so transparent. "It went really well."

"And?" She gestured with a hand for him to continue.

And...he didn't know what else to say. Identity was confusing. It was subjective. Some people were offended by the topic; others were defensive. How could he talk about something so personal? He hadn't yet been able to process it himself, that just three months ago, his food—and he, by default—was inauthentic. And today, a person that shared his DNA told him that he was 100 percent whole.

The only thing he knew for sure was that he was standing in front of this beautiful woman who he was undoubtedly taken with.

But he couldn't go there. He didn't want to burden anyone with his issues.

"And, I think we need to tell the Espiritus that I found one too many cigarette butts on this trail. Which means we have to somehow enforce our no smoking rules and keep a special eye on that at the next event. The last thing we need is a fire." He took a step down the trail and thank goodness found something to pick up.

"That's disconcerting. I'm definitely going to bring that up at the next meeting." She trudged after him. "I appreciate you mentioning that, but I know there's more you're thinking about. Have I mentioned I'm a pretty good listener?"

He took her in. He loved the fact that she had two sides to her, the strong and the soft. The guarded and the open. And at all times, she was honest.

He leaned in and took her lips with his and wished everything was as easy as that.

"What was that for?" Matilda asked after the kiss.

"I was just thinking how lucky I am."

"Yeah?"

"Yeah. To have someone here that cares about the way I feel."

She looked at her feet. "It's my job to care. I manage this place."

He didn't object, because he knew he was pushing her comfort level. "It's still something. And I'm hesitant to tell you not because I don't trust you, because I do, Matilda. From day one you could have said something to Eva but you haven't. It's just that I don't know *what* I'm feeling."

She took a step forward, and they began walking down the path, at first in silence. She picked up a couple of pieces of trash, and spun toward him. "Try me. I've got ten years on you—"

He rolled his eyes and groaned. "The age thing again."

"It's a real thing."

"You don't know what I've gone through and vice versa."

She bit her bottom lip. "Okay, that's fair. How about this then—try me, because I might have gone through something similar, even just a little bit. People don't have to be in the same situation to understand. There's empathy. And I can have that."

They had gotten to the middle of the trail, where the canopy of trees lent a chill to the air. Jared shivered in response as he gathered his thoughts about his time with Frankie.

"I…felt seen by Frankie." He glanced at Matilda, and she met his eyes. "I had the same experience with Gabby the other week, and it was one of the things that spooked me.

"I don't know the Espiritus at all, and yet I see something of myself in each of them. In Liam, even. All my life, I always felt a little bit out of place. I mean, I don't want you to think that life was doom and gloom, because it wasn't. I have a good life, Matilda. I'm lucky to have the family I have. This is not about being accepted by my family or friends, because I am. A lot of my feelings have to do with the discovery that my birth father died and was out of the picture, though it didn't really hit me until a few months ago, when my mom handed me Louis's things. Up to then, I had denied it to myself that Louis was important."

They'd come upon a large rock, and Matilda perched on it. She gestured to the empty space next to her. "This cooking lesson must have been wicked."

He laughed, taking a seat.

"Seriously, though, it's good to feel understood," she said.

"It's not just good. I needed it. Here's the thing, though—I'm not sure what to do with that. It took me till now to want to know more. I was convinced that seeing this part of my family wasn't important. That blood didn't matter. Now that I'm here, I'm wondering if I waited too long. Am I too late?"

He looked down at their feet, stretched out in front of them. At his own hiking shoes, at how new they looked compared to Matilda's worn boots. Apparently his father loved to hike. And Frankie, Gabby and Eva all possessed a part of him that Jared would never know about.

"There's so much I don't yet know. And I'm scared. I'm afraid of what I missed. I'm afraid of them finding out the truth of who I am and I'm afraid that…dammit I can't even put it into words…" Jared trailed off. He felt as if he'd come right up to a wall, and he couldn't push past it. Something was on the other side and he couldn't see. That by refusing to face his past, his heart was preventing him from doing so out of spite.

Matilda bumped him gently, so it knocked him out of his momentary spiral. "Hey. It's okay that you can't put all of it into words yet, because I think I understand."

"You do?"

"I think so." She looked off into the distance. "Is it maybe that you're afraid that if you do find out all these things, that nothing comes out of it? That there's no solution, or reunion, or…real connection?"

Her words seemed to chip away against the wall. Jared could see a pinprick of light through the brick. "That, and that maybe—" he swallowed against the ball in his throat "—that I didn't matter anyway."

The words, said out loud, acted like a sucker punch. His insides folded over and pain dashed through him. It was the same sensation he felt when he'd thought about Louis in the past, when he'd first met the Espiritu sisters, and Liam. Except that back then, he would snap himself out of it with a joke, with a grin.

Matilda took his hand into hers and whispered, "You matter. Despite what happens with the Espiritus. It is independent of that."

"What are we but who we are to other people?"

"That's deep, Jared." She squeezed his hand.

"Sometimes I even surprise myself." He sniffed a laugh.

She scooted closer, so the warmth of her body was right up against his, and it abated his fear that he had said too much. That he'd dragged her down to his drama.

"Look, Jared. If we based who we are against what people thought of us, my gosh, how do we all improve as people? Not everyone had a great life. Some folks fall into tough situations. And sometimes, it's up to us to get ourselves going. Sometimes, improvement and growth doesn't happen in a straight line. You are your own person."

He took her hand into both of his, mulling her words. She had echoed Frankie, and he was overwhelmed with her words. He couldn't process it all the way through, but her touch and presence had calmed his racing thoughts. He snickered. "I bet you didn't expect this while picking up trash."

She looked afar and hummed. "Look, as long as you aren't

complaining about what more you can slip into the menu… When I was your age…"

Her tone had lightened, and it lifted the heaviness from his heart. He groaned playfully. "Here you go again with your age commentary." And despite being alone, he leaned in to whisper, "Then again, I don't think you mind my energy in bed."

The tops of her cheeks reddened. "I could do with more, actually. Don't you know the forties is a woman's sexual prime?"

He laughed. "You're too much." But as he said it, he knew it wasn't true. Matilda was enough in all the ways that mattered.

Chapter Sixteen

A few days later, Matilda finally received the call that Allie was home from the hospital, settled in and ready for visitors. Now, she, Bess, Krista and Helen were hanging out in Allie's kitchen, plied with tea and snacks from Allie's mother, awaiting her appearance. Each possessed a bag or a basket of gifts, with Matilda bringing by chicken tinola, a Filipino-style chicken soup courtesy of Jared.

"Look, Brianna, your aunties are here," a voice said from the staircase.

Matilda turned to her friend, who had descended the stairs, with her baby in her arms. On her face was a smile, but she was tearful.

The flurry began. One took the baby—Krista had won out this round—Helen got the recliner ready, and Matilda and Bess helped Allie to the living room.

Allie snickered. "You all know I can walk on my own right?"

"Just shush," Bess said. "Let us spoil you."

Matilda took the closest seat next to Allie after sneaking a peek at the baby. Though her friend was undeniably tired, to Matilda, she looked beautiful and brave and strong. Yearning shot through Matilda, at how momentous an occasion this was, though she stifled the temptation to pepper her with too many questions. "How are you?"

"Sore. She came out so fast." She went on to describe her

birth story, the quick trip to the ER to almost deliver there. Matilda was rapt.

"She was amazing," her mother said from the kitchen.

"Of course she was," Matilda said.

"I can't tell you how often I went outside to soak in the sun yesterday. In a couple of days I think I'll be able to hit the garden."

"My turn for the baby." Bess stood, but Helen beat her to it with a bump of the hip, scooping her up from Krista.

"Nope. Me first."

"I'm going to patiently wait my turn, but look at you, Helen," Matilda said teasingly. Of the three, Helen was most prickly about kids. The first to comment about kids on planes, kids in restaurants and how town square was crowded with them.

Eyes on the baby, she said, "This is different. Brianna's special."

Allie raised her eyebrows at Matilda and whispered, "Who knew?"

Bess sighed. "I can't wait to be a mom. But my ovaries are on a different schedule than my preferred timeline. MBA first. And perhaps a ring." She shrugged. "But this is why you and Krista have kids. I can come over and get my fix."

"So tell me, what's up with everyone? What's going on in the outside world?" Allie asked.

Everyone took a turn to catch Allie up. Krista was all booked for the spring for wedding updos, which she wasn't looking forward to. Because bridezillas. Helen, a boutique jeweler who owned Valley Gems, was having a spring sale the next couple of weeks, and she expected a rise in marriage proposals. And Bess, who ran the after-school teen center, reported that 100 percent of those placed in her charge were in cahoots to prank her every chance they could.

Soon they were all cackling and checking out the teenagers on social media, where Bess's jump scares were recorded and streamed.

Allie turned to her. "And how about you?"

"Me? Oh, the same-o. We had our eclipse event the other day, which you all avoided." She waved a hand in the air. "You were excused, Allie, but these other three?"

"Why would I pay and subject myself to a crowd when I can see the full thing right in my backyard?" Krista shrugged.

The other two hummed an agreement.

"And it's interesting that you say 'same-o,' when it certainly is not." Allie gave her the side-eye. "Our friend Matilda Matthews has been making house calls."

Helen passed the baby to Bess, wide-eyed. "What?"

Matilda gritted her teeth, knowing where this was going.

Allie continued, "House calls to someone who she happens to be working with, at a certain rental property I can see from my bedroom window."

"Oh my God, Kite Flyer?" Krista gasped.

Bess squealed. "Jared?"

Denying it was futile. She sighed. "Yes. But it's casual."

Allie objected with a snicker. "At least two nights in a row casual..."

"And a secret." Matilda leveled everyone with a glare.

"Everyone of importance is in this room." Helen rolled her eyes. "Though now I'm wondering why you haven't said a thing."

"I don't know. I guess I wanted to keep things simple."

"No. I don't believe it," Bess said. "Look at you. You're not vehemently denying it." She pressed a hand against her chest. "Our Matilda's growing up."

"Okay, let's stop."

"To be honest, I'm a little relieved. I was feeling guilty about taking too much time off work for bed rest and postpartum.

Now that I know the chef's working out, I can make my announcement," Allie said.

The air crackled with change.

"It's been a rough couple of days," she continued. "Sad to say, it wasn't even sweet Brianna who was causing it. In fact, she has been perfect. It's like we're partners already."

"Oh dear." Krista had been handed some water bottles and she set them on the coffee table. She unscrewed one and handed it to Allie.

Allie took her time to drink. Meanwhile, concern shot through Matilda. There was more than the exhaustion of motherhood on her friend's face.

"It's Eugene," Allie said, voice breaking. "He's been offered a job in a hospital in Northern Virginia, pending he passes his boards. Apparently he received it a couple of weeks ago, but didn't tell me until after Brianna was born."

The room stilled.

Matilda frowned, sorting through her friend's words above her running thoughts. "Northern Virginia? I thought staying around here after his residency was the plan?"

She shook her head. "Apparently the opportunities here don't interest him."

"So you *didn't* know he was looking?" Bess asked.

Allie bit her lip, a tell.

Matilda looked up at the rest of her friends, who all bore shocked expressions. She waited for someone to call that part in. Wasn't this a red flag?

Krista snorted a laugh. "He said no, right?"

Allie half laughed, her gaze migrating to meet Matilda's. "He said yes."

"What does this mean?" Bess whispered, her cheek pressed against the baby's temple.

"It means that after my postpartum recovery, we're putting the house up for sale and we're moving."

* * *

"I think we should do more open to the public events."

Gabby's declaration knocked Matilda out of her thoughts. Her mind had been back at Allie's. At the fact that her best friend was moving and the B & B chef was leaving. Permanently.

Allie's announcement had flipped the tone of their visit a full one-eighty. But it had been unanimous, though unsaid, that grilling Allie about how she really felt about moving wasn't yet appropriate. Instead, Matilda, Bess, Helen and Krista had retracted their claws and curiosity to celebrate the baby.

Matilda would need to update the Espiritus about the situation today, but first things first: her thoughts on public events. She refocused to Frankie, Gabby and Eva, all sitting around Eva's meeting table in the front room.

Matilda raised a finger. "Three quick thoughts on my end. One, there were times when it felt a little out of control. Perhaps we admitted too many people. Two, the state of the property the day after was horrendous. At cleanup, Jared found cigarette butts on one of the trails, which is concerning because it's an obvious fire hazard. If we continue to do public events, we'll need extra security or eyes in all parts of the property. Three, I don't think we served our B & B customers well that day."

"But the effort is worth the extra revenue, don't you think? With ticket sales, we could afford to outsource the deep cleanup and increase security," Gabby countered.

A knock on the front door silenced them. They all turned to Jared, who was carrying a tray. "Sorry to interrupt. But I thought you might need some sustenance."

Seeing Jared brought back a flood of images of their lovemaking the last few nights, of the afterward, sitting up in bed eating whatever leftovers he had in the fridge, watching television and talking.

Yes, she'd changed her mind about meals in bed. It was a luxurious treat, made romantic by Jared.

The afterward was sometimes the best part, the most fun part. Not that the sex wasn't good—it was amazing—but the afterward, as she thought of it, was the cherry on top of the sweetest and richest full-fat ice cream. It was the afterward that she carried with her throughout the day.

"We are the luckiest ever." Gabby echoed Matilda's thoughts and shot up from her seat. She pushed aside all of their papers and devices, to make room in the middle of the table.

Jared set down a charcuterie board of meats, cheeses, crackers and some fruit, eliciting *oohs* and *aahs*. But it was Jared who Matilda was looking at the whole time. She could very well get used to this, their lovemaking and the afterward for the long-term.

Could he stay for the long-term?

That would mean the Espiritus would have to accept him for who he was.

Would they, knowing he'd stayed under false pretenses?

"Matilda?" Gabby asked.

She shook herself from her downward spiral. "Yes, sorry. I think it's me that needs a little sustenance. Can you repeat that?" For good measure she stood and helped herself to a couple of pieces of cheese.

"Jared just agreed that a few public events throughout the year is doable from his side of the house."

"He did, did he?" She pressed her lips together and gave him a teasing smile.

"That's my cue." He backed away, waving.

She looked down at her iPad and scrolled through the long-range calendar. "Do you have an idea when some of these events would happen? Though many of these weekends appear open, shouldn't we leave them free for upcoming weddings? And don't forget college events—parents love staying with us for parents weekend."

"Since the solar eclipse was a success, here are some possibilities." Gabby read out dates for lunar and solar eclipses in the upcoming twelve months. Matilda marked them on her calendar. "Or, we can do a fall festival. Maybe an adult-only fall festival?" Her eyes lit.

Eva stood up and looked out one of her windows, deep in thought. After a breath, she said, "Matilda's right. I think we'll need to compare our profit from an average wedding versus the SE to see where that lands. No matter what, I want a consensus among all of us."

Matilda jumped in to squelch her own rising discomfort at being the lone dissenter. "I'll go with what you all decide," she said. "We learned a lot from our first event, and so long as we can make changes, I don't see why we can't level up."

"Great!" Gabby clapped. "So, my last order of business are the upcoming weddings."

"Gabby, that's not until later in the agenda. Matilda's next with B & B topics." Frankie sighed, shaking her phone, which displayed their emailed agenda.

"But I need to get this out before I burst. There's two things actually."

"As a reminder, you asked me to hold my issues at our last meeting. I mean, what's the point of writing an agenda?"

"It's because you're generally all over the place."

"And you aren't?"

"Girls," Eva said.

Truly, the difference between the two Espiritu sisters was like a solar flare and a solar eclipse. One was hot and fiery, and the other methodical.

Eva sat back at the table. To Gabby, she said, "Go ahead, honey."

Frankie rolled her eyes.

"First—the Roland-Shim nuptials. You all know how the bride, Carly, is a social media influencer. Well…brace yourselves…the wedding is being sponsored by Maggie Thurmond Weddings."

"Maggie Thurmond?" Eva breathed out.

Maggie Thurmond was the quintessential all-about-weddings guru. A lifestyle business from back in the eighties, Maggie was the original wedding influencer.

"Maggie hosted a contest for couples to send in their dream wedding idea, and Carly made a compelling pitch. Now, it doesn't change anything. All plans remain, but Maggie's going to be footing the bill. And, there will be a media crew coming to cover the event."

Frankie lifted up both palms. "Wait, when you mean cover this event—"

"Video, photography and the whole affair is going to be featured on the magazine, print and online. And on their socials, of course. Though, we'll need to meet with the Maggie Thurmond legal team. We'll have to give approval, sign permissions, etcetera."

"Of course we're giving approval." Eva placed a hand over her mouth. "Oh my gosh. That means that the B & B will be—"

"Everywhere."

The table erupted in joyous conversation, and while Matilda joined in, she couldn't allow herself to feel the excitement. She was caught on the details and the stakes. "We'll need to have all of our ducks in a row. Hire a larger security team, and perhaps a valet system instead of a parking crew."

"It all sounds good. All of it!" Eva exclaimed with both hands in the air. "This is fantastic."

"There's a second thing. We have a wedding inquiry. A big one. Huge." A giggle escaped her lips.

"Wait," Matilda said, now with urgency biting at her heels. "Before we talk about anything else. I need to mention something."

"Go ahead, Matilda," Frankie said, lifting her phone. "Technically it *is* your turn."

"What I have to say is relevant to everything." At their silence, she pushed on. "Chef Allie is not returning."

Jaws dropped.

"Why not?" Gabby asked.

"Her husband is taking a job in Northern Virginia."

"Oh no. We're going to miss her." Eva frowned. "I'll call her straight away."

"How long is Jared staying?" Frankie asked.

"He's flexible up to several months." She swallowed against the fear rising up her throat; his availability would depend on how the Espiritus would react to his secret. "Most of the candidates I interviewed picked up permanent positions elsewhere because I was only looking for a temporary hire."

"Can Jared stay?" Eva asked.

"I don't know. I haven't asked because I wanted to bring this to you all first."

"Ask him, please, as soon as possible. I'll think about how we can make the salary competitive and how to make the offer more appealing."

Matilda nodded. Little did Eva know that she would be the one to determine if Jared stayed.

Matilda shifted in her seat, uncomfortable.

"To turn this moment around," Gabby interrupted, "I received a high profile wedding request. The future bride, Jane Gardner, is the daughter of the fifty-third Speaker of the House. Jane is marrying a former Peak resident. Talk about neat. It's a quick event, in four months because she's pregnant. But, we happen to have room that weekend. I'm meeting with the couple in a few days, and they want to view one of our weddings before they sign the paperwork."

"Who's the resident?" Matilda jotted down notes.

"Noah Phillips."

The sound of her ex's name dragged Matilda out of her head. Out of her body.

A knot formed in her throat. This had to have been the reason why Noah was trying to reach her. He was coming back to Peak. To marry his pregnant fiancée. In the B & B she worked in.

What kind of luck was that?

Horrible, horrible luck.

"Why does that name sound familiar?" Frankie asked.

"We're going to pass on this wedding." Eva spoke up, glancing at Matilda.

Gabby went wide-eyed. "For what reason? This is an incredible opportunity."

Matilda met Eva's stare, wishing this moment away. Wishing that she had called Noah two weeks ago to mitigate this situation. Wishing that she didn't have to explain her history.

Frankie looked between the both of them. "Mat. The groom. Is he your ex?"

"Wait. What?" Gabby frowned. "This is *your* Noah?"

"Was..." Matilda corrected, though unsure how to proceed. She wanted to gain control of the situation, to take back the power of the moment. But she knew that putting words to what she had kept back with a lock and key, hidden behind her work ethic, would cause her pain. Physical pain.

It had been five years, dammit. Shouldn't that have been enough time for her to forget him? To not have this power over her?

"Noah and I...we were married, for eight years. It didn't work out and five years ago, I left him and came back home to Peak."

"How did I not pick up that this was him?" Gabby asked.

"It's because I never talk about him," Matilda said.

Their faces indicated they were waiting for more, but she let the silence fall among them. What she'd said was the gist of it. The most important gist. There were other details that she'd shared with Eva, and that was only because Matilda had been so down on herself. Such as why she hadn't been gainfully employed at thirty-five, why she hadn't had a grown-up résumé when she'd applied at the B & B.

As the seconds passed, though, the implication of her admission became clear. Eva would continue to protect her, even if it was to the detriment of the B & B's bottom line.

Matilda couldn't do that to them.

"But it's fine," Matilda said, with a smile on her face. "That was so long ago."

Eva pressed a hand against the tabletop. "Matilda, we don't have to take this on."

"But this wedding will link us to DC networks," Gabby protested.

"It's fine. Really," Matilda said firmly. "Eva. I'm over it. And Gabby's right. Even if this all still bothered me, I wouldn't let it mess with business."

"Are you sure?"

"Yes." Matilda waved a hand in the air. "Promise."

But inside, Matilda winced, wondering if this promise wouldn't come back to bite her.

Just like another one she'd made.

Chapter Seventeen

Jared, standing on Kite Flyer's back porch, breathed in the morning, invigorated by the chill. In the nearest tree, he noticed a pair of birds perched on one of its branches and heard the cheerful knocking of a woodpecker.

He just knew it was going to be a great day.

Since arriving in Peak, the fog that had settled into his bones had lifted a little each day. His appreciation for the slower lifestyle came with getting to know Kite Flyer's quirks and this view. Louisville was a stone's throw from the country—so it wasn't that he had been lacking nature—but his proximity to it every day reminded him to be thankful for these small joys.

The ambience enhanced how hot the coffee was in his hands, though not an espresso but from a decades-old coffee maker. The wind against his cheeks, grounding him to himself, and the way he had been able to sleep soundly, especially with Matilda next to him.

Speaking of Matilda…

Jared padded over to the window and looked in at Matilda sleeping, with the covers up to her shoulders. Her dark hair was splayed against the pillow, face turned to the right. Unlike him, she slept perfectly still, and her body was cocooned in his covers like he'd tucked her in. And while the bed was tiny—a double though that would be pushing it—not once did he feel crowded with her in it.

As if feeling his presence, she stirred, turning all the way to her side, toward the middle of the bed. The blanket shimmied down, exposing her shoulders and upper body and the profile of her breasts. She was captivating even in sleep.

Then, he watched as she reached out to his side of the bed.

She was searching for him.

Whatever part of him was cold from the weather warmed at the sight. Matilda was such a professional at work. To her word, though she remained communicative at the B & B, she was sometimes aloof to his lingering gazes. Yes, he was a kid with a crush, doing just enough to make a fool out of himself. Like making a full charcuterie board just so he could walk into a meeting she was attending.

It was irrational, knowing that he wouldn't be here forever. But he hoped that she was feeling the same way about him.

Her eyes fluttered open, and he tapped against the window.

She sat up, holding the sheet against her chest, and turned toward him. Upon meeting his eyes, her lips curved into a smile.

Jared's heart soared higher than the trees in his backyard.

He raised a finger, as in "wait for it."

Back into the kitchen he went, and he started on her oatmeal breakfast and poured her a cup of coffee. This had become a routine too, reaching for the tub of dry oatmeal and turning the burner on. Grabbing her tiramisu-flavored creamer from the fridge. He was a personal chef in the most intimate of ways, because he was going to get to serve her too.

It was a simple breakfast, and in making it for someone he cared for, allowed him to remember why he loved cooking to begin with. Or, better yet, it peeled back the last bit of hesitance and doubt with his cooking. Sprinkling brown sugar over Matilda's oatmeal had become a kind of therapy. Making her coffee just to her liking gave him purpose.

He brought the tray of breakfast to Matilda, who was scrolling on her phone. It was both their days off today, a rare event, but she, unsurprisingly, had a harder time disconnecting.

A wrinkle had formed in between her eyebrows, but it cleared when she lifted her eyes to his. "My mouth's watering already. Yum."

It was all the thanks he needed this morning, for the rest of the day. Matilda's expressions continued to be the validation of her emotions. What she couldn't say, he could read.

He set the tray on her lap. "Everything okay?"

"Yeah. We're planning out all the seating areas for the Roland-Shim wedding." She sipped her coffee and moaned.

The satisfaction that rolled through Jared was too much, that when she set her cup down, he kissed her on the lips.

"What's that for?"

"For nothing. For everything."

"That's…specific. Though I won't complain. I'll take those kisses anytime." She kissed him back, and their lips lingered seconds more. "Though my tummy is grumbling, and I need caffeine to function. Aren't you seeing Liam today?"

"Yep. As promised."

"What are you planning to do?"

"Fly kites. Right here." His voice lifted at the announcement. "It was Liam's idea, and surely there was a reason why Chip named this place Kite Flyer. We're going to head out to the knoll just down the backyard trail. Liam should be here in a couple of hours."

"That's sweet, Jared."

"Not like I could say no to the kid. He's quite convincing, just like his mother." He nudged her knee, noting that she wasn't quite present. "But hey, I can tell you have something else on your mind."

"Yeah…won't it be hard to get so close to Liam, and then…"

Her words trailed but he finished the sentence in his head. *And then you have to go.*

They had both been true to their agreement to one another. That they wouldn't create pressure over their relationship. But the pressure was already there. It was pervasive.

"It's one day of flying kites. Not like I'm trying to be his uncle or anything," he said playfully, though inside he was struck with the absolute opposite. Technically he *was* Liam's uncle.

She met his eyes. "What if there was a chance you could hang out for more than one day?"

"What's going on?"

"Allie isn't coming back after maternity leave. She's moving to Northern Virginia, and Eva wanted for me to feel you out. If you would be willing to stay, permanently."

His jaw threatened to hit the ground as he tried to process that news. "A permanent position."

"Yes. It was a consensus. They love you." She bit her lip. "They wanted me to report back on your thoughts ASAP."

"Well, I can't stay unless they know about me."

She nodded solemnly. "You were already planning on telling them."

"I know, but this feels…different. I'm not sure what to say." He shook his head. "Not about telling them about me, because I knew that was upcoming. But the fact that they want for me to stay. This is—" he looked for the word, but nothing rose from his thoughts "—wow."

"You sound like Mountain Rush Jared."

The thought of that night appeased the rising tension within himself and he half laughed.

"Jared, I'll tell them whatever you want me to. But I *am* worried about telling them before the wedding." She bit her lip and paused. "We talked about this. If things don't go well, not that it won't but I have to think about the worst-case scenario, I don't think I have the ability to replace you should—"

"Should they kick my ass out of here?"

"Yeah." Remorse laced her tone.

"Well, that was a mood killer."

It was Matilda's turn to bark out a laugh, though it was humorless.

He needed to think. Some place besides Peak. "We should go out."

"That was random." She did a double take. "Wait. You're serious."

"Yes. I want a good meal that I didn't make. Maybe talk through what I'm going to say."

"It'll take one person for the entire town to know what's up with us. One person and one hour."

"Then let's go somewhere else. To Charlottesville. It's a big enough place. My buddy's restaurant is up there. It's private and intimate, and they even have parking in the back just in case."

"That's an hour away."

"And so?"

"What if the B & B needs me?"

He gave her a look. "You can tell them it's your day off."

"I can't do that."

"You can't? Are you saying you haven't taken a day off in five years?"

She frowned, thinking back.

"No freaking way." He found this preposterous, though at the same time, it was so Matilda. "Then you're in serious need of a night out." He linked his fingers with hers. "Let me show you a wholesome good time."

"Wholesome, huh?" She stuck the spoon in her mouth, clearly deliberating. Then, a smile grew on her lips. "What if I don't want wholesome?"

"Whatever you want, you get." Magnetized, he climbed into bed. He plucked the spoon from her hand and tossed it on the tray, which he took off her lap. Her fingers rested on his shoulders as he eased her on her back.

"Okay." Her answer came quietly at first. "Let's go to Charlottesville. But first…"

She peeled off the covers to expose her naked body.

His decisions were going to have to wait, for now.

"Fly a kite they said. It will be fun they said," Jared grumbled.

The day wasn't turning out the way Jared had hoped it would. Number one case in point: a few hours after he and Matilda had their final quickie of the morning, he was standing on a tree branch trying to untangle kite strings from a smaller branch.

"What's that, Chef?" Liam asked from the ground. The safe, solid ground. Next to him, on that said ground was his kite.

"Nothing. But wait. You have a phone, right?"

"Yeah."

"And if needed, you know how to call 9-1-1?"

"Uh-huh. Why?"

"No reason," he grunted, continuing under his breath with, "You know, in case I fall to my death."

"Do you need help? I can climb up."

"No. No, I'm fine." Because what was worse than getting his kite stuck in a tree but having a little kid to save his said kite?

"You really shouldn't have let go of the holder," Liam said. "First rule of kite flying. Don't let go."

"Thanks, dude." Jared reached over for what was a couple of inches though felt like ten feet. Then, finally, he grabbed the handle and flipped it around the branch. Methodically, he repeated this action until it untangled from the branch and landed on the ground.

"Yay! I'll reel it in," Liam said.

Jared carefully shimmied down the tree, to a lower branch, and hesitated before the final leap to the ground.

This situation was going to end triumphantly or land him in the hospital.

Liam appeared below him, now holding both kites. "I believe in you."

Damn, the kid was sweet. He could tell that he was loved, that someone had said those same words to him, most likely Frankie or his father.

For a beat, he wondered how Liam was like when he was a baby, a toddler. Frankie and Gabby too. Had they felt a little out of place as Jared had? Did they bicker like Jared and Emma?

"Wanna count backward from three?" Liam said, snapping Jared out of his thoughts.

"What's that?"

"At three, hang on the branch. Okay?"

He allowed himself to come back to the moment, and grinned at Liam. "All right. Let's do it together."

In unison, they said, "Three, two, one."

Jared lowered himself onto the branch and hung for as long as he could, then let go, landing on his feet.

"I knew you could do it." Liam threw his arms around Jared's waist. The kites poked him in the back but he didn't move a millimeter.

It was as if Jared had waited his whole life for this hug.

Then, he realized, this was his first hug from an Espiritu.

Slowly, he lowered his hands and patted Liam on the back. Something had lodged itself in his throat and he had to clear it. "I'm never climbing up a tree that high again. If a kite gets caught up there, then it's going to stay up there."

"So this won't be the last time." He looked up at Jared with hope in his eyes. "No one likes to fly kites with me. Mom thinks that it's boring. Tita Gabby doesn't like exercise, and Lola Eva's too busy."

All of Jared's insides turned to mush. Every part of him wanted to say yes. Not necessarily for Liam, but for himself too. Even if he did have to risk life and limb for a kite, it was one of the best things he'd done thus far.

But he was going to leave, because would Eva allow for him to stay after he revealed the truth? Then again, he didn't have a timeline yet, so he ruffled Liam's hair and said, "Yeah, bud. We can do it again."

"Great! Because I think you need practice."

"Noted." Jared laughed. "C'mon, that's enough kite flying for the day. Wanna go inside? I have stir-fry I can whip up."

"Yum. Can I help?"

"If you want to." They began striding across the knoll toward the back side of Kite Flyer. The sun was high, blue and cloudless. From their vantage point, it felt never-ending. Jared felt swallowed up in it. At the same time, he felt free, unboxed.

"Can I tell you a secret?" Liam looked around, as if someone were going to surprise them in an open field. "I like someone."

For a beat, Jared was stunned. "How old are you again?"

"Eight. Third grade."

"Practically grown." Jared fought to keep a grin from bursting out. The last thing he wanted was for Liam not to think he was taking him seriously. "The person you like—are they nice?"

"Yes. But I need advice."

"All right. I can definitely do my best. What's up?"

"So, her name is Daisy. Cute, right?"

"Super."

"But she hangs out a lot with Drake during recess. I can't get a word in."

"Ah." *Grin, get thee behind me.* "They're good friends, I assume."

"Sort of. But he likes her too. He told me *after* I told him that I liked her. So, Chef, how do I get her to notice me?"

They slowed as they climbed the final hill to Kite Flyer.

"Well, one way to get her to notice is by hanging around her, by going out of your way to talk to her. Ask her questions. Find out what you have in common. But if that doesn't work, you might have to do something else to grab her attention. Can you think of any ideas?"

He hoped that he wasn't going against anything Frankie had taught Liam. Sure, he wasn't around a lot of kids, but at the restaurant, he'd learned real quick that when a kid asked for something, the server's first action was to double-check that it was all good by the parents.

Liam was breathing hard. "Oh, oh! I could get her something."

"You definitely can. Do you have the funds?" He gave him the side-eye.

"I'm broke. But—" a grin spread across his face "—I can make her something."

"Even better."

"Chef," he said, as if realized something. "Will *you* help me make something?"

"Oh," he choked out. This kid was going to be the cause of all of his emotional outbursts. He steadied his voice. "Sure We'll have to ask your mom, though."

"She'll say yes. She thinks you're a cool guy."

"She said that?"

"Yup."

He swallowed back his joy. "Wait. But what do I get out of it?"

"You get to hang out with me. And, I'll tell you another secret in return."

"A secret? Why do I need to know about this secret?"

"Because it's about you." He lowered his voice. "Someone likes you. Her name starts with an *m* and ends with an *a*. But you didn't hear it from me."

"There are a million people with names that start with an *m* and ends with an *a*. It could be anyone. Maria?"

"No."

"Martha?"

He laughed. "Not even close."

Jared's lips were betraying him now; he was smiling so hard his cheeks hurt. But when they climbed onto the back porch, Jared found that he hadn't unlocked the back door. "We have to go through the front."

"Okay." Once they made it around the house, Liam said, "So do we have a deal? You help me and I'll tell you the secret?" Liam raised a hand for a high five.

It wasn't so high for Jared to reach. "You've got yourself a deal."

Just then, a car honked. Not a car, but Matilda's Bronco. She slowed and rolled down the window. "Hey, you two."

Liam giggled.

"What's going on? What did I miss?" Matilda was laughing already—Liam's was that contagious.

"Nothing," Jared said. Though he couldn't wait to tell her about all of this later on. "What are you doing in my neck of the woods?"

"Allie needed some cheering up, so I grabbed her some flowers." She lifted a packaged set of blooms from the passenger seat.

"That's really sweet, Matilda."

"Well, I try." She shrugged, though Jared could see a bit of shyness cross her face.

Next to him, Liam was still giggling. It was both embarrassing and cute, and very much felt similar to when one of his friends gave him a hard time. Never mind that Liam was eight.

"I'd better let you go. You have your hands full," she said.

"Who, this? This…monster?" Jared lifted Liam and slung

him over his shoulder so he was upside down. The giggling intensified.

"M… M…" he said in between laughs.

Jared made a sign with his right pinky and thumb to Matilda, in a "call me" motion.

When Matilda nodded, he felt an uptick in his already great mood.

"Bye, you two," she said.

And as Jared watched the Bronco drive away, he couldn't imagine how else the day could get better.

Except that he was going to see Matilda tonight.

Chapter Eighteen

"I want to know more," Allie said to Matilda while arranging the flowers in a glass vase. They were in her kitchen while Allie's mother, Greta, was in the living room rocking Brianna.

"There's nothing much *to* say," Matilda said. "We're going on a date tonight."

"Then why did you walk in here with a big ole goofy grin?"

That grin threatened to bust out of her now as she thought of Jared and Liam in front of Kite Flyer. The wholesomeness of it all was overwhelming. "Liam was there at Jared's when I drove by, and they were both having a good time. It was... sweet to see them together. Jared is so good with him."

Allie nodded. "What were they doing at Jared's?"

"They were flying kites."

It wasn't hard to imagine them on the knoll with how close they were at his front porch. When she had driven away and caught a final glance through the rearview mirror, she saw how they continued to laugh even as they entered his front door. It tugged at every part of her, at every part of what had been her before Noah. Someone who'd been innocent and hopeful and wanting a family.

"Oh... Mat." Allie sat down and gazed at her through eyes that Matilda knew meant trouble.

"Oh no...what's going on in your matchmaker brain?"

"You like him. Like really like him."

"I think I do." It felt good to say it. "I mean, I wouldn't go out on this date if I didn't. There's too much at stake."

"What's at stake? Everyone knows that there's something between the both of you."

Matilda looked away—she and Allie had remained open books, and she hated that she couldn't tell Allie about Jared and who he was. But this wasn't an ordinary secret. It was about family. His family, and she didn't have a right to tell that story.

So she said what was more accessible. The fact that seeing Jared with Liam showed her that he had so much of his future up ahead, and well, she wasn't there anymore. "Even if things are going well—we're just not in the same place."

"How could you say that?"

"Seeing him and Liam. He's totally dad material, and I..."

"You're not mom material?"

"I haven't even considered it. Not really, not until you had your angel. You know me, I'm on the slow side of getting things together."

"You're not on the slow side. You are on your own path, just like I am and Jared is and everyone else in the world. And as for being a mom—only you know what you want—but this is the beginning of your relationship. You don't have to plan everything ten years down the road."

"Right. Do you even know me?"

She considered it with pursed lips. "You might be on to something there. And then you have to consider actually talking to him about it before making assumptions."

Matilda shook her head. "Feelings. They are so inconvenient."

"But necessary."

"I don't want to talk about it anymore. Besides, my role right now? It's to be an auntie to Brianna." She pressed a smile on her face to move them forward. "I'm here for you, too." She reached out to squeeze her forearm. "How are you feeling?"

Allie winced as her finger got caught on a thorn. “I just don’t think I’m doing anything right.”

“Are you kidding, Allie? You’re an amazing mom.”

“How do you know that? You’re not here in the middle of the night when I’m frustrated out of my mind. And you’re not here especially when Eugene and I are arguing about our move to Northern Virginia.”

“To be honest, I was hoping that all that moving business was a joke.”

“It’s so real that it’s painful.” She paused at one of the blooms and touched a petal.

This was hard. Matilda wanted to make her friend feel better. But what did Matilda know about being a mom? She didn’t even know if she wanted to be one; nor if it was physically too late. From what Allie had told her at the beginning of her pregnancy, she had been considered high-risk. And that sounded scary as hell.

“You asked me how I know that you’re an amazing mom, Al, and I’ll tell you. You were the only person who continued reaching out after I left Peak. Fourteen years later, you were the person who picked me up from that bus station in Charlestown when I decided to leave Noah. You didn’t think twice about getting in the car. You didn’t ask questions.”

“That’s not motherhood.”

“That’s every person-hood.”

Allie snorted. “That’s not a real word.”

“At this second it is.” She allowed her message to sink in, when Allie somewhat settled in her chair, when she looked like she was open to more. Allie and Matilda were alike in this way. They were both headstrong, and sometimes Matilda needed to hold back her opinion, just until Allie softened enough to listen. “You’re thoughtful and caring. You’re empathetic, and even when you’re not feeling your best you’re always thinking of the other person. You’re pretty important to me. You’re important to everyone in this room." She glanced over at Allie's mother, who nodded. It was a signal.

Matilda just wasn't there to bring over flowers and to gossip about her love life. She was there to take care of the friend who took care of so many others.

"But… Al, when you mentioned that you don't feel right. Do you think…do you think you should talk to someone about it? Your doctor maybe?"

Allie's eyes narrowed. "Why do you say that?"

"Because. Hormones, they shift. I mean, they shift anyway in our forties, but even more so after you have a baby. There's stress. Sleep deprivation."

Allie leaned in across the kitchen island. "Did my mother say something?"

She gave a small nod but added quickly, "I saw it when you were on bed rest. And you have been so hard on yourself. With the move, you seem resigned. And I've rarely seen you that way before."

Allie snorted. "I don't need to see a doctor. What I need is sleep."

"Sleep, too, of course. But maybe someone to talk to?"

"I'm talking to you right now, and from a woman who barely tells anyone her own feelings, that's a stretch of an ask."

Matilda recoiled but held her tongue. She knew that Allie had felt blindsided.

Allie's gaze darted downward. "I'm sorry. I shouldn't have said that."

"It's okay."

"I'll think about it. Only because it's you who asked." Except there was a definite chill in her tone.

Matilda nodded, satisfied. She would need to try to make her friend laugh throughout the rest of the visit, but she couldn't quite purge Allie's words: *from a woman who barely tells anyone her own feelings, that's a stretch of an ask.*

People didn't say things to hurt people unless there was at least an iota of truth in it.

And the truth hurt.

Matilda hadn't been always this way, and part of her wished that she still had her old self back.

"I was fun once," Matilda said, realizing a beat too late that she'd interrupted Jared in the middle of a sentence. It was a couple of hours later, and they were sitting in a private corner of an outdoor patio of a French restaurant in Charlottesville. Next to them was a heating lamp radiating much-needed warmth and the perfect amount of light.

Despite the serene surroundings, Matilda couldn't forget her afternoon with Allie. While she and Allie had quickly turned around that awkward conversation and ended up soaking in some sun in Adirondack chairs in the backyard, Matilda was still left with the sting of Allie's statement.

Matilda jumped back in to explain. "I wasn't always this… cold."

Jared's eyebrows stitched together. "I don't think you're cold."

"You're being nice."

He put his fork down. He'd ordered a coq au vin and was halfway through it. Matilda hadn't really been present since arriving; she had a mild remembrance of their drive to the restaurant and being sat and served. Her own ratatouille was untouched. She'd just been moving the vegetables around on the plate.

"I'm telling the truth. I don't think you're cold. You're direct and straightforward."

"You mean brash."

"Nope, and this might be the first time your synonyms have failed you. Honest is more like it." He grinned, then reached over to touch her arm. "What's going on?"

"I just thought I needed to explain myself."

"Why?"

"Because of this." She gestured to the table. "We're here, together. Alone. On a date."

He beamed. "That we are."

"And you—" she gestured to his face, at the hope and the innocence "—and that look."

"The look of a person who's damn lucky to be out with you?"

"And that. How can you say things like that?"

"These things you're pointing out…are these good things, or bad things? Because I'm not sure what you're trying to get at."

"These are good things. All good things. But how is this even happening? We're so different." She sighed. "Can I start over?"

"Yes."

"What I was trying to do was explain myself. That it's easier for me to keep people at arm's length. It hurts less if I don't let them get under my skin."

"You're defensive."

"Resistant."

"Resistant, then." He nodded. "But the people who understand and respect you accept you for who you are. As I do. You don't owe anyone an explanation."

"I feel like… I want to give one to you anyway. So you understand who I am. Who you have in front of you." Matilda felt the words wanting to burst from her chest. She couldn't explain why, except that she didn't want him to misconstrue her. Because he mattered to her.

He mattered to her.

Oh my gosh, he mattered.

He wasn't just a fling, a temporary thing. A momentary lapse in judgment. These days spent together had meant something to her and would continue to have meaning.

But after she explained herself, would he be as happy-go-lucky around her? Would he still want to spend time with her?

In getting to know someone, in really knowing them, one saw their faults. It made one vulnerable to getting hurt.

Five years after her one big hurt, she wasn't sure if she could do it again.

She set her utensils down and took a sip of her wine, allowing the liquid courage to flow down her throat.

"I was not the same person before my relationship with my ex," she said. "I was…a people pleaser. I did anything, everything to make people happy. I spent a good portion of my life following my ex, all the while not realizing how much I had given up. Years, Jared. Years had passed me by without a spark of a dream for anything else but to make a family with him."

Lines appeared on Jared's forehead, and a rare serious expression had fallen across his face. His arms rested on the table. "Did he hurt you?"

"Not physically. But there was no doubt our relationship was toxic. With him I was drained, used and sad, always. Needy. Every opinion of his mattered to me. My life became a stagnant mosquito-infested pond. I had no agency, or at least I thought I didn't.

"I was with him for fourteen years. It took a lot for me to come back home, and it was Eva who hired me and got me on my feet. She even let me stay in one of the cottages on the property, just for me to save a little face. Because this whole place knew how I lost myself to Noah. They watched us date in high school, and they saw how I changed. My parents and friends tried to tell me, but I didn't listen. I was so caught up, so eager to please.

"This is my first real date in five years, Jared. I like you so much, but I don't know how open I'll ever be. Sometimes I wish that I could be like you and show you the same things you have shown me. I wish I could express how you make me feel, because you deserve it."

He reached out and took Matilda's hand, which she hadn't

realized had been shaking. His skin was warm, and comfort pulsed through her. "Thank you, for sharing all this with me. I know it took a lot. I have my thoughts about your ex, though I'll keep them to myself, except to say that I'm so sorry you had to go through some of those experiences. For what it's worth, though, I want you to know that I like you because of exactly who you are. I don't compare you to anyone else I've dated, and I don't wish you were a certain kind of person."

"But you're so young."

He half laughed. "C'mon. We're back on that again?"

"Because it matters." Gathering her thoughts together felt like she was trying to catch the pollen being blown through the trees. "You and Liam are amazing together. I saw it in the couple of minutes when we chatted in front of Kite Flyer. And I just know. I can just tell that you would be a good father. And I'm forty."

He shook his head. "Being a father isn't in my purview right now."

"But the future—"

He grinned. "So you're thinking of me in the future."

"Jared, be serious." Matilda half laughed. "Even if it's just one date, or a little fling for a couple of months. That's time spent with someone that might not be able to give you what you need down the road."

"I think I know what I need, Matilda. But what are you trying to say?"

Seeing their server in her periphery, Matilda quieted. In their conversation, she had forgotten where they were, which was this beautiful restaurant picked especially for her. They'd driven over an hour to get here. He'd planned the entire night.

This man was thoughtful, kind and deserving of a woman who didn't have all this baggage.

At the very least, he deserved the truth of how she felt at that moment.

She reached over to Jared, and thank goodness, he didn't pull away his hand. She offered him a smile, as weak as it probably was. "Jared, I'm not trying to do anything here. You are…something else. You do something to me. You make me smile. You make me laugh. You make me food every day and I go to work like I can conquer the world."

He squeezed her hand. "My food is magic."

"More than. It's like a life force. For all the doubts you had about your food, I'm telling you that you shouldn't have an iota of it. This was just to make sure you knew where I was coming from. So that you're not surprised or disappointed."

It took a long while for Jared to answer but he finally squeezed her hand. "I appreciate you opening up, Matilda. I didn't realize how much I needed it, for you to give a little about yourself. And now that you have—" in the pause, Matilda's heart began to ache, anticipating words of a breakup "—it doesn't in any way scare or worry me. I care about *you*, and that means everything that brought you here."

"Really?"

"Promise."

"Don't say promise," she said. "I'm not a fan of that word."

"Okay then, I won't say it. I'll just have to show you."

Matilda was overcome. Shortly, she was flooded by relief and an incredible appetite. There was nothing more she wanted to do but show him, too. She smiled and nodded toward his food. "Then you're going to need that sustenance."

Chapter Nineteen

At the B & B early the next morning, Jared turned on the exhaust above the oven and flipped the pancakes in the cast-iron pan. The side was perfectly browned and the chocolate chips emanated a sweet scent that made his stomach growl.

He was hungry again. As if second dinner last night and his pre-sunrise breakfast hadn't been enough. When Matilda had warned him that he'd needed the sustenance, she hadn't been lying.

A smile wiggled onto his lips as scenes from last night replayed in his head. He and Matilda had hardly slept, but he was wide-awake.

He wondered how she was doing. It had been hours since he'd seen her.

Hands wrapped around from behind him and he startled to see that it was Matilda. "Whoa. Won't someone see? Not that I'm complaining."

"Everyone's outside running around like there's a fire. I wanted to sneak in a hug since we had to rush out this morning."

Eyes darting for any movement, he kissed her on the forehead. She smelled of sun and her shampoo, and this simple kiss alone, done in a place outside of Kite Flyer, felt more intimate. That what they had wasn't just a figure of his imagination. Much like their date last night, it made him feel like they were a bona fide couple.

They weren't in the same place as they had been in the beginning of their relationship—she had said as much at their dinner last night. Something had changed between them that made Matilda finally feel safe enough to tell him about her ex.

He was ecstatic, but the stakes of his presence here had now been catapulted to stratospheric levels. Besides the Espiritus, he had a whole home and family he had to contend with in another state. And now Matilda, who he didn't want to leave.

"Jared, the pancakes."

Jared woke to the moment and he swiftly turned to flip the pancakes onto a serving platter. "Whew, near miss." He glanced backward. Matilda was leaning against the island with the phone in her hand. "So, to what else do I owe this pleasure?"

"Can't a girl come by and say hi?"

"Um, sure they can, but with your calendar and all…surely you're foregoing something else to hang out with me." He poured another generous ladle of batter into the sizzling, buttered pan. As he wiped his fingers on a rag, he turned around.

"Eva's on her way here to ask you to stay."

"Oh."

"She followed up with me this morning, to see if I had felt you out, and I said that I couldn't tell where you were on the decision. She's eager, to either claim you as a permanent staff member, or to find a new person quick."

"Wow."

She nodded. "Wow indeed. Um, do you think you're going to tell her?"

"To be honest, I don't know what to say. I'm still riding high from last night."

A blush rose to her cheeks. "I know what you mean."

He stepped up to her and whispered, "It was nice."

"A nice escape. But reality calls."

"Damn reality." He turned and tended to the pancakes and

mulled over his answer at whether he could tell Eva his whole story today. "And we have a wedding in two days."

"Here's what I was thinking. Why not serve the meat loaf on Thursday instead of Friday, and offer an extra vegan option since it looks like half of our guests are vegan or vegetarian?"

The change in subject was sudden. "What—" Jared turned his head to Eva walking into the room. A wide-brimmed hat sat on top of her head, and her face was shadowed. She pulled her plate-sized sunglasses off her face.

"R-right. I think that's a great idea. I'll make that change right away. Hi, Eva."

"Sorry to interrupt, but I was wondering if I could grab you as soon as you're free, Jared."

"Absolutely. I've got another ten minutes, fifteen at most."

"Perfect. I'll be back from my walk-through. See you at the cottage then. Bye, Matilda." She walked past them to the back door.

Wordlessly, Matilda wiped imaginary sweat from her forehead, lips pursed.

That was close.

And he didn't have much time.

The bell from the front desk rang out, and Matilda left to take care of it. As Jared plated the last of the pancakes, Chip walked into the kitchen with Matilda. Both were sporting smiles.

"Chip. Hey." At first, his presence confused Jared. He had firmly associated Chip with the grocery store, and a week ago felt like ten years. Then, he noticed that he was wearing a backpack bursting with contents.

"As promised." His voice boomed through the room, and it had the same easygoing and eager tone. He unslung the backpack and handed it to him after rounding the corner of the island. "It has everything you'll need for the hike on Sunday. Granted, if you're free."

"Sunday is his day off but hold up." Matilda raised a hand. "You're going hiking?"

Jared gritted his teeth into a smile. "Didn't I mention it?"

"I would have remembered." She nudged Chip. "He's a beginner, you know that, right?"

"Hey, I'm not *that* kind of a beginner. I'm on my feet every day."

"Jared, have you ever carried a pack for more than a mile?"

"No, but it shouldn't be so bad, right?" He slung the backpack on, and he felt his smile fade. The pack was heavy. "How far are we going again?"

"Twelve miles."

"Twelve?"

"Six hours max. No biggie."

"Great. No biggie," he whispered. Behind Chip, Matilda bit her bottom lip, presumably suppressing a laugh.

"So you're good this Sunday?"

"Yep. I guess so."

"Great. I'll pick you up bright and early." Chip walked backward shooting a finger gun at him.

"Where does the trail start?"

"Two hundred yards that way, right in your backyard. Alrighty, talk soon." He spun on his heel and jogged out of the kitchen.

Matilda burst out laughing once they were alone, and had it not been for that, Jared would have been tempted to chase after Chip and toss him back his equipment.

"You find this funny?"

"Very. Twelve miles? Most people need to work up to that."

He peered at her, taking in her relaxed posture, and how he loved it. This was what he wanted to see more of. He'd seen snippets of it at Kite Flyer, but to be open about who they were would be sublime.

"Know what? I can think of a way I can work up to the twelve miles. A little cardio, a little strength training."

Her eyes rounded and she broke out into a giggle. This time it was she who looked around. "Shh."

"I'll shush you." He backed her into the butler's pantry and shut the door.

Jared's internal temperature was still at fever level when he stepped out the back door. He and Matilda had spent a max of five minutes in that butler's pantry, and though they'd only shared a kiss, it was enough to set his imagination on fire.

The idea of them getting caught only heightened the excitement.

Outside was a stark contrast to the inside, with preparation for the Roland-Shim wedding at full throttle. Though much of the planning had not changed for the wedding since Maggie Thurmond's people came on scene, everything felt a little more extra. Gone were the wildflowers to adorn the space, which were replaced by an array of roses and peonies. The DJ would be supplemented by a harpist and an accompanying jazz ensemble during the reception. The B & B's standard white chairs were upgraded to teak. The caterer, he was told, was switched out to Maggie Thurmond's beloved event chefs. Tomorrow would be a one-of-a-kind celebration.

He couldn't appreciate any of it though, not until he met with Eva.

It took longer than expected to get to Eva's cottage, since the road was paved with people who stalled him along the way. The truck bringing in more tables and tents for the reception. Another with bales of hay as part of the decor. Gabby, darting here and there with a phone against her ear.

Eva's front door was open when he climbed up the porch steps, though he lingered at the threshold. She was looking out her back windows.

Though this was not his first time in Eva's cottage, he'd rarely been alone with her since his interview almost three weeks ago. At the time, the adrenaline of finding Louis Espiritu's family had allowed him to sail through it without overthinking.

But now, he was assailed with thoughts he'd properly denied on that first day.

This was Louis's proper wife and Jared's stepmom. Sharla Sotheby had been the other woman.

He cleared his throat.

"Come in," she said without turning.

Shoes were lined up to the left of the door so he toed his off, then walked across the hardwood floors to join Eva. The cottage was neat and sparsely decorated, with nothing on the walls. It brought all the attention to the view of the trees outside. And with the way Eva was leaned forward, he couldn't help but ask, "Something going on out there?"

With one last lingering look, she said, "Sometimes I see the occasional through-hiker and it's always kind of neat. Makes you wonder why they would want to hike so many miles. Not that I haven't hiked my share of trails. But I very much appreciate being able to come home after a couple of days of camping. The full twenty-one hundred miles, though? I can't even imagine it."

"I could see how it would be a pilgrimage. Kind of a search." He glanced out the open window and sure enough, from that view, one could see where three paths intersected. "I haven't been in that direction yet."

"It's farther than one thinks. From our trail it's probably another half mile. See that path to the left? It winds so it juts right up to my cottage. Someone had created the trail but it hasn't been maintained. There's even a trail shelter back there."

"What's a trail shelter?"

"A lean-to made of wood." She looked up to him with a

smile. "You said you weren't much for the outdoors. Have you taken a hike since arriving at Peak?"

"Nope. Although I have been coerced into a twelve miler the day after tomorrow. Which means I'm going to be limping around the next day at work."

She laughed. "I always tell new hikers three things. One, wear sunscreen and bug spray. Two, bring extra socks. And three, water is king. But I'll add in what my late husband used to say."

"What's that?"

"Never stray off the path." Then, she smiled. "The advice was definitely something a thirty-something would say, because my whole life since then had been beating down a new path. So, only take that advice when you're on the trail. But off it? There are no rules."

He couldn't quite nail down Eva's mood, but he remembered Matilda's statement long ago, about Eva's stoicism.

Eva had needed to be a strong woman to raise Frankie and Gabby as a widow. To have built the B & B. And to run it now, on top of everything else. Jared was aware of how much sacrifice it took– Sizzling Platter would not have survived had it not been for Yamamoto's blood, sweat, tears and years of toil and ups and downs.

He remembered his own mother, slightly older than Eva. Equally as serious and as stoic, but in a different way. Sharla's heartbreak occurred early in her life, when her parents disowned her after she'd gotten pregnant with Jared. Whereas, Eva's had occurred later in her life, when she lost Louis.

It was all so bewildering how life dished out its gifts and struggles. As a bystander, Jared felt ill-equipped on how to handle it.

Around Gabby and Frankie, Jared felt a connection. But how was he supposed to feel about Eva? Should he be grateful for her kindness? Should he feel sorry for her because Louis slept with his mother? Was he supposed to care at all?

And yet, he risked having to end all of these relationships in one swoop.

"Come sit." She gestured to a lounge chair.

He sank into it; seconds later, she took a seat across the way. The quiet was unnerving.

"Have you enjoyed working here the last few weeks, Jared?"

"I have. Yes."

She nodded. "That's good. The guest feedback has been through the roof. It's clear that you've made a difference, that people love you. That you fit in. That transition issue we discussed a week back seemed to have disappeared altogether." She linked her fingers on her lap. "But I've run into a problem. Our chef is no longer returning, and while we know you only planned to be here temporarily, we want you to stay. *I* want you to stay. While we are, as you know, a small operation, I want to shoot my shot to keep you here.

"I'm offering full-time employment, with health benefits, with the option to live on the property. We have a couple of cottages that, though would need some work done, would make a great home. So, the cottage of your choosing would be included in the package." Her voice rose and she stood, grabbing a folder from behind her, and handing it to him. "It's rare we offer full-time employment. But the true judges, my daughters, agree that you're a part of the family."

Jared opened up the folder, to an official letter. Inside were handwritten notes from Gabby, Frankie and Liam too. Yes, he'd known about the upcoming offer, but this was another thing altogether. "I wasn't expecting this."

"I know, it's emotional manipulation, but Liam insisted that he weigh in, too. Not to add more pressure, but I'm thoroughly convinced that had my husband met you, he would have thrown the whole bank at you."

Jared's breath left his body. "Really?"

"Yes. You remind me so much of him. Before he left for that last deployment, we were talking about having another baby. He wanted a son." Her eyes glazed over, but she blinked it away. "And at the risk of sounding way out there, I feel like you belong here. That something must have brought you to Spirit of Shenandoah. Besides a job that is."

It was Louis, he should say. It seemed the next step, the perfect step, to reveal who he was. And ideally, after his revelation, this new job, a new life with Matilda.

And then what? A gradual blending of the two families? A true acceptance into the Espiritus? Was that even an option if they found out who he was? How would they treat his mother?

The Espiritus would hate him. They would hate his mother. He would be cast away from them. Those notes in the folder would be rescinded, and so would his offer.

No, he couldn't admit who he was. Not now, not with the wedding preparation. Matilda was right—the upheaval would ruin what was supposed to be the B & B's step up into being a renowned wedding venue.

"Can I...can I think about it?" he spit out.

"Absolutely. I know you have to consider a permanent move to the Shenandoah Valley. Though I hope it's going to be a yes." She stood and offered a hand.

He took it, and though he provided a confident handshake, he had no idea what his next step would be.

Chapter Twenty

"What can I help with next?" Matilda sidled up to Gabby, who looked ethereal yet professional in a floral sundress. Though not the bride, it was Gabby's big day too, tasked with executing this feat of a wedding. With T minus six hours till the event, she was handling it as Matilda thought any bride would: with frantic anticipation. Currently, the Roland-Shim nuptials had swept up every single person on the property.

It was a flower-filled, white lace and organza-lined hurricane.

Gabby was thumbing her phone. "If you could make sure that no one sets up chairs where the band's dais is going to be, that would be amazing."

"Not a problem."

"Thank you. I can't tell you how much I appreciate you helping without complaining. Everyone's being a bridezilla, even the B & B guests. Every person I've run into has had a complaint or a suggestion." She raised a hand to the spectacle in front of her. "You're like the only calm one. You and Jared."

As if summoned, Jared appeared with Maggie Thurmond's catering manager. While the manager wore a chef's jacket in contrast to Jared's casual apron and jeans, Jared was still the winner in the looks department. Then again, Matilda was biased.

Matilda noted that his smile was distracted, though; his

mind was elsewhere. She could only assume it had everything to do with his conversation with Eva, which he had avoided discussing last night.

Discomfort pricked against her skin.

Her phone trilled from an unknown number. She stepped away from Gabby and took it. "This is Matilda."

"Mat."

The sound of Noah's voice shot tension through her body. "I'm sorry, you have the wrong number. I can give you our wedding planner's number if you'd like."

"Look, we need to talk, right this second. It's important."

She corralled her voice with precision and calm. All her feelings about Jared and the vulnerability she had allowed herself to feel when around him—she pushed that deep and down. "I'm unavailable to speak at this time."

"We are in front of the B & B—"

"Excuse me?"

"My fiancée is walking up the drive as we speak. I stayed back in the car and said I needed to take a call. We were invited to view the wedding. Did you know?"

"No, I didn't."

"Surprise," he said without a lick of warmth. "It's to determine if Gabby and the B & B can give us the wedding we want."

Her first thought was that she had to get out of there. "Thank you for this information."

He heaved a breath. "We have to talk about us, Matilda."

"There's nothing to talk about."

"I need you to reassure me you'll be able to work with my fiancée should we sign with Spirit of the Shenandoah."

"Technically, I'm the manager of the B & B and not the wedding planner."

He groaned on the other end, but Matilda wouldn't succumb or make this easy. "But you *will* be there, and especially when we stay at the B & B for the wedding. I don't want you and my fiancée to have any extended contact with one another."

She guffawed. For all that she couldn't express, this was easy. "Ah. She doesn't know about your controlling behavior?"

"Listen, if I had a choice—"

"Did you not tell her about me?"

"She knows. And she's not a bit bothered. I've finally found a woman who's confident and understanding, but the question is, can you be the same?"

"If you have an issue with my presence, you'll have to take it up with Eva."

"So you want me to tell Eva that I have a problem with you working with us, because she's going to side with you? I don't think so. Surely we can settle this between ourselves."

The tone in his voice was making her head spin. It was the kind that doubted her and dared her all at once. It was the precursor to his gaslighting.

Though she knew his MO, her heart began to beat that steady drum of dread.

Matilda shook her head. Eva was like family. Eva would stand by her if something came to a head.

Then again, it had been Matilda keeping secrets from Eva. It had been Matilda not telling the full truth. It was she who couldn't keep her promises.

Noah was right. She had to do what he said. It was the best thing.

"Fine. I'll stay out of your way."

"I knew you'd see it my way. I'll see you in a few minutes."

A few minutes.

Matilda tore her eyes away from her phone screen and scoped for an escape route.

"Eeep! They're here," Gabby did a little hop, eyes alight. "Matilda, Jane Gardener is here. I'll be right back."

"Great. I'll check on those chairs." But when she turned to leave the patio, Clark stopped to ask her about the hedges.

Meanwhile she had bitten her cheek raw. It was a bad habit, an old habit, and of course it was back in full force, when the oldest and worst habit she ran away from found her.

This wasn't how she was supposed to be acting. Jane Gardener could become their next big client. As the manager, Matilda should be at Gabby's side to greet her and Noah and to answer questions about the B & B's amenities. She was supposed to be a professional.

She would be a professional.

She would prove to herself that she had grown from that doubtful and fearful woman of five years ago.

Then, Noah stepped on to the patio, freezing her in her tracks.

Five years had changed him, or perhaps it was all lipstick on a pig, since he was no longer wearing worn jeans and a sweatshirt. He looked like an adult, with slacks and a knit sweater.

The shock of black hair, the slim build. And were those aviator glasses hooked on the neckline of his sweater?

But, undoubtedly, his nature was still in full display, not wearing a proper suit to a formal outdoor wedding. She'd once had to convince him to wear jeans instead of basketball shorts to a work dinner at a fancy restaurant.

Years she had done his laundry, cooked his meals with her own meager skills. She'd mothered him, and here he was, looking like the man she had wished he'd become.

From her right someone brushed against her arm. "Oh my gosh, they're here. It's showtime." It was Frankie rushing by, in her own flowing dress and her hair trailing down the back.

To her left was Eva, who was unabashedly staring at her. "I don't like this."

Matilda looked straight ahead. "It's been five years."

"I more than most understand that there isn't a timeline to manage grief."

"I'm not in grief. He's still there."

"You don't have to lose people to experience grief. But in this case, it's not just him, but the idea of him, and time."

She turned to Eva, seeing her as she'd appeared when they'd first met five years ago. Back then, Eva appeared frailer, less comfortable in her skin, untethered by grief. Now, she was a force at fifty. Like she had been forged in steel by her loss.

It wasn't the same, was it? Matilda's regret was nothing compared to Eva losing Louis.

But yes, in the fourteen years she'd been with Noah, she had been in a state of desperation to keep him, to please him. She'd put herself last. She was still catching up.

Now, he was getting remarried. He was going to become a dad.

"Matilda, talk to me." Eva placed a hand against her forearm.

"I'm fine, really." Though, at the moment, she was sipping in breaths, because Noah's fiancée had stepped out to join the group.

Jane Gardner was blonde and lithe, with a small bump showing through her long dress. Something in the way she carried herself communicated a possessiveness, that this entire B & B was for her. Jane took Noah's hand and they spoke briefly to Frankie and Gabby, before all of their faces turned Matilda and Eva's way.

Matilda's legs felt like they were shot with adrenaline. She pulled her phone out of her pocket and said, "It's Clark. He needs me in the gazebo." She hiked a thumb over her shoulder, inwardly wincing at the lie.

She didn't wait for Eva's answer before spinning and speed-walking away. Instead of heading into the gazebo, she stepped off the path and high-kneed it into the brush.

Finally alone and surrounded on all sides by foliage, she breathed out the heaviness in her chest.

It's fine. It's fine.

No, it's not fine. You can't stay here the whole time.

"Did I miss a text for a rendezvous?" At the sound of the familiar voice, she turned, a smile curving her lips. Just the idea of Jared banished all of her confusion.

She threw her arms around him. "Thank goodness it's you."

"Hey. What's up?" He spoke into her hair while wrapping his arms around her waist. Along the scent of pine and outdoors, she detected cinnamon, sugar and his cologne, all of which should have been a comfort. But all of these things, mixed with Noah and Jane Gardner's presence and this talk of grief spun her emotions around like a tilt-a-whirl.

She wanted for all of it to go away. "Just kiss me."

Excitement flashed in his eyes, and his fingers buried themselves in the hair at the nape of her neck. He captured her lips with an expertise she had grown to appreciate. She lost herself in how he took the lead, in the firm grip he seemed to have of her, when all she felt was fragile.

The Roland Shim wedding went off without a hitch, a blur of white and of a harp's chords, R & B music and bubbles. There was laughter and tears, macarons and cake slices.

Matilda moved through the event in a kind of haze, perpetually scanning the crowd to avoid Noah and his fiancée.

Hypervigilance and inattention—it was a sickening combination, when she knew she wasn't doing her job correctly. Throughout the ceremony, she'd had to be reminded of her duties, sometimes asked twice.

And yet, much like the dichotomy of hypervigilance and inattention, while her insides were a tornado, her outsides were a beacon of calm. No one had been the wiser.

She was so good at this, at pretending everything was okay.

It was the story of her life. Of so many years hiding the fact that she had been living in a state of emotional chaos with Noah. And now, in perpetuating that she had it together.

She was jostled back to the present with a hug from Gabby. "Ack. Can you believe it? We did it."

Matilda's brain rallied to the moment. "You. *You* did it, Gabby. You did such a good job."

"I mean, Maggie Thurmond's people helped."

"Sure. But you're the mastermind. Look at this." She gestured toward the crowd, of beautifully dressed people, now dispersed with their drinks in hand. The white tops of tents perched all over the property. The soothing music that set the jovial mood. "It's breathtaking."

"Call me silly, but I just have a feeling." Gabby took a deep breath, and her cheeks puffed up with air. "That this is the start of something big. Huge. First, today with Maggie Thurmond, and fingers crossed, Gardner-Phillips in four months. Jane Gardner will be our first pregnant bride. It's going to be so special."

At the sound of Jane and Noah's combined last name, a sign that the two had all but finalized their decision to wed at the B & B, Matilda's smile froze on her face. "Only the best, Gabby."

She sighed. "Speaking of, they have loved this wedding thus far."

"Where are they?"

"They're on Mom's porch." She shrugged. "Technically they aren't guests and I didn't want Roland-Shim to feel like we're violating their space."

"It makes sense." Still, it felt too close for comfort; rarely did Eva allow guests at her cottage.

"I thought so, though Mom wasn't keen. Anyway, I hope we'll have a contract from them at the end of today." She looked at her phone. "Mom just texted. Looks like they're coming down." She gave Matilda a double take. "You're sure, though, that this is all right with you, with Noah being here? I was thinking about it the other night, and if it was me, if it was my ex, I wouldn't be sure what to do with myself."

"You and Nathan broke up six months ago, Gabby. My relationship with Noah was five years ago. Can you imagine yourself five years from now?"

"Gosh, I sure hope I'm over Nathan after five years."

"Right? That would suck." Matilda attempted to infuse levity in her tone, but her voice cracked at the sting of the comment.

At a distance, she spotted Jane and Noah with Eva heading in their direction. She glanced at her watch and frowned for good measure. "Well, it's time for me to do the rounds. You know how it is, especially after the SE and the cigarette butts we found. It takes one stray group of folks."

"I'm glad you can play the bad cop. I'll see you later?"

"Yep." She hightailed it to one of the B & B's side entrances. With her key, she opened it and stepped into the storage closet.

All around her was the smell of bleach and pine, and she welcomed it.

This was getting old, this running away.

Then, she heard someone call her name, followed by footsteps and the appearance of Jared at the storage room door.

She felt all her worry melt away, and a giggle escaped her lips. "Hey."

"What are you doing here?"

"Doing rounds."

"Rounds, huh?" His eyes narrowed playfully. "First in the brush, where you kissed me at risk of being seen, and now the storage room?"

"That's what rounds is. Checking everything out."

"So this is not about your ex being here?"

She looked at the ground, guilt catching up to her. "I'm sorry."

His lips quirked into a smile. "There's no need for you to be sorry. I'm just wondering why you didn't say anything."

Matilda toed the linoleum floor. "Because it shouldn't be a big deal."

"And is it?"

"No." She shook her head. "I mean yes." Matilda couldn't find the words, but she was trying. With Jared, she wanted to meet his vulnerability. "I hate this so much."

"Hate what, exactly?"

"That he still has the ability to trip me up." She looked up at him, realizing that what she was saying could be misconstrued. "It's not that I still have feelings for him. But seeing him is…just really upsetting. It's ridiculous, right? That I could be like this five years later? You must think I'm pathetic."

"Hey." He closed the distance between them, then placed both hands gently on her shoulders. His right thumb grazed the line of her jaw, and it somehow unlocked the holes in her explanation.

"I wish you weren't seeing me like this. This is not me."

"You look to be the same smart, gorgeous woman I see every day."

"Jared." She attempted to look down, but he lifted her chin with a knuckle.

"For what it's worth, I appreciate seeing you like this."

"A mess?"

"Not a mess."

She peered at him, challenging.

"Okay, a little bit of a mess, but it doesn't make me think less of you. This is another side of you that I'm grateful you're sharing with me."

"I don't like feeling like this."

"I'm sorry." He brought her to his chest without a word and hugged her tightly. "I'm here to listen."

Matilda melted into his arms, thankful that at that moment he didn't have a wise word to say, that he didn't have a suggestion on how to fix it. That he knew that what she needed was to feel like she was grounded to the present, and that she was accepted for who she was.

As the seconds passed, Matilda's world righted just a little: her breathing settled, and her heart rate slowed.

She stepped back, though she continued to clutch the sides of Jared's shirt. "Something is going on with you, too. You're usually pretty forthcoming, and you haven't said anything about your meeting with Eva."

He nodded, though his expression had turned contemplative. "She offered me a permanent position as you said she would."

"And?" She was blasted with a mix of hot and cold. "Did you tell her who you are?"

"Not yet, though I was tempted. She said I was already part of a family, and selfishly, I didn't want to ruin it. But every time I remember that I'm lying through my teeth, I feel a little sick inside. It will all be okay, won't it?"

"You're asking me?"

"You know the Espiritus best."

"You're giving me entirely too much credit." But in seeing the worry on his face, her insides constricted. Once Jared confessed, then Matilda would surely feel the consequences in some way even if she was spared from blame. "Am I worried about what's going to happen when Eva finds out? Yes, but I have to believe that they won't be angry forever."

"I hope so."

But there was hesitancy in his tone. Still she said, with hope in her heart, "You and I are going to take it day by day."

"Do you mean that?" He heaved a breath, seemingly gathering newfound energy. He wrapped his arms around her body.

This, this made it all better. "It's going to be hard. But I mean it."

"Well then, that's all that matters." He stepped back and lifted her chin with a knuckle and kissed her deeply, silencing all of her worries, that perhaps hard wasn't quite the right word to foreshadow what they would soon face.

Chapter Twenty-One

"I'm sorry. Could you repeat that again, please?" Jared's head swung to face Matilda. They were standing on his front porch after a speedy getaway from the B & B. He had been chomping at the bit to bring her back home, to be with her. Throughout cleanup and a quick meeting with the Espiritus, his only thought was to follow up their break room conversation with action.

She had said she wanted to be with him. Her mention of "taking it day by day" had been said without hesitation.

With that commitment, he was more than ready to tell the Espiritus who he was.

"I think…that we should go back to my place," she said once more, with a grin. Then she guided him by the hand back to his car. "You should drive."

"You're sure?" He rested a hand on his car door, pausing. This felt like a gift, knowing how much Matilda valued her privacy. He had naturally adjusted to her coming to stay with him; it never bothered him.

"I'm sure. I feel kind of bad, saddling with you with all of the cleanup, cooking and groceries the last three weeks."

"You don't owe me anything."

"I know, but I also want you to see my house. Show you the nonfood I have in my pantry, and see what I have on the walls. I know…that I've held back."

"No explanations needed. It's your right to do so, especially since we both thought I wasn't staying."

"Well then, it's my right to finally share it with you." She kissed him, lips soft against his.

"Screw chocolate," he said, after coming up for air.

"What's that?"

"That was the sweetest thing I've ever tasted."

"You're so cheesy." She laughed. "And I love it."

"Good. I've got more where that came from. Let's go." He opened the passenger door for her and jumped into the driver's seat.

It was the fastest three miles he'd driven, if but a bit dangerously, up and down the two lane roads.

When he entered Matilda's house, he gasped.

It was cozy.

He hadn't known what to expect. Her nature, her personality—it had given him the impression that her life was the same way, and her home would be sparse and neat and maybe even Spartan.

But it was full of warm, fuzzy things. A couch one could plop into, covered in pillows. A quilt draped across the arm, wrinkled and worn, as if she'd used it recently. A book, opened and face down on the cushion, with more spread around on the marred wooden coffee table.

Instead of overhead lighting, lamps lit the space. Rugs of different patterns lined the floor, and in the air was a mingling of scents; candles in decorative jars were perched on every surface.

"What is it?" she asked, drawing him in. Her hands were already at work, unbuttoning his shirt. And he, of course, allowed this without objection.

He had been hers since the beginning, and for the first time, now seeing her home, he truly felt that she belonged to him too. "It's so..."

Jumbled words caught on his tongue and he looked into Matilda's deep blue eyes.

Then, he knew.

Of course her house was warm, cozy and full of pretty things. Matilda was kind and thoughtful. She cared in the deepest of ways, so much that she pushed her own feelings aside. She was personal and insightful in all the ways that mattered. She also cared for the things she loved; she cherished them.

As she'd cared for the Espiritus and her friends.

As she'd cared for him.

"You," he continued. "It's so you."

"Do you like it?" Her face lit up. "It's not exactly coordinated."

He pulled her toward him, a hand on each of her shoulders. "It's perfectly you."

The words that left his mouth hearkened what Emma had said of him.

Perfectly her. Perfectly him. Despite who he was, and what had happened in his life, he was exactly as he should be, just as she was.

He leaned in and kissed Matilda, taking her wholly.

Soon they were wrapped into one another, and she was leading him up the stairs, to her bedroom. On the way, he caught glimpses of who Matilda was from the hanging pictures on the wall. He followed her to her bedroom, which was all white. Another surprise.

She didn't give him time to think; they were stumbling to bed, sheathing on a condom and making love. Her skin was hot against his, and he became lost in the sound of her voice, the way she moaned his name. They moved, sometimes in tandem, sometimes not, but together they worked themselves into a groove until his release was too much to bear.

He wanted her. He wanted to show her how much this meant

to him, being here. Because this felt different. Looking up at her, in the way she stared down at him, he saw something else in her eyes.

"Matilda," he said, his voice gruff with attempted control, because could it be? Could this happen after a short month together? "I'm here. Every single day. Every goddamn night."

"I'm here, too." Her face contorted with a kind of relief. Still making love to him, she bent down and kissed him, the moment so intimate and intense that he could only shut his eyes and feel every sensation rushing through his veins.

Jared held on for as long as he could, until he could feel her coil into herself, until he could sense the rumble of pleasure against her skin, for him to finish.

In the end, they caught their breaths on top of the covers, both looking up at the ceiling, silent for a beat.

As if they'd both had to process that what had transpired between them had changed them both.

Then, she snuggled against his side, wrapping her arms around him.

The first time, too.

He couldn't let this go. He wouldn't let this go.

"Jared, Jared, let go...please. Wake up." A whisper cut through Jared's sleep, startling him from absolute darkness. It pulled him into consciousness, where he realized Matilda was trying to inch her way out of his arms.

"What's going on?" His eyes squinted against the light coming through the window. Dang, it was already morning. As he wiped the sleep from his eyes, Matilda sat up in bed, her back exposed. He reached up to touch the warmth of her skin, just in time to feel the urgency coursing through her, and before a shirt cascaded down to cover it.

Leaning down, she kissed him on the lips. "I woke up to

my phone buzzing. And then yours. It's Eva. She wants to see the both of us."

He inched up in bed, still confused. It was their morning off—Matilda had a part-timer covering for her until noon, and he was due to go hiking. "Now?"

"Now." Her face twisted into a frown. "Something is going on."

He rubbed his eyes and slid out of bed. His body was spent, and despite her tone, he wasn't going to let it squash what had been an important night. As she stood, he pulled her down by the waist, onto his lap. "Hey, hold up a sec."

"She doesn't summon like this. What do you think it is?" Her arm encircled his neck and the other draped across his chest. Sighing, she leaned her forehead against his. He felt her melt into his arms.

"Whatever it is, it's going to be okay." He infused optimism into his answer.

"Do you think this has something to do with my ex? Or something about you? Or did I do something wrong?" She shut her eyes, throat moving as she swallowed.

He scoured her face in the pause and calmed his racing heart. He had told the truth seconds before; he wasn't afraid of the future if he knew that Matilda was backing him up. He could withstand the consequences of his actions if he knew that she was by his side.

Her doubt and worry was disconcerting.

"Seeing my ex brought up a lot of reminders. About how happy I was with him and then completely devastated by the end of it," she said.

"Five years ago," he reminded her. He didn't like where this was going. The tone of her voice had changed.

"Five years ago," she repeated. "And my life since then had been on a slow rise, you know? My work at the B & B, mending friendships and then meeting you."

He felt his insides give. "Am I the devastating thing?"

She softened. "No. But seeing Noah felt like a lead up to this moment."

"I still don't understand."

"It just feels like that in my life, good things come to an end, and disastrously. My life had been so good lately, even knowing you have this secret. I just fear that this call is the disaster. That my time for happiness is up."

"I hear you, but do you plan to toss your happiness away?"

"What? No, of course not."

"Then why would you say it's up? It's yours. It's ours. It's mine. As far as I'm concerned, I'm going to be hanging on to it." He lightened his tone, adding good vibes, and whatever happy he could, because the look on her face wasn't inspiring optimism inside of him. "Look at me. I finally made it into your house. Who can say that?"

"But you still have to tell the truth, and what happens after that? What happens to you, and to me, and my job? We're in too deep."

"First of all, your job is safe. I said that I wouldn't involve you. But if we fall in too deep, then we're in it together."

"It's so easy for you to say. You're so young..."

"Here we go again, Matilda. Age isn't anything but a number."

She shook her head. "It is when you're talking about life cycles, when you're talking about starting over. You've got a whole decade where you can still make a million mistakes."

The sound of that word took him aback. "Mistake. Do you consider us a mistake?" He gently made to stand, which caused her to do the same. As if pulled, they migrated to different parts of the room. He needed the moment to breath.

"That's not it." She dug her hands into the crown of her hair. "I don't know where this conversation is going."

"Me neither." How could five short minutes bring up so much baggage, and after one of the greatest nights he'd had?

Downstairs, the doorbell rang.

"Don't get that," he said, sensing her inclination to flee. If she left, their chance to hash this out before the rest of the world weighed in would be gone. He needed to know what all this meant, and where it left them.

She checked her buzzing phone. "Shit."

"What?"

"Eva's texting again. It's her at the front door."

"Before we go down there, we need to talk this out."

"Jared."

"She can wait another thirty seconds." He pinched the bridge of his nose. "For some reason, this conversation has grown out of proportion to what this might actually be. We cannot panic. For all we know, this is strictly about the B & B."

She nodded, and after a couple of breaths said, "Right. You're right. It could be something simple."

After one last look, they both headed out the bedroom door and down the stairs.

All the while, Jared felt Matilda slipping through his fingers, like this entire thing had been truly a dream. And he was about to wake up whether he was ready to or not.

Chapter Twenty-Two

Matilda's instincts called it; the situation had been far from simple.

After she answered the door to Eva, who had nary a word to say to either one of them, they followed her back to her cottage. Eva had not wanted to leave their current part-timer on her own for too long with all the Espiritus needing to be present at this urgent meeting.

Currently, Matilda was seated at the meeting table while Jared stood by the windows. Frankie and Gabby occupied opposite corners of the room, and Eva took the head of the table, hands linked in front of her.

Matilda had tried to dismiss her worry; she hung on to Jared's optimistic words; she tried to bring back the bliss and comfort she felt last night wrapped in his arms. That all would be well. That all *was* well.

But these memories were all out of reach. Even now, as she spied Jared's profile, what coursed through her was the anticipation of disappointing Eva and losing ground with the woman she had become after her life with Noah.

"We're here because of this." Eva gestured to the iPad on the long meeting table, to a photo of Jared and Matilda locked in a kiss. The photo was slightly pixelated.

"Where did you get this?" Matilda asked, unwilling to confirm or deny. Though, it was clearly them in the brush the day before the wedding, shortly after she'd seen Noah.

"A guest tagged the B & B on their socials," Gabby said. "The person who took this thought it was cute—they didn't recognize either one of you, but I did right away."

Matilda bit against her cheek to contain that additional shock. That Gabby hadn't gone to her first. But she pushed it away with the next thought—Gabby had every right to point it out. This wasn't personal. This was business.

Except that to her, it was all intertwined.

It was the same for the Espiritus, and why they all lived on the property, why Eva asked Matilda not to have a relationship with Jared while working at the B & B.

It was a rule to keep some semblance of order when family go into business together. Eva had always said the full-time employees of the B & B were like family.

Her cheeks burned with shame.

Oh, God, what I have given up?

What did I just risk?

"We tried to stay away from one another at first." Jared turned from the window. "But one thing led to another. We did our best to keep it professional."

"Obviously not well enough." Eva's tone was clipped.

Her disappointment resonated with every syllable. It reached Matilda's ears and settled in the same parts of her heart that she'd thought she'd healed.

"I'm sorry," she said now. "We were in the wrong. We went against the rules, and I hope that you can forgive us. Forgive me."

Jared raised an eyebrow, but she didn't acknowledge it. This wasn't about him, not really. She was also trying to keep the context of their secrets somewhat contained. There were so many in this room, and now she wasn't sure if she wanted Jared to admit his truth.

Because that would mean…

That would mean that she could be fired, too. But more, that she could lose Eva.

Secrets and lies never could remain hidden. Even if Jared denied Matilda's involvement in the secret, Eva would surely be suspicious because of their romantic relationship.

"I hate lying. You know that." Eva's features darkened. "We work together and live together and because of that, there has to be boundaries. I have very few rules around here, and one is that we remain honest about our intentions and admit when we've done something wrong." Her eyes slid over to Jared, and as with previous days, came a moment when she just looked exhausted. "I'm not a fool. It's not that I think that all of this could be a utopia. But here, I want peace and communication. I would appreciated it if you could have told me when things changed. I wish I didn't find out on social media."

She might not have been Matilda's mother either, but by God, she was every bit an older sister. "I'm so sorry you found out this way, Eva. I regret it. I do. I'll do whatever you need."

"Regret it? Regret what? *Us?*" Jared asked.

She refused to look at him; she didn't want to see his expression. "We can talk about this later."

"No. I don't want to talk about this later." The volume of his voice dialed up. "It's out in the open now, so it's something that we should be able to talk about."

"Not now. Not with everything." Matilda was feeling herself crumble from all the pressure.

Pressure was something she could stand in this job, in all her jobs. In the past, she'd served a dozen tables while keeping personalities in check. During the B & B's busiest seasons and most finicky customers, she could handle the ins and outs without drama.

But this emotional pressure made her want to run away. It made her want to shut down. It made her want to hide in her house, and never come out.

"I've… I've got to go," she said now. Standing. "I… I just need a moment."

* * *

Matilda didn't pace on the back deck for long; seconds later, she heard the squeak and then the slap of the back door. And yet, she didn't turn. She took in the quiet of the woods to fortify herself. For a beat she imagined that she was all alone in the world, that there wasn't an entire town on the other side of the hill. That she didn't have four people inside that thought poorly of her.

"I'm sorry for pushing you." Jared's voice rose above the chirping birds. "But what you said in there, Matilda. Regret? That hurt."

"We can't talk about this here," she countered. "We can't talk about us, and regret, and consequences because you have bigger problems. You have your secret to tell."

"I'm ready."

"But I'm not. I… I didn't think all of this through. At how this changes everything for me, and probably for the worst. You're going to get fired, and you're going to have to leave this place. And then what happens to me?"

He recoiled as if Matilda had delivered a blow. "I thought we were going take things day by day? That we're going to be there for one another?"

"I am here for you, but you just don't understand." The heat in her body turned up to high. What she'd realized after leaving Noah, and what she was finding out once more, was that no one had walked in her shoes. She could try to explain what her life had been with Noah, but no one would truly comprehend what she went through.

He shook his head. "We're not doing that again. Don't assume I don't understand just because I'm ten years younger than you. It isn't just ageist but completely unfair, especially with what you know about me. And you're forty, Matilda, not someone who's twice my age. Even then, there's nuance."

Matilda's face burned, the callout adding embarrassment

to this pit of desperation that she was trying to climb out of. "Okay, fine. But we're seeing the difference now, aren't we? We are not in the same place. Not with our work, not with what we want. And definitely how we have to handle this situation."

"What are you saying?" He stuck his hands in his pocket, a tell that he was clearly trying to deescalate.

But there would be no denying what was happening now. Things were falling apart.

She lowered her voice to a whisper, the thought of saying the next sentence feeling like the doors shutting on another part of her life. "That they mean everything to me, and your secret will change that. If you tell them, I'm left, to what? At best, I pick up the pieces in yours and in their life? At worse, they don't accept you and they find out my role in it. And I lose everything again."

"So…you're saying that I shouldn't even tell them?" Then, his voice rose to a yell. "They're my family!"

The ring of those last words settled around them, and by how the backyard had gotten quiet, the entire forest had heard what Jared had said.

It wasn't the forest Matilda was most worried about.

She looked up then, to the back windows, of three faces staring at her.

Chapter Twenty-Three

Jared shut his eyes; he'd caught Matilda's gaze over his shoulder and had heard her gasp.

He reined in the fear and anger that he'd expressed just seconds before. He blew out a panicked laugh. "They heard."

"Yes."

He joined Matilda next to the railing. Her eyes were filled with pain, and her face was contorted into a grimace.

He hated that he was involved in causing that pain. He hated that they'd come so far in three weeks for it to all fall apart the last twenty-four hours.

"You were right from the very beginning," he said, thinking on the day after their one-night stand. "I should have told them from the start. This is my responsibility and my problem. I'll tell them now, and I'll make sure that they know you had nothing to do with it. Stay here, okay?"

"No, I should—"

He shook his head. "I have avoided this my whole life. I convinced myself that I didn't need to know more about Louis and his family. My family. When I finally got myself here, I stalled a good three weeks. Sure, it was because I was waiting for the right time. But I was also scared. In the end, all I really did was drag this out and wrap you up in it." He squeezed her hand. "I was wrong. Stay here, please. I have to own up to this. To them."

She nodded. "Okay."

He leaned down and pressed a forehead against Matilda's, willing himself to remember this moment. Then, he spun and entered the back door, to the office where Gabby, Frankie and Eva were waiting. "I have something to tell you."

Being a chef meant using one's senses. Sight, touch, smell, taste, hearing.

Being a chef meant keying into instincts.

When Jared revealed who he was, he picked up the minuscule shift in Eva's expression; he heard Gabby's gasp. He felt the tension in Frankie's icy stare.

It was Frankie who spoke first. Of course. "What the actual hell. You're…our *brother*?"

He could only nod, thunderstruck at the title.

"All this time," Gabby added. "You didn't say anything. All the conversations we had, not once did you say a word."

"I wasn't sure what to say."

"You could have started with, hey, we're related," Frankie snapped back. "That your dad is my dad. Holy crap. Liam has a tito."

"Wait," Eva said. It was first word she had uttered since he began his explanation. Her eyes narrowed. "How do I know you're not lying?"

The idea of it stunned Jared. That he could and would lie about something like this. "Because I'm not."

"How do I know you're not some scammer? People do that all the time you know. They find out who's passed away and take on their identity. What if you're just one of those people? Frankie. Get the sheriff on the phone."

"Wh-what do you mean?" Frankie said.

"Eva, I don't think that's necessary," a voice said from behind him.

Jared's turned; Matilda stepped through the door. His heart grew by double.

But Eva jutted a finger at her. "No. You don't have a say in this. You yourself don't know the truth. Better yet, I want everyone to leave."

"But, Mom," Frankie said.

Gabby raised a hand. "Wait."

"All of you, that includes you girls. Out. Out!" She turned her back, the refusal a rejection, one that clearly was felt by Gabby and Frankie, who both rushed out the door. Matilda backed away, and with her head down, walked out.

The silence was deafening. Being left behind was heart-wrenching.

"I'm sorry, Eva. I didn't intend...please know that Matilda had nothing to do with this. She didn't know until today." He swallowed against the pain of this lie. A part of him wished that she'd stayed to stand up with him, even if this was a term in their agreement. He pushed on, knowing he only had seconds left with Eva. "But for what it's worth, knowing you all has changed my life. And I wish we had more time together." With nothing else to say that could mend the situation, Jared left Eva's cottage.

Matilda's Bronco was gone when he returned to the B & B.

Jared would need to forfeit his security deposit for Kite Flyer, given how he was leaving it. He hadn't stripped the bed, nor had he emptied the refrigerator. The dishes weren't done, and the pantry was full of dry goods.

This was not his MO. He cleaned up after himself. He didn't saddle people with his mess.

He heaved a breath as he stuffed his suitcase with clothing, his phone blowing up with texts from Emma. He'd called her with the CliffsNotes, and as predicted, she had bombed him with texts, knowing he wasn't in the mood to take a call.

Nor did he want to hear an "I told you so."

Clean, dirty, he didn't know what each article of clothing's status was, so long as it was packed and quickly so he could get in the car and onto the highway ASAP, before he fully allowed himself to think about what just happened.

"Knock knock." The front door opened and Chip walked in. The sight took Jared aback, until he remembered that he should've been meeting him for his hike.

"Argh." Jared's shoulders drooped. "I'm sorry."

"Dude, the hike's about to leave in ten minutes."

"I meant to call."

Chip looked around the room. "This doesn't look like you're just backing out of the hike. I thought you were staying at least till the end of the month."

"Don't worry, I won't be asking for a refund for the partial month."

"That's not what I mean…hold on—" he fished out his phone and texted "—Jared, I'm getting all sorts of bad vibes. What is all this?"

"It's complicated."

"Says everyone. You realize I'm a bartender right? That's everyone's disclaimer, and well, sometimes it might seem complicated, but it all boils down to simple syrup."

"Is that bartender speak?"

"Very much so." He grinned. "Try me."

"Don't you have a hike planned?"

"I texted my boss to say I'm staying back."

"Aw, man, you didn't have to do that." Jared was making a mess of everything.

"Nope." He moseyed over to the counter and hopped on a stool.

The guy looked like he wasn't going anywhere until Jared told him something, and admittedly he needed to speak to someone who had zero skin in this game. Someone who could just listen.

So Jared explained everything. All of it, starting when the critic called his sisig inauthentic to today. It all spilled out of him in one mad rush. At some point, Chip retrieved a bottle of whiskey from a pantry Jared hadn't explored, met him at the kitchen table and poured themselves a shot. Then a second, and a third.

Jared lost count after that.

"You're right, it is complicated," Chip, now glassy-eyed, said.

Jared burst out laughing. Then, they were both laughing; Jared clutched his heaving stomach.

As he did so, the last three weeks flipped through his mind. His arrival, his impulsive decision to work for the Espiritus. At how despite his best intentions he had grown to like the Espiritus. To how he felt a part of them.

And Matilda, who he'd fallen in love with.

"This is so messed up." Jared cradled his head in his hands. It was full of whiskey, of memories both good and bad.

Chip gripped his forearm. "At least you have nothing else to hide." His words slurred, and yet, it reached Jared's ears as clear as a spring Peak day.

"That's not true. I didn't tell Matilda that I love her."

"Then stay and do it."

"I'm not welcome here anymore." He pressed the heel of his palms against his eyes. "She made it perfectly clear that the Espiritus would always come first. And I don't blame her. They're great people. I just wish I didn't make a mess of things."

"Look. Eva might not want you at the B & B, but you're welcome *here.* At Kite Flyer. And in Peak. I'm no brooding, gorgeous B & B manager, but I wouldn't mind it if you stayed."

"You just like having someone here paying your mortgage."

"No lies detected. But I don't know. I've liked hanging out with you."

He snorted. "Chip, this is the first time we're really hanging out."

"I know, and hasn't it been great?"

Jared smiled, nodding.

"That's more like it." Chip stood and cleared the glasses, setting them in the sink. Then, he approached Jared. "You might not know me from Adam and vice versa, but I pride myself on being a good judge of character. Leaving might seem like the next best thing because yeah, it's tough. But you're a good person, even with all this swirling around. And if this feels like home to you, then I hope you stay." He stuck out a hand. "Will you call me when you come back?"

"If." Jared shook his hand, and to his surprise Chip pulled him into a hug.

"Whatever." He stepped back. "I'm out. Don't be a stranger, man."

"Wait, I hope you didn't drive."

"I didn't mention it? I'm next door. Quarter-mile walk up the street. And hey, load up the dishwasher, okay? Or I *will* take that security deposit."

"I'll clean up," Jared said. Though he knew that in his case, he could only do so much.

Chapter Twenty-Four

After three days, only one thing had been able to make Matilda smile, and it was Allie, showing up at her front door with Brianna.

And that smile quickly turned into tears.

"Oh no." Allie stepped in with the car seat wrapped around her arm. After setting the car seat down, she hugged Matilda.

Matilda let herself go. The tears that she had held on to spilled out into a waterfall of regret and sadness. It rivaled what she'd felt when she'd left Noah long ago; in this case, she knew deep in her soul that she and Jared should be together. That it hadn't been their time to say goodbye.

And yet, she had pushed him away. Not only did she come up with a million reasons why he hadn't been right for her, including their age difference, she'd left him at Eva's.

Worse, she'd let him drive out of town without stopping him, and since then, she'd continued to carry on at work like she hadn't been a part of the ruse.

"Let it all out, Mat," Allie whispered into her ear.

After the sobs died down to the occasional hiccup, they both stepped into her living room and plopped down on the couch.

Brianna remained asleep in her car seat.

Allie picked up a book at her feet. "Wow, I haven't seen this place so…"

Matilda winced at the books scattered all around, some

on the floor, and the half-empty cups of tea, coffee and wine perched on every surface. "I was thirsty."

"I can see that. And looking for something to read."

"I couldn't find the right book."

"Ah, disassociation by literary devices."

"I tried," she sniffed, feeling her heart lighten. For all the hurt she had been feeling, Allie's presence was a reminder that there were people in her life who still loved her, despite all of her faults.

"I'm just glad you opened your door."

"Did I have a choice?"

"Nope. Besides, I have a key, for emergencies."

"Remind me to ask for it back."

"You wouldn't dare." Her face softened. "I know all about what happened at the B & B with Jared, and that he's gone."

"I dare ask how the news made the rounds."

"Gabby was at Mountain Rush."

Matilda grimaced, guilt rushing forth.

"I was out with the girls and heard her tell everyone what happened. She was so upset. We tried to keep things in control."

"You were there, with the crew?"

"Yeah. Krista encouraged me out, in cahoots with my mother, of course. It was a shock for me to find out that you weren't there. Why didn't you tell any one of us what was going on?"

"Because." *Because I took part in the lie but left him to fend on his own. Because I should have kept him from leaving.* She shook her head, debating what to say. She was sad, and lonely, and upset with herself most of all.

The truth. I can tell the truth, too.

Matilda swallowed the fear welling up inside her. "There's more to the story."

"Oh no." Her jaw dropped minutely.

"I knew all about it. I knew who he was the first day he was hired. He asked me to keep it a secret. And because I needed a chef, I agreed."

Allie covered her mouth with a hand.

Seeing the shock on her friend's face sent her to her feet. "This is why I didn't tell anyone. Everything is awful."

"Matilda, sit down, please. You're going to wake Brianna." She gestured to the baby.

"That is emotional manipulation."

"I know. And I'm going to milk it for what it's worth until we get to the bottom of this."

Matilda sat back down. "I'm already at the bottom—I messed up. Not only did I keep that secret for Jared, but when he finally admitted who he was, I ran like hell."

The line in between Allie's eyebrows deepened. "Now, I admit, keeping that secret from Eva was probably not a good idea."

Matilda grunted. "No."

"Nor was not admitting you had a part in it."

"Especially that."

"And you're going to have to make up for it, but shutting everyone out is not the answer. You're doing this now."

Like you did before, she finished in her head.

Allie scooted closer to Matilda. She took one of her hands into hers. "When you were with Noah, I didn't have the wherewithal to tell you outright to leave him. I said that you changed, and that I missed you, but not the cold hard truth. I thought that it wasn't my place to judge your relationship. After, though? I promised myself to tell you the truth, no matter how terrible it sounded.

"You cannot keep holding yourself up to who you were when you were with Noah. But if you insist on doing so, hold yourself up to the person who came home bravely."

"Bravely? Hardly."

"Mat. Stop. You coming home was the bravest thing. You

rebuilt a life. If you're going to insist on comparing yourself to someone, then do it to that woman. That woman who overcame. I promise that you will overcome this, too. You don't have to do this alone."

Shutting everyone out is not the answer. Allie's words came back to her.

"I shut Jared out, didn't I?"

Allie's expression was grave. "Not only that, but you had the audacity of going three days without telling us. That's not allowed in our friend-book, Mat. You are not allowed to disappear on us again. Have you tried to reach Jared since he left?"

"Sort of. I called the restaurant he worked for before. He had mentioned he was taking leave, so I thought it was worth a try."

"And?"

"I asked for him by name, and when they told me to hold, I hung up."

A buzz sounded between them. "Perfect timing."

"For what?"

"Reinforcements."

Allie stood and went to the door, opening it.

At the threshold were a man and a woman she hadn't seen except over FaceTime the last year.

"Mom? Dad?"

Her mom lifted a bottle of prosecco with one hand, and her father offered a hardback novel, a new thriller she'd mentioned on their last call.

As her mother hugged her, she said, "Let's figure things out, okay?"

Matilda *still* took another couple of days to decide that today was the day, and as she drove her Bronco up to the Spirit of the Shenandoah B & B for her usual shift, she pumped herself up for what would be one of the hardest conversations she would ever take part in.

Entering the B & B's oak double doors, she was greeted with its usual vibrant energy of guests milling about and breakfast being made.

From afar, she heard Eva's voice.

It was now or never.

Matilda walked deeper into the dining area, and spotted a person in a chef's jacket at the stove. It was Chef Mason Griffith, a clutch hire, one of Maggie Thurmond's chefs discovered by Gabby at the Roland-Shim wedding. He had been looking for a side gig until his next opportunity as a super yacht chef. The strangeness of another chef occupying where Jared had been was another stab of pain in Matilda's heart.

There'd been more moments of painful learning. In the last couple of days with her mom, and an emergency session with the therapist she'd worked with after breaking up with Noah, she had begun to understand when and where she could have changed perspective and course. She'd also accepted that nothing could be remedied if she simply hid from the truth.

Speaking of…

Eva walked out of the butler's pantry, a pedestal platter in her hand. Her face was gaunt, despite the smile she was wearing. "Good morning, Matilda."

"Morning." She swallowed against her fear. "Is it possible to chat in private?"

"Sure." She set the platter on the island and wiped her hands on a kitchen rag. "Your office?" She took the lead and stepped out toward the hallway.

"Um. Okay." Following behind, she winced at the chosen location. "Just a warning that it's tight in there."

It was more than tight. It was…

"Whoa," Eva slipped into the black hole of what had been an impeccably kept, though tiny, space.

Now, inside with her boss, Matilda saw her office in a stark lens. Her papers were everywhere. Her whiteboard hadn't been updated since the wedding.

Matilda cleared her things off a chair, relocating them to a random shelf, and gestured for Eva to sit.

"I'm glad you called for this chat, Matilda. I've been meaning to talk about what happened with you, though honestly, I didn't know how to approach it. As you can imagine, I'm still in shock."

She swallowed the ball of nerves in her throat. "How are the girls?"

"They're doing better than me. More curious than angry. They want answers, of which I can't really give them. All I could tell them was my side of what I think happened, if Jared is truly who he says he is. Louis and I married so young. Nineteen!" She looked amazed, even now. "And if you can imagine, after the short honeymoon period, of me being away from family because we moved to North Carolina, I wanted to go home. I wasn't prepared to be an army wife.

"We split up…for about six months, maybe seven? I didn't intend on us getting back together, and I told him to move on. But I missed him. So I came back home, and I was soon pregnant with Frankie. Not once did he say there was anyone else. And again if Jared was telling the truth, then Louis and Jared's mother would have…met…when we split up." She cleared her throat while her fingers wrung themselves in her lap. "But this conversation is about you. I haven't checked in with you, at the shock you must have felt, too. I know you're working out your own feelings right now, like we are. Are you okay? I hear your parents are in town."

Matilda had held her breath while listening to Eva's story, and now she was feeling light-headed. Here her boss was, concerned about her, when she was about to drop another disappointing truth. "Yes. They've been staying with me."

"They're such great people." She heaved a breath. "I owe you an apology for taking too long to ask how you are doing."

"Eva," Matilda said, no longer able to sit there with her guilt. "I should be the one to apologize."

"Oh, there's no need—"

"Yes, there is. I'm just going to say it outright, and I fully accept that there will be repercussions. But I want you to know that…that I made mistakes. I…kept my own secret too."

Confusion crossed her friend's expression. "What do you mean 'too'?"

Everything. Matilda was risking everything.

But was living a lie living at all?

"I knew who Jared was."

Silence met her statement, so she pushed on. "I knew who Jared was, from the very beginning. All he wanted was to get to know who you were, in exchange for working for us."

Eva shook her head slightly. "You knew," she said in an eerily calm tone.

"We were stuck without Allie, and Jared was more than qualified. And… He was desperate to know Louis's family."

"So you gave him access to us." Her voice was as still as the air in the room. "You gave a stranger access to *my* family. A stranger. Who lied."

"Eva, I don't think he lied."

She stood. "And yet you're not sure. Did you see any verifiable documents?"

"I mean…no…but he passed a background check. He came with credentials. He's not any more dangerous—"

"That's beside the point, isn't it? I trusted you, Matilda, and you…you gave it all away, for what, someone to fill in a role?"

Matilda knew that Eva had meant the role of the chef, but what she heard was that the role was for a bed-buddy.

Or maybe Eva had meant that, too.

In both cases, the statement was a sword in her heart.

"I'm sorry. I should have told you."

"You think?" She laughed sardonically. "From the jump, and especially after Jared had admitted who he was. But instead, you kept quiet. To think I felt sorry for you as the person he left behind, when you were actually part of the whole damn thing."

"I wanted to tell you, but I didn't want to lose you all."

"Well…we are too far down that road. The U-turn was miles and weeks ago." She went to the door and opened it. "You should go. I need to figure out how to effectively transition you out of this job. Please leave your keys on the kitchen counter."

Matilda nodded, though her body was numb. She didn't feel the ground as she walked away from the office, though she jumped as the door slammed shut behind her.

At the kitchen counter, she fished her keys from her pocket and uncoiled her house and car keys, the two of the bunch that belonged to her. As she set the B & B keys on the counter, Frankie burst in, already midsentence. "So glad I caught you, Matilda. I just finished up the website but wanted to make sure our reservation dashboard was seamless and…" She slowed. "Everything okay?"

Matilda shook her head, overcome with regret. "I'm sorry for everything, Frankie."

Then, she did what she never thought she would ever have to do.

She walked away from the Espiritus.

Chapter Twenty-Five

"I need a dragon fruit mai tai and an orchid martini," Jared yelled over the crowd hovering around the bar and the music piping through the speakers.

"You got it," Mike, one of the bartenders, said, though didn't look up from his task at hand, which was putting on a show slinging drinks. The crowd was captivated, a couple even pausing their conversation to watch.

If Jared had not felt envious, he would have clapped alongside the spectators. As it was, though, all Jared wished for was to be back in own element. He missed the pressure and the heat of the kitchen. The intricacies of seasoning something just right. Of knowing something made from his hands provided joy and physical satisfaction.

Two weeks had passed since he left Peak. It had been about ten days since he jumped back into work at Sizzling Platter, though this time as a server. Yamamoto had hired another sous chef since Jared's departure; there was no room at the inn, or so the story went.

But he took the job, because Yamamoto had welcomed him with open arms. Bouncing back to a former restaurant family seemed like a good salve from being kicked out of another one, at least until he found a chef's position elsewhere.

And since Emma had somehow made his home hers since she was on the outs with her band, work became the quieter of the two.

Had it really only been two weeks?

It felt as if he had been sad for a long, long time.

Matilda ruled his thoughts. Eva, Frankie, Gabby and Liam too. But Matilda above all.

"Jared, drinks are up!" Mike snatched him from his thoughts, gesturing to the two cocktails.

"Thanks." He set the drinks on the platter and made his way to a table, dropping them off with a smile, noticing that he had a guest at one of his tables.

When he turned to the booth, the tray almost slipped from his fingers. "Mom?"

"Hi, son." Sharla Sotheby was holding the menu almost an arm's length away, face tilted upward. Her gray hair was coiled in a loose bun. "I forgot my reading glasses." She harrumphed. "How about a white wine to start—you pick whatever's good."

This scene, how she was acting—that she was there, in Kentucky—felt like the start of some alternate universe reality. He didn't know whether to take her order, or to scoop her into his arms.

He chose the second option, because this was his mother, and she was a sight to behold. Like she had somehow intuited that he'd needed her. Slipping into the booth, and ignoring the stares of other diners around him, he allowed his mother's hug to console him.

"What are you doing here?" he asked.

"I guess I should ask first—what are *you* doing serving?"

"Oh, where do I even start?"

"From the beginning."

"Can we talk tonight? After my shift? It's jumping here tonight."

"There's no time like the present. Besides, I called you out of work."

"What?"

She extended a finger to something behind him, and Jared turned, to his boss at the other side of the dining room. He raised a hand in greeting, which Sharla returned. "He was kind enough to give you the rest of the night off. I told him it was a reunion and he more than obliged. He's supposed to send over some food too."

"That's more than kind. He only just hired me back."

She pressed her heart to her chest. "When I heard that you left this job in the first place, my heart skipped a beat, but in a bad way. Wanna catch me up? Apparently I missed out on a lot."

"Are you sure you don't want your drink first?"

"Might as well rip that Band-Aid off, I say."

After heaving a breath, Jared told his mother everything. He realized this was the second time he'd recounted the story—the first was with Chip—and though he still mourned his loss of the Espiritus and Matilda, he no longer felt like he was drowning.

These days it was more like he was wading in a stagnant lake.

"Did you find what you were looking for?"

He paused to think on it—he had been ruminating on that same question for days now. "I found them, which was part of what I wanted. Did I get to know Louis? Not really. But his family, on the other hand—"

"*Your* family."

He felt sucker punched by the statement. It was easier to let some of his attachment go, knowing that those relationships wouldn't continue.

"You could have told me about your plan. I could have helped you," she said matter-of-factly, and without malice.

"I know. Especially since Eva Espiritu doesn't believe me. Eva was Louis's—"

"I know who she is. I did my own research too. I had so many years to connect you with your father, and by the time I did, it was too late. I regret not looking for him sooner. Then again, I was a young mom just trying to survive. Since then, though, I promised myself I would rather know than not."

"I don't judge you for not finding him sooner, Mom. Hell, I knew about his family but it took me until now to get brave enough to find them."

"All we can do is try to do better. Next time, though, know that you can count on me."

He met his mother's eyes. They were a bright blue and fierce, and he was hit with another dose of remorse. He had underestimated Sharla. "I was worried that involving you would complicate things."

She raised both eyebrows, making her point that he'd done a fine enough job making things complicated.

Food arrived for them, and Jared made introductions between the server and Sharla. As he watched his mother interact, her words returned to him: *Since then, though, I promised myself I would rather know than not.*

It was very much something Matilda would say.

Then he wondered: had he told his mother of his plans first, would he have met Matilda under the same circumstances? And would he have left Peak with memories of Matilda, as laced as they were with his own family drama?

When the server left, and he and Sharla were alone once more, he said, "As hard as it was with all that happened, at least I met Matilda. She was something, Mom. She was fully herself, and with her, I felt that I was enough. Maybe it was okay for me to do this on my own."

Sharla smiled wistfully. "You are definitely my boy." After a pause, she said, "Telling my family I was pregnant after a one-night stand was one of the hardest things I had to do. Up to when you were born, it was a struggle. I dropped out of college. I didn't know how I would survive. But then you were born and made all of the challenges worth it. I found my purpose, and I fell in love with you and being your mom. While I wish I found Louis sooner, when it comes to you, I have zero regrets."

She reached out and squeezed his forearm, the act grounding him to that moment. That he was loved, he was wanted, that his family would always remain so. And that his identity was the sum of all of his experiences.

I am enough.

He would need to say it more; he would need to feel it. He was whole and not part of himself, as Frankie had told him.

"Now it's my turn to confess," she announced.

Jared had taken a sip of water and coughed. "Okay?"

"I knew about what happened before I came here, and it wasn't through Emma. Eva contacted me. Actually, it was her daughter Frankie, first, and then Eva."

His jaw dropped. "How did they…"

"Find me? They looked you up on your socials, followed through to Emma, which led them straight to my social media." She blew out a breath. "I had no idea it was that easy. Anyway, Frankie messaged me on Facebook. And then I went to Emma to confirm. Eva and I connected on video chat. She wanted to know the truth, and I gave it to her. I also showed her the one picture of me and Louis, at Myrtle Beach."

Questions mounted, though he could only ask, "Did she believe you?"

She shrugged. "I don't know. It's up to her to decide what to believe or not believe. At the very end of the day, your truth is what you accept. That is, in your case, until you and one of your half sisters decide to take a sibling DNA test."

Hope flared inside him. That perhaps not all was lost. That maybe someday, he could return to Peak.

As if reading his mind, Sharla said, "The peace is in knowing that there are no more secrets, Jared." She raised her wineglass to him. "Onward and upward?"

Could he move on?

Could he one day think of Peak without feeling regret?

Could he find the same joy he'd experienced being with Matilda?

He would need to. He would try, anyway.

He clinked his glass against hers. "Onward and upward."

"Ready to go in?" Krista nudged Matilda. They were parked in front of the B & B, and had been for at least fifteen minutes.

Matilda shook her head. Still, she opened the passenger door.

It had been three days since she'd turned in her keys to Eva. Three days in which she'd anticipated what she knew would be her official firing.

Matilda still wasn't ready for it.

Hence, Krista as backup.

"I'll be right here," her friend said as a sort of nudge. "Go, Matilda."

"You're such a nag," she told her.

"You're welcome."

In truth, had she not had Krista, or Allie, or her parents, she wasn't sure that she'd have gotten dressed in the morning. They were pushy, insistent and stubborn, and she loved them for it.

She slid out of the seat and straightened her clothes once she got out. She was wearing the B & B uniform, because until she was officially fired, she wouldn't not wear it to work. And with a final nod to Krista, she entered the B & B.

As usual her eyes darted everywhere. She double-checked the cleanliness, the faces of the guests for their satisfaction, whether the windows were sparkling clean and if the temperature were comfortable.

Everything appeared normal until Gabby raced past, the phone against her ear. She had a panicked look on her face. Then she turned, and when their eyes met, her body seemed to collapse into itself. She stuffed the phone back in her pocket.

"Oh my God, you're here." Gabby threw her arms around Matilda, and she all but melted into Gabby's embrace. They hadn't really spoken since Jared's confession, and Matilda had missed her. "I'm so sorry. About the social media post. We saw it together, Mom and I. And I couldn't *not* say anything once she saw it. And then came the fight, and you and Jared. I meant to come over, to sort things out, but I promised Mom."

"It's okay." That social media post felt so long ago, and it was such a small issue as compared to the enormity of the real secret that she and Jared had kept. "It's me who's sorry, about everything."

"I love you, Mat. You're like a sister to me." She was squeezed harder, then Gabby stepped back. "But we don't have time. We have to go. How did you know?" She started for the back door.

Matilda followed her. "Know what? I'm here to do my final meeting with your mom."

"That's the thing, though. She's in the honeysuckle." Her voice came out in a panicked wheeze, and together they jogged up the hill to vista point two. As they crested the hill, they were met with noises of a struggle.

Frankie was pleading. "Mom, please."

"Go, Frankie. Just go!"

Those words were from Eva.

Matilda and Gabby slowed; Matilda's heart thumped like a bass drum as she tried to catch her breath. When they rounded the corner, Eva's back was to them. She was wearing a robe and wielding a bush trimmer on the highest setting. Honeysuckle blooms were scattered on the ground. When Eva turned, her face was red and full of tears. Behind her, Frankie hands were cupped against her mouth, with a stricken expression on her face.

"Eva," Matilda yelled, her tears now giving way. "Eva!"

With a thumb, Eva shut off the trimmer and set it down on the ground. As if drunk, she tottered to a nearby bench.

Matilda took a knee in front of her; she gazed up into Eva's eyes. Eva, her boss, her mentor and her guiding light the last five years.

"It's true," Eva whispered. Her face was contorted into pain. "It was all true. Jared is Louis's son. Frankie found Jared's mother. We got on video chat and…and she showed me a picture of him. My… Louis."

"I'm sorry. I'm sorry. I'm so, so sorry," Matilda said, over and over. She had never doubted Jared, but she sympathized with Eva. She knew what it felt like to have the veil parted, to see what was on the other side of something that she thought was solid and real. Her heart broke for Eva. "I wish I could make this better. I feel so responsible."

Eva sniffled and wiped her cheeks, though it was stained black from her mascara. "It wasn't your fault that Louis betrayed me. And it wasn't your fault that you fell in love with his son."

"This isn't love. Love is supposed to be natural. It's supposed to be easy. Love is me loving you and Gabby and Frankie. Love is me loving Peak and this land. And I shouldn't have felt anything for him. After finding out who he was, I should have told you right away. I don't have a single excuse."

Eva lifted up Matilda's chin with a knuckle. Matilda squinted at the glaring sun just to the right, and still it stung her eyes. The heat of its glare warmed her cheeks. The scent of honeysuckle overrode it all. "No, Matilda. This was Jared's truth to tell, not yours. You were respecting that." Her voice softened. "Love doesn't have those rules. That's the problem. That's the problem," she repeated. "And also the amazing thing about it all. Love doesn't have rules. And it sure as hell doesn't have a road map for something like this. But what you have, what I saw on your face, on his, too, was love."

Matilda thought of their last moments together, at Eva's house. She had been so afraid of losing the Espiritus, of disappointing them. She had been terrified to slide back to who she was with Noah, that it clouded what was right in front of her.

Jared, who cooked for her, who cared for her, who accepted her for who she was.

"I do love him," Matilda said, and in voicing those words, her conviction rose above the doubt she harbored. "I love him, and I let him go."

Eva pressed both of her hands against her face. "I let Louis's son go, too. My son." She heaved a breath in her palms. Heavy, deep breaths, a yogic breath. Then, she lowered her hands, as if making a decision. "It's not his fault either that he was born to this situation. Nor should you two be blamed for falling in love with each other."

She looked up at her girls. At Frankie and Gabby, who were now holding hands. "Ladies, help me up. It's time to plan a road trip."

Chapter Twenty-Six

This time, Jared knew what to expect, and he brought backups.

He squinted across the studio from under the warm, bright lights to his parents and Emma, standing off to the side. Simultaneously, they all gave him a thumbs-up. So cheesy. So typically Sotheby, and just what he needed.

That, and some makeup. Some touch-ups under his eyes to hide the lack of sleep, a little blush on his cheeks, because he looked like death, as Emma said.

In truth, he still felt like death. Loss continued to course through his body, and it was layered. Loss of love, of newfound family. It was the loss of Louis, too. The idea of him, the legend of him.

Jared been back in Louisville for about three weeks, and the recovery was ongoing. Thankfully, his family was patient. And in the last week, one of the line cooks at Sizzling Platter quit, and he was back in the kitchen.

As well as in front of a camera.

The opportunity mirrored the very first video segment, down to the fact that he was, once more, a substitute. He'd agreed to appear because what else was he supposed to do?

It wasn't as if he had any plans on his calendar.

"Good morning, Louisville, we are back for our next food segment with Chef Jared Sotheby, who's here to show off his own version of chicken soup, Filipino-style." The anchorwoman, wearing bright pink, enunciated her words with a bright smile.

Then, the camera cut toward him.

Filipino-style.

His thoughts jumped back to the Espiritus. Of being around Gabby and her enthusiasm for numbers, Frankie and their cooking lesson. Flying a kite with Liam. And Eva, who pushed him to step up at the B & B.

With that rush of memories came an important thought. This opportunity was a mirror except for one thing. Months ago, after that first segment, he'd doubted his ability to cook something Filipino-style. He'd been plagued by imposter syndrome.

No longer.

Someone cleared their throat, and Jared snapped to, taking in the silence. He jumped into the spiel he had practiced. "Chicken tinola is a salve for anyone who's ill, and a comfort food for homesickness."

He was starting to sweat. Beads had collected in between his shoulder blades at his mention of homesickness, because he missed Peak. He missed Kite Flyer and the forest in his backyard. He even missed the guests at the B & B who hovered around him while he cooked.

His actions went on automatic, and much like in his kitchen, or even at the B & B, he sliced and diced, instructing along the way. He put his all into each step, for a beat imagining himself cooking for Matilda in her cozy house. A minute later, he pulled out an already made chicken tinola from a makeshift oven.

Two minutes were up and over before he knew it, and he exhaled.

The next segment was already queued, but inside, Jared felt triumphant. And he would take this win, as small as it was.

He exited stage left, finding that his family was gone, replaced by one woman. Matilda.

He was stunned silent and halted midstep. Then, Matilda gripped his right hand into both of hers and tugged him toward the exit. Her skin was warm; he wasn't dreaming.

"Are you real?"

She smiled. "It's me. I'm here."

Matilda's choice of words created a sliver of clarity in the haze, and the curtain rose to reveal that she was in fact, in front of him.

He wrapped her in his arms, and to his relief, he felt a squeeze against his torso. "I can't believe you're here."

"Not just me, the Espiritus are here, too."

"Really?" Stunned he asked, "But…why?"

"Oh, I don't know, we thought driving five hundred miles would be fun."

"Okay?" He was still in shock.

She stepped back. "There's a whole room of people who are waiting for you, but I wanted to talk to you first. Not that these few minutes are going to cover everything I want to say." She paused. "I'm sorry I didn't stand up for you. I'm sorry I let you go. You. Who I love."

Jared's mouth had gone dry. "You love me?"

"I do." She shut her eyes and inhaled. "I did things that were unforgivable. I was ageist and unfair, and I didn't give you or us enough credit. I was convinced that we weren't in the same place, but I realized that no one is when they first meet. It's about two people meeting somewhere in the middle.

"And we did. We found our middle, but I walked away when I should have stood next to you. I should have stood up for you. And maybe it's too late, but I wanted to make sure you knew that I love you, and I'm a better person because of you. You reminded me that I could trust myself and what I feel. That I can share these feeling, too."

Jared cupped her cheek with a hand and brushed her skin gently, her words sinking into him and spreading warmth across his chest. "You love me."

She nodded.

Jared heaved a breath and gathered the tendrils of his thoughts. He hoped it would all make sense. "It was part of the plan that you wouldn't be blamed for my decision."

She shook her head. "Plans change."

He pressed a thumb against her lips. "I made decisions that I didn't think through, Matilda. All my life I chose comfort. It's what I do, it's what I like. Why I didn't look for my father sooner. It took that critic to say something to me that sent me running to look for people, and I didn't consider their feelings on the matter. All I knew is that I hated feeling different. I hated not exactly fitting in. But as soon as it got uncomfortable at the B & B, I took off.

"I should have stayed to work it out with you. To see through the bomb I dropped on Eva. But I don't want any more secrets between us. Because I love you, too."

She wrapped her arms around him, squeezing tight. It was the best thing he'd felt since he'd left Peak. "I want things to be okay between us."

"It will. It already is, though it won't be perfect. My God, daddy issues, am I right?"

"Ex issues." She snorted and looked up at him with those gorgeous eyes.

He bent down and pressed his lips against hers and it was like coming home. It was a reunion. It was acceptance.

And he would never let it go.

Minutes later, she led him to the hushed voices in the waiting room. A step in, he was bowled over by Liam, who wrapped his arms around his waist. "Tito Jared!"

Tito Jared. *Uncle* Jared.

"Hey, buddy." His voice croaked and he let it, lifting his

nephew up by underarms. Liam wrapped his legs around Jared's waist and hugged him tightly.

"We missed you. I went to this kite store and got another kite for us to fly."

"Of course. Anytime, bud." He looked around then, finding Frankie and Gabby, who leaned in for a group hug. Stepping back, Fred was hanging in the periphery. And steps away was his mom, who was standing next to Eva.

He stilled.

Do you see this, Louis?

It was a whisper in the air. The very first time Jared spoken to Louis, or the spirit of him anyway.

"Jared, I hope you don't mind that we're here," Eva said.

"No." He startled at the question. "This is great. Really great."

Apparently he was back to being so articulate.

"Sharla and I spoke. I'm sure she told you."

He nodded.

"I didn't believe her at first, just as I didn't believe you when you told me who you were. And I owe you an apology, Jared. A big one."

"Eva, I chose to keep it a secret—"

Eva raised a hand. "No. This was *Louis's* secret… and something for me to take up with him."

The room went silent. Jared had no doubt that wherever Louis was, Eva would find him.

"Now you have three sisters. What are you going to do about that?" Frankie nudged him with an elbow. It broke the tension, and a laugh bubbled through the space.

"More to keep him in check," Emma said.

"More to feed." Gabby grinned, leaning into Jared.

"More to love," Jared said, looking straight at Matilda.

Epilogue

Four Months Later

"I can't handle this stress," Matilda muttered under her breath as she stared up at a tree, where Jared was precariously standing on a branch unraveling the last bit of kite string. "Please be careful, Jared!"

Next to her, Liam was laughing. He had been giggling all afternoon at gosh knew what. She gave him the side-eye. Something was up.

The idea quickly evaporated when she heard a grunt from above. She'd only gotten Jared back to Peak a couple of months ago and refused to let the newly rehired chef and unrepentant city boy get hurt, not under her watch. The idea alone threatened to break her heart in two.

Soon after she'd admitted to Jared that she loved him, she was bowled over every day by the overabundance of feelings. From joy to worry, to tears. It was as if by allowing herself to love, she'd opened the gates to the rest of her emotions that she usually kept locked away.

She knew this was all good, but it was overwhelming at times. So much, that she'd admitted to the Espiritus that she would not feel comfortable being in the same space as Noah while he and Jane were staying at the B & B. Matilda took an unprecedented staycation—three days off. The wedding was yesterday, hence Jared's day off today.

And since a promise was a promise, it was also a kite flying day with Liam.

"We could leave the kite. Surely the wind will take it down sometime," she called up. It was a thirty-five-dollar purchase that didn't warrant this kind of attention.

Jared called from above. "Got it! I'm coming down."

She held out her arms, as if that would assist. While she was working on lots of things in therapy, one that she knew would take time was her attempt to control situations. And well, she didn't want her boyfriend to go splat without her trying to save him.

Boyfriend. It was a title she wasn't used to, but found that it gave her the shivers, in a good way.

To her relief, Jared shimmied down. His forehead was covered with sweat, which wasn't helped by the summer humidity. But his smile was bright and expecting, and contagious as it was, she grinned back.

"I like this better. You on the ground."

He leaned into her ear. "In bed is better for me."

She pushed him away playfully, all of her worrying thoughts dissipating.

"Ew, did you just whisper sweet nothings?" Liam asked.

Matilda bit back a laugh. "Who told you about sweet nothings."

"Mom did. She said that's what people who love each other do. Whisper sweet nothings. So did you?"

"Yes, that's exactly what I did." He ruffled Liam's hair. Then, to Matilda, he said, "Wanna take a walk?"

"Um sure. I mean, aren't we already kind of walking?"

"Do you always have something to say?"

"Yes."

"Good. Don't ever change. C'mon." He offered an elbow. It was odd, but she went along with it, and he walked her to the edge of the knoll.

The sun was on its way down. Not quite the golden hour, though the horizon was orange. The valley was luminous with it, and for a beat Matilda lost herself in the view.

"Do you remember the song we sang our first night together?" he asked.

"Of course. '(I've Had) The Time of My Life.' We kicked butt that night."

"We sure did. And every day since then has been an adventure."

From afar, she heard the start of a song. The tune was familiar, and sure enough, it was "(I've Had) The Time of My Life." Looking toward the house, she spotted Liam on the porch with Jared's portable speaker, waving it in the air.

Then, Jared began to sing the lyrics. She giggled at first, until she realized that he was singing it *to* her, and without a lick of irony or humor. She was entranced by it; it felt like a full circle. From that first night and first song, from which they'd overcome fear and struggle, to now. To love.

When he got to the last line of the first stanza, the music faded, and he got down on one knee. From his pocket he retrieved a jade-green velvet box.

The signature velvet box of Helen's jewelry business in downtown Peak.

"Matilda," he started.

The emotions Matilda had been contending with? They all spilled out of her in one go. She didn't need to see what was in the box, nor did she wait for the question. She got down on her own knees and met Jared with a kiss and a promise in her heart that she knew she would keep.

* * * * *

Don't miss Eva's story, the next installment in
Spirit of the Shenandoah,
the new Harlequin Special Edition miniseries
by USA TODAY *bestselling author Tif Marcelo.*

Coming soon!